THE HEART REMEMBERS

THE HEART REMEMBERS

Faith Baldwin

Chivers Press • Thorndike Press
Bath, England • Thorndike, Maine USA

This Large Print edition is published by Chivers Press, England, and by Thorndike Press, USA.

Published in 1997 in the U.K. by arrangement with the author's estate.

Published in 1997 in the U.S. by arrangement with Harold Ober Associates Incorporated.

U.K. Hardcover   ISBN   0–7451–8832–X   (Chivers Large Print)
U.K. Softcover   ISBN   0–7451–8833–8   (Camden Large Print)
U.S. Softcover   ISBN   0–7862–0917–8   (General Series Edition)

The text of this Large Print edition is unabridged.
Other aspects of the book may vary from the original edition.

Set in 16 pt. New Times Roman.

Printed in Great Britain on acid-free paper.

British Library Cataloguing in Publication Data available

Library of Congress Cataloging-in-Publication Data

Baldwin, Faith, 1893–
    The heart remembers / by Faith Baldwin.
        p.   cm.
    ISBN 0–7862–0917–8 (lg. print : c)
1. Large type books.   I. Title.
PS3505.U97H44   1997
813'.52—dc20
                                                    96–38776

This is for
Mildred and Richard Crooks,
two very special people, with my love

CHAPTER ONE

Crossing Park Avenue in the brilliant spring sunshine Carol congratulated herself. She had waited for the light, she had been sedate, she had not hurried. Walk, do not run, to the nearest entrance. Entrance, not exit. A new job, a new world, a wider opportunity.

She smiled at an officer of the law who responded with a broad grin, white teeth, weather-beaten face, blue eyes, alight for the brief moment with unspoken compliment. Carol's heart lifted, it felt tight in her breast, it beat like a drum.

She looked at her wrist watch. She was on time. She was meeting two men for luncheon but she was on time. These were not men whom you kept waiting, this was a business engagement, not cocktails for two and a discussion of the ballet while you regarded the menu and said eventually, with pleasing flattery, 'You order—'

She reached the Waldorf. The doors engulfed and spun her. She walked up the broad stairs, and her hosts rose from the cushioned chairs to greet her.

Mr Richard Maynard. Fifty-six. Ten pounds overweight. Good gray hair and tired brown eyes. Bulldog jaw and a beautiful, controlled mouth. No one had called him Dick since he was seven. Senior partner in the firm his grandfather had founded ... Maynard Company, Publishers.

Mr Stephen Hall. Forty-eight. Several pounds underweight. Scant reddish hair and bright blue eyes with laughter lines starring out around them. A square, cleft chin and a thin, amused mouth with a scar in the left-hand corner. Everyone called him Steve. Junior partner in the present firm ... Maynard and Hall, Publishers.

An old firm and a good one. Fiction, nonfiction, juveniles; a solid backlog of textbooks, religious books, scientific books. Maynard and Hall had published three of the seven great best sellers which had appeared in the last decade. They moved with the times, they conceded that tastes change, they allowed themselves an occasional artistic failure or a fine edition. They permitted a smattering of fine poetry. They admitted new schools. Their quota of Books of the Month was gratifying, their advertising conservative, their authors as satisfied as authors ever are. And their publicity had dignity.

Too much dignity, they had decided recently.

Stephen Hall regarded Carol's approach with interest and curiosity. He had never met her. He had her dossier at his finger tips and he and she had undoubtedly been under the same roof at one time or another, at a big party perhaps or lunching in the same restaurant. But to the best of his knowledge he had never before seen her. Now he saw her and liked what he saw. He was a happily married man with a seventeen-year-old son who made him feel his age, but he was capable of deriving pleasure from pleasurable things. It was pleasant to look at Carol.

Maynard was performing the introductions. He did so in the worried, rather shy way which sometimes misled new authors. They felt that Mr Maynard was not quite sure of himself, which made them very confident. They soon learned how mistaken they had been.

Hall's glance, impersonally friendly, was absorbing Carol ... a tall girl, not too tall, slender without appearing starved. When you looked at her you did not think of dessicated breads and salads thrown together without oil. He liked her navy-blue suit, the short flaring skirt, and the dusty-pink sweater. He liked her silly little hat, with the bird's wing which repeated the pink tones. He liked her dark hair, her clear skin, and the direct regard she accorded him from very fine dark eyes.

He asked:

'Shall we have our cocktails here?'

'If I may,' said Carol, 'tomato juice...'

Stephen Hall lifted an eyebrow slightly. Carol flushed. She knew what he was thinking. Smart girl makes sober impression on prospective employers. Her mouth, which was

3

generous, full and not too red, tightened, but she said nothing. Maynard said it for her, in his slow, almost hesitant way.

'Miss Reid's a sundowner, Steve,' he said mildly; 'I tried to tempt her when we lunched together last week. But it appears that she doesn't indulge until dinner-time.'

'She's wise,' said Steve, sighing. He smiled at Carol. 'I wish I had learned that lesson at your age,' he remarked. He crooked a finger at a hovering waiter and ordered. Tomato juice for Carol, Scotch for himself, a Manhattan for his partner.

Her age. He knew how old she was. Carol Reid was thirty. She looked younger. But then most women did nowadays ... if, like Carol, they were sundowners, got all the sleep they needed, took care of their skins and were restrained when it came to make-up. He looked down at her hands. Nice hands, long and firm, almond-shaped nails, pink with health and nothing else.

The drinks came. Across the room someone waved and Steve said, waving back:

'Laura Thurston. You'd better go over, Richard, she's very much annoyed with me.'

Carol turned, slightly, in her chair. She had seen Laura Thurston many times but always at a greater distance. She was curious about her. She asked, as Maynard rose and lumbered across the room, 'Is she one of ...? Oh, of course, how stupid of me.'

4

'Mrs Thurston,' said Steve grimly, 'is Maynard and Hall bread and butter. She and half a dozen others. Now and then we find we have a jam pot under contract. But bread and butter is vital.'

Carol looked over at Mrs Thurston's table. Mrs Thurston was drinking something, straight. A younger woman was with her. Carol said:

'She's quite beautiful, isn't she?'

'Yes. It's sheer propaganda that female authors must look like something out of a haystack. Of course,' he mentioned, setting down his glass, 'some of them still do. Several haystacks. But the majority of them look like Carnegie *cum* Arden. You must have learned that during your magazine experience.'

She said, smiling:

'A news weekly doesn't run to beautiful female writers ... but I have encountered a few.'

'Richard's very enthusiastic about you,' Steve told her. 'You did an amazing job with *Facts*. I remember when the first issue appeared on the stands. No one thought it would last, considering the heavy competition from older, established magazines. You put it over.'

She said, 'I had good help, a good staff.' She looked at him, very directly. 'You aren't forgetting that *Facts* folded?' she inquired.

'No. But that's no argument,' he said

5

instantly. 'There wasn't enough money, even the circulation jump couldn't alter that. And, when Dennis committed suicide...'

She said thoughtfully:

'He was a fine person. I learned to appreciate him during the two years I worked for him. It was a hideous waste, Mr Hall. I suppose he felt it was the only way out. The magazine wasn't doing as well as he had hoped, he had sunk all his personal means in it. He had a wife and two young children. Also he was incurably ill. But he had managed to carry, over a long period of time, a large insurance policy.'

Hall was interested. He asked quickly:

'You're condoning suicide?'

'I'm not condemning it, in this case,' she said. 'How can any of us judge unless we've faced a similar situation?'

Mr Maynard came back, looking startled. Laura always managed to startle him although he had known her for over fifteen years.

They went in to luncheon. During it, Hall said, smiling at Carol:

'You're going to find this job rather different from *Facts*. There will be considerable personal contact with our writers. You may find some of it wearing.'

Her heart hammered. She thought, Baldly, that means I'm hired. Maynard, the first time she had seen him, had expressed himself as satisfied with her qualifications. But Stephen Hall was on the Coast. Nothing would be decided until he returned.

She remembered that day in Maynard's private office ... and how frightened she had been, almost as if this were her first attempt at personal salesmanship. When *Facts* had folded, Jimmy Ellis had told her about Maynard and Hall. Jimmy was top rewrite man on *Facts*, brilliant, hard-boiled, slightly younger than herself. He had written one book, the result of several years as foreign correspondent for a New York newspaper. Maynard and Hall had published it. She recalled the day when they knew that *Facts* could not continue. Ellis had come into her office to sit on her desk, with his long legs dangling. He had taken a cigarette from her pack, lighted it and asked:

'Any plans, Carol?'

'None,' she had admitted.

'Any dependents?'

Carol shook her head. She and Jimmy Ellis knew each other well, in the office. Outside the office they knew very little about each other. She answered:

'My mother died over a year ago, Jimmy.'

'Well,' he said, 'that's that. A man's a fool to get married.' He had added that he had accepted an offer to return to his paper. Not that his wife would like it. He couldn't take her with him, if he was sent abroad again. Not with that hell's brew going on. Then he had told her that he'd heard that Maynard and Hall were

7

considering a change in their publicity department.

'Hogan ran it for years; a nice guy, Hogan. He's retiring ... came into some money and a bad heart at the same time. It's a swell outfit, you'd like it there. If you like I'll call up Richard Maynard.'

She had liked, he had telephoned, and she had had a letter from Richard Maynard, on the solid letter-head of the firm. She had gone to see him, and the following week they had lunched together. Now, Steve Hall had returned from the Coast.

Luncheon was over, the coffee cups stood on the table. Steve refilled his. He put his hand in his pocket and strewed a dozen dingy memorandums on the table. He shuffled them as if they were cards, found the one he wanted, and looked at it. He crammed it back in his pocket again and the older man laughed. He said:

'You'll get used to that, Miss Reid. Steve has the finest collection of notebooks in the world ... most of them given him by long-suffering authors who have witnessed what you saw just now.'

Steve grinned. He said:

'I was trying to refresh my memory. I've an appointment sometime today ... I thought I'd written it down.'

Carol said, smiling:

'Your secretary must have her hands full.'

'She's used to me,' said Steve. He looked at his watch. 'I've remembered. It's in ten minutes, at the office. Coming, Richard?'

Maynard paid the check. He said:

'Of course . . . and Miss Reid?' He looked at her inquiringly. 'Would you come with us, and we can settle the final details in comparative peace and quiet?'

They went out together and walked over to Madison and downtown. It was a superb day. Carol walked as if she liked walking, lightly, freely. Her clear skin glowed, her eyes shone. Steve, next to the curb, said, 'I'm glad you don't like taxis. I hate them, they scare the living daylights out of me.'

'I do like them,' said Carol, 'in bad weather.'

The big brown building was on a corner. The elevator took them to the eighth floor, where the editorial offices were situated. The firm occupied three floors in the building.

A small waiting room, uncomfortable enough to discourage importunate people. A reception clerk in a sort of wooden cage. A switchboard. A narrow lane between open spaces to right and left filled with earnest people at typewriters. Another corridor at right angles, flanked with glass doors opening into private offices.

Maynard's office was on the corner. It was ample in size and comfortable. No modern furniture, no Picassos. Bookshelves, crammed with books in bright jackets. Autographed

9

photographs. A big desk. An ante-room in which a ticking typewriter was operated by a small middle-aged woman. 'Miss Harris,' said Maynard, coaxing her out of her lair, and presenting her, 'my right hand, also my left. This,' he added, 'is Miss Reid, who is taking Mr Hogan's place.'

As easy as that, as simple.

Sitting opposite him at the big desk, 'You and Mr Hall understand,' asked Carol, 'that I have not had any experience in this particular branch—?'

'We do. All the better,' said Maynard, leaning back in his chair, 'you'll come to it fresh, you'll have perhaps a new angle. We need it. I hate to admit it, but we do. For years we've gone along with the usual releases to the book pages and the trade magazines, and an occasional party for one of our authors. But it isn't enough, in these days.' He sighed. 'I'm a die-hard,' he confessed, 'I don't like a lot of this circus pony and ballyhoo business. I still believe that the profession of publishing should maintain some dignity—and that even authors are entitled to private lives. If only they themselves keep 'em private,' he complained. 'I deplore the methods of many of our competitors, and I deplore the fact that there are times when publicity issued by a publishing house is partly to counteract the bad publicity which the authors themselves attract. Not all of them, mind you,' he said hastily, 'not, by any means, the majority. However, there it is.'

She said, 'You know I'll do my best, Mr Maynard. I'm most grateful for the opportunity.'

Two hours later she was ready to leave. Hall had come in again, and she had met a number of people with whom she would work. Olga James, the juvenile editor, George Heckman, textbook editor, several of the salesmen, Stephen Hall's pretty secretary, Mitty Lenard, and John Hogan.

Hogan was a lean man, approaching sixty … a nervous face, a good handclasp, quiet, appraising eyes. His assistant was a woman of about forty-five, Elsie Norris. Miss Norris was flat-chested and redheaded. There was also a secretary, Miss Owen.

The office which Carol would occupy was of good size. It had two windows, and was strictly utilitarian in furnishings. She would share it with her assistant, Elsie Norris. Dorothy Owen had her own small cubicle.

Miss Norris, Hogan assured her, would be of the greatest possible help, as she knew all the ropes. Miss Norris smiled, a taut, pinched grimace. Her eyes were definitely hostile. She was looking at Carol's suit and comparing it to her own tweeds, sufficiently undistinguished for a duchess.

Carol smiled at her. She thought, This woman hates me. She must have wanted the job herself, perhaps she rates it. Life's a mess, you don't get anywhere without stepping on someone's neck. It is important that she become an ally, not an enemy, important that she grow to like me. That's my first big job.

She said:

'I'll need a lot of help—and I'll be very grateful.'

Back in his office, Maynard said briskly:

'That's that, then. I'll have Hogan get up some data for you and send it along with the books—the current list—to your home. Some clippings too, perhaps, which you may wish to glance over at your leisure. I hope we are going to work happily together. I feel confident that we are. But I am quite aware that we are doing you an injustice, from a financial standpoint, at least.'

She said quickly:

'*Facts* paid me a great deal more than any of my other jobs had paid. Mr Dennis was overoptimistic, and enthusiastic. I didn't expect anything like his figure, Mr Maynard. This is exactly the opportunity I've wanted.' She glanced around the office and added slowly, 'There's a sense of security here, friendliness ... and I feel that I have something to contribute. I'll work hard. And I'll be here on the fifteenth,' she added, smiling.

Later he walked down the corridor with her, through the busy room. People glanced up from the typewriters as they passed. He said, as they walked along:

'You've met quite a few of us ... our West Coast salesmen of course come in only biannually and others of the sales department are out on the road. There's the accounting department, the various typists, filing clerks, on the editorial, production, advertising and publicity side. We aren't as departmentalized as we used to be. When Stephen Hall came in with me some fourteen years ago he changed things. Everyone has, as you put it, something to contribute, often quite outside of what people would call his or her field. Peter Tarrant—our advertising head, who isn't in the office this afternoon—has, for instance, as keen an eye for fiction as anyone in the editorial department. One of our production men writes poetry and I may say understands other people's better than most of us. Everyone in the organization reads ... we have no so-called regular readers. Our editor in chief, who is really my assistant, does a little bit of everything. He's on vacation now, but will be back shortly before the end of the month. Normally you would have heard from him, initially. But Hogan's resignation took place after Morgan left on his cruise, so the very pleasant task of selecting his successor was left to me and Stephen. One of the objects of Morgan's vacation was to get him away from office detail, so we shall cable him merely that John's leaving and you've consented to take his place.'

'Morgan?' she asked. No premonition troubled her.

'Andrew Morgan.'

She was pale, but he did not notice. She repeated, 'Andrew Morgan?' and Maynard looked at her.

'Yes,' he said. 'Do you know him?'

She answered quickly:

'I once knew—but perhaps it's not the same. It isn't an unusual name.'

The girl at the switchboard spoke to a harried young man, who was waiting in the reception room. She said, 'Mr Hall will see you now, Mr Peterson.'

Peterson, clutching the brief case which contained the Great American Novel, scurried past them on his hopeful errand.

'Monday, the fifteenth,' said Maynard, smiling.

Carol shook hands with him. Presently she was in the crowded elevator. It smelled of stale smoke and staler people. Two men were arguing about the administration. A messenger boy whistled, off key. A tall lad got off at the next floor, with a great pile of books under his arm.

When Carol reached the street the afternoon sun spun a golden net over the city. It was quite cool, the wind blew the idle dust, the scattered papers in the gutters.

She thought, I'll go home and write Mr Maynard that I've reconsidered and concluded

14

that we've both made a mistake, and I find that, after all, I cannot accept the position.

CHAPTER TWO

Carol lived in the Seventies, on the East Side. Her small apartment of bedroom, living room, kitchenette and bath was high and relatively quiet. From the living-room windows you could see the river.

Shortly after her mother's death she had moved from the home they had shared, a big, old-fashioned apartment downtown, off Fifth Avenue. Her mother had liked the location, the high-ceilinged rooms and fireplaces. They had lived modestly but comfortably on her annuity and Carol's contribution to the family budget and they had not had to touch their backlog of government bonds which was, with the annuity, all that had been recovered at the time of Mr Reid's death.

The annuity had ceased with her mother's death but Carol would derive a fair income from the bonds, and the former dividends, which had piled up in the saving bank, were sufficient to take care of expenses. She had sold much of the furnishings of the apartment, as they had come from the Connecticut house and were heavy, massive pieces for the most part. She kept enough linen and silver and china and

15

kitchenware for her needs, and a few things which she loved, a graceful desk, a wing chair, the small love seat, some good water colors which her father had collected, some books, rugs and lamps. Her own bedroom furniture was too big for the new place so she bought lighter, small modern pieces, a day bed for the living room and a little, portable radio. She had managed to make her rooms attractive and pleasant. Bess Manners, who had worked with her on *Facts*, had suggested that they take a place together. But Carol had refused. She was very fond of Bess, sprightly, gay, wise and loyal, but she could not imagine sharing an apartment with her. She had said anxiously:

'You won't be hurt if I say I think I'll try living alone for a while?'

'You won't like it.' said Bess, 'no matter what the books say.'

'I think I will—after I get used to it.'

Now, she was used to it. She found that she did like it. After all these years . . . how many—well, thirty really, of not living alone, she discovered that solitude has its uses.

She put her key in the door and went in. The house supplied maid service if desired, and there was a good restaurant downstairs. Carol got her own breakfast and, often, her dinner. Or, she could have something sent up. If she had guests, dinner could be well served on the gate-legged table in the corner of the living room. It was a pleasant, easy way to live. She

16

need not worry over part-time maids, their dependability, the difficulties of their family lives, their frequent miseries. When she reached home after work her bed was made and the apartment cleaned and for that impersonal, practically invisible service she paid a certain set sum, supplemented by a Christmas present. And was well content.

She tossed her hat on the love seat and went into the bathroom to scrub the dust and grime from her face. Presently, in pajamas, she came out and sat down in the wing chair by the window. It was a big chair, well worn. When she had curtained this apartment she had considered having the chair reupholstered, to match the love seat. She had not done so. It had been her father's chair. He had loved it. The worn place was made by his head, leaning back. When he sat in that chair with his feet on the matching gros-point stool, smoke had arisen like a halo, strong, sweet pipe smoke…

She thought, If you had any sense you'd get up, go to the desk and write to Richard Maynard. He'll think you're crazy. Perhaps you are.

There must be dozens of Andrew Morgans.

Andy used to say, 'Welsh, that's me. Taffy was a Welshman. That's why I sing in the tub. All Welshmen sing. Carol, did they invent Welsh rarebit?'

She had not seen Andrew Morgan for almost ten years. She did not know where he was. She did not know whether or not he lived in New York, or what work he did. Once, looking up a telephone number, she had chanced on the Morgans, a lot of them. There were several Andrews and several A.'s and one A. L....

Over nine years ago.

She remembered Tuesday, October twenty-ninth, and Andy's drawn young face and his tight voice saying, 'Wiped out, I tell you—and people going crazy ... a man I talked to yesterday shot himself this morning ... And Carstairs—you remember Carstairs?—I saw him last Thursday. He came in, just after noon. He said, "Everything's going to be all right"; the bankers had formed their pool, the selling halted. He's dead too, Carol. There's one thing to be said for skyscrapers, there's always a high window...'

He'd called her that day and asked her to meet him at Luigi's, on the East Side, with the parrot in the cage and the murals on the wall. Luigi's knew them very well, when the panel slid back and big Joe looked out he always grinned. 'Glad to see you,' big Joe would say, and jerk a thumb, open a door and they'd be inside. Crowded, smoky place, low ceilings and smoke, good food and fair liquor, everyone they knew went to Luigi's. Andy had sent dozens of people there ... 'Tell them Andy Morgan sent you.'

Then suddenly it was December and they

18

were going to Connecticut, Christmas Eve, to her people. Andy hadn't a job yet and he'd come in, very drunk, with that defiant look which shut her away from him, and they hadn't gone to Connecticut together after all. She'd gone alone.

She hadn't thought of that Christmas for years.

Carol rose and went over to her desk. She sat down, took a sheet of paper and fountain pen and wrote:

'Dear Mr Maynard:

'I have been thinking things over and have come to the conclusion that I do not, after all, fill your requirements for—'

She crumpled the sheet, which blotted in odd shapes, and threw it in the metal wastebasket.

'Dear Mr Maynard:

'Something has happened which I feel will make it impossible for me to accept—'

She tore that up too.

It needn't be Andy. Why should it be Andy? Dear God, don't let this man be Andy.

She did not love him. She rarely thought of him. He was a stranger to her, someone once loved in a dream. She had awakened years since.

She had so liked both Maynard and Hall, the old unpretentious offices, the possible scope of her work. The drop in salary did not matter, she had expected it. With her own small income she would get along very well. She was not—at

19

least not now—an extravagant person.

The telephone rang. It was Bess Manners.

'What's new? Did you see the big shots?'

'Yes, I saw them,' Carol said.

'You sound strange. Are you tight or just coming down with something?'

'Neither. Bess, what are you doing tonight ... now?'

'I've been stood up,' said Bess tragically, 'Jerry, blast him, had to go to Cleveland.'

'Come around,' said Carol, 'I want to talk to you. We'll have something sent up from downstairs. Still lamb-chopping?'

'*And* raw vegetables,' said Bess. 'I've lost two pounds. Peace, it's wonderful. Order me a salad. I'll be along.'

Carol hung up and called the house restaurant. Lamb chops, a raw vegetable salad, pot cheese, pastry. Bess might reconsider, and as for herself, her weight never varied.

She went to the hall, picked up the newspaper lying on the floor outside the door and returned to the wing chair. Now the room glowed with light, it was a comfortable room. The wind was rising, it was cool, more like September than May.

Bess had a new job, Bess never worried about jobs. One of the competitive weeklies had taken her on, in the research department. Bess had worked since she was eighteen. She was forty now. Good days, she looked thirty; bad days, she could have been sixty. Carol had known her for six years, it was Bess who had coaxed her away from the publicity work in the big charity organization and made her apply for the berth on *Facts*.

Bess came in. She was plump, with untidy, graying hair and small, neat features. She wore clothes badly and lipstick well. She had tiny feet of which she was inordinately vain, an enormous appetite for good food, which she tried to curb, and an infinite capacity for Scotch which she ignored as the fatal factor in her dieting.

'Two pounds,' she said, and smote herself, hip and thigh. 'Behold!'

'You look elegant. You can qualify for the Powers Agency presently,' said Carol.

'What's wrong with you?' asked Bess, shedding her outdoor things, 'you look as if you'd seen several ghosts.'

'Perhaps I have. Sit down, dinner will be along presently. Have a cigarette. Bess, do you remember the speakeasy days?'

'Who could forget 'em? Lord, all I've lived through ... Free love, soap boxes and rickety stairs in the Village. The old days, when, corn-fed and pretty as a girl on a calendar, I came to New York to be a writer. Salons and talk, and we didn't ask to be born and the world's our oyster, with a pearl necklace coiled up inside. You wouldn't remember, you're a decade younger. Clamshells for ash trays and good old rowdy evenings. I had a dress I made from

21

curtain material. It was a green velvet business. I cut a hole in the middle and sewed up the sides and recited Edgar Lee Masters to an admiring throng. Street fights and garlic, and Italian babies like dirty cherubs—until they opened their mouths. Then they were just dirty. Gallons of red ink ... and no money, those were the days. And after that,' said Bess, taking a lungful of smoke, 'war and a uniform, the Y hut at Camp Upton, flag waving and parades, don't eat sugar, and brave little Belgium ... and the Liberty bond you couldn't afford. Then prosperity plus a pheasant in every pot, life on margin, and Mr Coolidge in a ten-gallon hat. Them were the days, ducky...' She laughed and shook her head. 'I miss the speakeasies. They were terrible, they bred a generation of ulcers—the doctors have a lot to be thankful for, they owe much to Amendment Eighteen ... but it was fun, we all went to hell and gone, and it was fun.'

She crushed out her cigarette. 'What made you think of speakeasies, darling? I like your pajamas, you ought to wear that nice dark red a lot more. You don't look as if you were old enough to remember.'

'I'm old enough. I remember my first,' said Carol. She was thinking aloud, she wasn't looking at Bess. 'I was eighteen. It was a hole in the wall. I forget its name. Tony's, I suppose. It was standard. There was a mechanical piano. You put a nickel in the slot and it did its stuff.

There was also a radio. You turned it on, and there was Rudy Vallee—or am I ahead of myself? Also a cocktail in a teacup. Pink tea ... a Jack Rose. Funny, wasn't it?'

'Screaming,' said Bess, 'like a geranium in a tin can. I remember that too. Outside people's windows, and on fire escapes. They still exist. But I remember a geranium in a shack near the Hudson. Hoover City. That wasn't as much fun.'

Carol said:

'Tony's was. I felt so adult, darling, so excited. I'd cut classes and come to New York. And there I was in a speakeasy, eating minestrone and ravioli and spumoni, drinking a cocktail in a teacup. And Andy said, "See Naples and die" and we both laughed.'

'Oh,' said Bess, 'so that's it.'

'What?'

'So it's Andy. I haven't heard you speak of him for—it must be three years. Do you remember? I hadn't met Jerry then and I'd seen Sam on the street and I went out and got plastered and you took me home and put me to bed, very quietly, so your mother wouldn't know, and you sat beside me and held my hand while I wept about Sam and what a heel he was and how much I had loved him and how much I hated him and how I wanted to murder that little blond Borgia. And when I stopped crying you said something about Andy. But not since.'

23

Someone knocked and Carol went to the door. The waiter and the tray. The gate-legged table was ready, she pulled it out, she had set it while waiting for Bess.

'Want a drink?' she asked Bess, when the waiter had gone.

'This is my week on the wagon.' Bess looked at the salad. She remarked dourly, 'Another week of this and you can skin me and make me into an ermine wrap at forty-four-fifty. I don't know why I bother. Jerry likes me fat.'

'When are you and Jerry going to be married?'

'New Year's Eve,' said Bess; 'why not?'

She cut into the chop and said, 'Yes, another week and I can count myself going over fences. It will make insomnia so personal. Have you *seen* Andy?'

'No.'

'Then what's on your mind? Maybe he's married, maybe he's dead, maybe he lives in San Francisco, maybe he's tired of it all and has gone to the South Seas. What's happened, or is this just one of those times when you start singing the remembering blues?'

'I thought I ordered coffee,' said Carol.

'You did. It's here. I'll pour. Come clean, baby.'

She said:

'When I left the Maynard office today—'

'I'd forgotten. Hired or eased out, gracefully?'

24

'Hired.'

'Why didn't you say so in the first place? This calls for a celebration.'

'Wait a minute. As I was leaving, Mr Maynard told me that I had met almost everyone in the shop except Andrew Morgan.'

Bess's jaw dropped. She set down her coffee cup. She said incredulously:

'Not Andy?'

'I don't know. There must be others.'

'Well, good Lord,' cried Bess in exasperation, 'didn't you find out?'

'How could I? Could I ask Mr Maynard to give me a blow-by-blow description, like a Man Wanted handbill in a postoffice?'

She thought, How old? Thirty-four, six feet in his shoes, brown hair—gray eyes, very good teeth. He broke his nose playing football, Mr Maynard. It's a funny nose, now. When he laughs his eyes almost disappear. He has a nice voice. He could do almost anything with it. I can't tell you any more about him because I don't really know him. Perhaps I never did.

'Didn't you say *anything*?' demanded Bess. 'For heaven's sake, don't sit there staring into space.'

'I—repeated his name. Mr Maynard asked if I knew him. I said perhaps it wasn't the Andrew Morgan I had known.'

'Well,' said Bess, on a long breath, 'if it is—how are you going to explain your reticence?'

25

'Must I explain it?' asked Carol. She looked very tired. She added, 'Before you called up I was trying to write Maynard, to explain that, after all, he needn't expect me on the fifteenth.'

'Have you lost your mind? You'd chuck up a job like that on the off chance—?'

Carol shrugged. 'But it would be awkward, wouldn't it?'

'Why should it be? Unless you're still in love with him. Are you?'

Carol laughed with genuine amusement. She said:

'No, Bess, I'm not. I haven't been for a good many years, over nine ... well, let's say eight and a half.'

'Then what's the matter? This is today, it isn't eighteen-eighty. It isn't even nineteen hundred. Don't you know anybody he knows?'

'Not any more,' said Carol. 'At first I saw a good deal of our mutual friends. After my father died, I stopped. Now and then I'd run into them. I still do occasionally. We grin insincerely and exchange season's greetings. We pass on. That's all.'

Bess was searching frantically in the cluttered attic of her memory. She dug out a trunk and pawed through it. She found what she was looking for and asked:

'Didn't you tell me that Andy was a classmate of Jake Fellows ... remember? You came into Reuben's with Jimmy Ellis—that was the night he decided to get married but

26

wanted your advice first, everyone's advice—poor old Jimmy. Must have been, let's see, about eight months ago. So we joined forces. Later you told me Fellows and Andy had been at college together, you remembered Andy had spoken of him, but you'd never met him before?'

'That's right,' agreed Carol, 'why?'

Bess went to the telephone. She picked up the book, thumbed through it, flipped it shut and dialed a number.

'Hello ... Jake? This is Bess Manners. No ... nothing of the sort, my good man, I'm getting married come the New Year. Just information, please. You were in Yale with a guy named Andrew Morgan, weren't you? That's right. Ever see him, these days? Never mind why I want to know, perhaps I want to blackmail him, it's none of your business. You do see him? ... that's fine. All I want to know is what does he do? Do, I said. I don't care if he does shoot eighty at golf and swims like Weissmuller and likes the comics. How does he earn a living? Oh. Thanks ... Sure, give me a buzz someday.'

She hung up and swung around.

'Your hard luck,' she said. 'He's with Maynard and Hall. Jake sees him because Jake's on the advertising staff of the *Times*. That's that.'

'I thought it would be,' said Carol. 'Long arm of something or other. Millions of people

27

in New York, millions of jobs, plenty of publishing houses, and this *would* happen to me.'

'You're scared,' said Bess. 'You're scared green. You're shaking-scared. You're terrified.'

'I'm not, you idiot!'

Bess asked thoughtfully:

'Going to tell Maynard ... if you go through with this?'

Carol shrugged. 'It doesn't make any difference,' she said. 'I don't know how Andy feels about it.' Her eyes widened. Once she had thought that she knew how Andy felt about everything. Now she realized she didn't know anything about him, except, according to Jake, that his golf was still good if not spectacular, that he still laughed at the funnies and still liked to swim. She didn't know if he still liked football and disliked baseball. She didn't know if his politics had changed, or his taste in food, wine, women. She didn't know *anything*.

Bess said:

'Going with Maynard and Hall's a swell break. Are you going to pass it up because of something that happened a million years ago? Because if you are—'

'I'm not,' said Carol. 'Why should I?'

CHAPTER THREE

On the morning of Monday, May fifteenth, Carol went to work for Maynard and Hall. Every new job holds all the elements of adventure . . . and she approached this one in a spirit of excitement, trepidation, uncertainty, and determination. It's something like getting married, she reflected in the elevator, a step into the unknown. Well, perhaps that was a trifle farfetched, she thought, and chuckled aloud to the interest of the friendly elevator boy who was a rich milk chocolate hue and whose name she discovered, by asking, was Fred. But new jobs open up all sorts of possibilities, vistas, pitfalls, dangers, and rewards.

She had spent a quiet Sunday, Bess had dropped in with Jerry during the afternoon and found her in a welter of closet cleaning, clothes pressing, button sewing.

'Good Lord, domesticity rampant!' Bess exclaimed, in horror. 'What's come over you?'

'A clean sweep,' said Carol; 'it's the influence of the new job.'

'I hope,' said Bess, 'that it wears off soon. This place looks like a New England boiled dinner.'

They tried to make her go out with them for a quiet pub-crawl—'nothing spectacular as the better boîtes are closed on Sundays'—but she refused. Reluctantly, they departed and a little later Kim Anderson called up. 'How about dinner and a movie,' he asked, but she refused. She was tired, tomorrow was the big day and she thought she would go to bed early, she told him.

Somewhere Jerry and Bess had found a florist open, and a chaste horseshoe arrived at the apartment with a purple ribbon around its middle bearing the gilded word *Success*. Carol laughed until she cried. Thank heaven, they had refrained from sending it to the office tomorrow! she thought, standing it up between the living-room windows and admiring the effect. Kim's gardenias arrived a little later. 'Good luck,' he had written on the card, 'but please don't fall too much in love with the new job.'

Fortunate girl ... home, friends, work. She did her nails, set her hair, creamed her face, feeling excited and alive and wide awake. She inspected her dress for the morning, cool, dark, excellently cut, with soft dressmaker touches to save it from being too strictly utilitarian. New gloves, good shoes, and a disarming little hat. She'd do, she thought, and went to bed convinced that she would not sleep and, of course, slept almost instantly.

It was pleasant to walk into the office Monday morning and discover that the girl at the switchboard remembered her name. Elsie

30

Norris greeted her in the office they would share. She was the reverse of fulsome, but Carol believed she was trying hard to be pleasant, and said, smiling:

'Well, here I am ... for better or worse. I hope, with your advice, it will be for better.'

Elsie endeavored to look mollified and Dorothy Owen, their mutual secretary, appeared from her own small cubicle with a bud vase containing one rose and put it on Carol's desk, by way of greeting.

During the morning almost everyone dropped in to see her and she had a long talk with Richard Maynard in his office. He said, as she rose to leave:

'I hope you're going to be happy with us.'

'How could I help it?' she replied. 'This is the friendliest place.'

'We have our ups and downs,' he admitted, 'slight outbreaks of office politics, an occasional rash of gossip, but in the main you'll find us loyal and co-operative. Do you remember seeing Laura Thurston at the Waldorf, when we lunched there together? She is coming in today and I want you to meet her. The sooner you get to know our authors the better. Some of them run in and out like— like—'

'Mice?'

'Exactly. A few, of the rarer sort, turn up only occasionally. Many of them live out of town, in near-by suburbs or scattered all over

31

the face of the United States. But sooner or later you will encounter them all. Don't be intimidated. They are just people. Many are quite human and do not labor under the delusion that a special gift—for which, by the way, they are not responsible—brings special privileges with it. But you will find some not so easy to handle; those who deal in, shall we say, exaggerations of behavior. But you'll soon learn all this for yourself.'

Laura Thurston arrived at the office, shortly before noon. She was lunching with Maynard. Carol, summoned to his office, was aware of an immense curiosity. Miss Thurston was one of the writers who made the news. She occupied a Fifth Avenue penthouse when she was not traveling or living in her French peasant cottage in Connecticut. She had been married twice, and twice divorced. She was an indefatigable first-nighter, and could be seen when in town at the more expensive restaurants, cafés, night clubs. It was reported that she danced beautifully, shot eighty at golf, was skilled in drawing to a straight flush and was ten years older than she admitted, and fifteen years older than she looked.

She was fashionably profane, and extremely beautiful in a dark, streamlined way. She wrote sophisticated novels of the type which used to be called daring. She was, in fact, a modern, female Robert W. Chambers in his middle phase, and one of the few women writers who looked like her books.

Later, Carol was to meet Mrs Peckworth who wrote innocent romances, in which the wages of sin were generally matrimony, and whose heroines were blond, sweet, and air cooled. It was a shock to find the celebrated Mrs P a large, masculine woman who smoked, privately, small cigars and went in for breeding horses and dogs. Also, she was to encounter Avis Norton, whose books were written with a hammer and sickle. Avis wrote of the antics, biological and emotional, of large families living in squalor in city tenements or on the wrong side of small-town railroad tracks. The things they said, the things they did, on paper, were incredible and appalling. But how true, cried the critics, praising her photographic eye, recording ear, and stark realism. Avis, however, to Carol's amazement, was under thirty, looked about fourteen, wore her mouse-brown hair parted in the middle and coiled at the nape of her neck. Her eyes were large, blue, and guileless. She affected low-heeled pumps, and little girl suits with white collars and her conversation was guiltless of so much as 'damn.'

But, today, meeting Laura Thurston in the practically ethereal flesh, Carol was wholly satisfied. Laura was just as Carol had pictured her after following her circulation-raising serials in the slicks.

Laura looked her over. She commented calmly:

'She's very pretty, Richard. Should cause quite a flutter. Is she married?'

'Not to my knowledge,' said Maynard, smiling.

Carol shook her head, feeling suddenly schoolgirl under the impact of Miss Thurston's startling eyes.

'Yearn to write?'

'Heavens, no,' said Carol, sincerely shocked.

'Good, we'll get on,' said Miss Thurston. 'I loathe pretty girls who yearn to write. I'm always afraid that they will—successfully. There's far too much competition in this business already.'

She qualified the word 'business' in a hair-raising manner. Mr Maynard's hair did not rise. He considered Laura's profanity a form of exhibitionism—like the prize fighter she bought one year, and the tenor for whose singing lessons she had paid. At that, she lost nothing through these harmless amusements, for whatever her original interest in the pugilist or the tenor they had come through handsomely, the lightweight having won every recent match, the tenor having landed an excellent radio spot. If her emotional urge had required no contracts, her financial sense had seen that they were signed and sealed and Laura was enjoying a pleasant income on the side through her devotion to the Cause of Youth.

After luncheon, Laura returned to the office and went into a huddle with Carol. New pictures, a new publicity slant. What could Miss Reid suggest?

She departed, well content, stopping to inform Maynard that Carol would 'do.' Maynard suffered this gratuitous information pleasantly as Laura was one author who, heaven knew, could afford to speak her mind within the sacred precincts of her publisher's office. Many a work of literature sitting glumly in the red had been offset by Laura's statements—which were always bold and black.

Carol's first week on the job was crowded with incident. So many people to see, so much to assimilate. She took the office home with her, she worked at night, was adamant to Kim Anderson's telephone calls, to Bess's warning ... 'if you kill yourself during the first month, Maynard and Hall won't pay the funeral expenses.'

'I'm thriving,' Carol assured her; 'I eat it up.'

All through that first week she found herself wondering what it would be like when Andrew Morgan returned to the office. Suppose he found himself so personally embarrassed by her daily presence that he fired her? No, Andy was too fair for that. Yet he might find fault with her work—he might honestly believe he had cause—and sooner or later his opinion would carry weight with Messrs. Maynard and

Hall. When he learned—as he would, of course—that she had known he was part of the ménage and yet had elected deliberately to take the position, would he be amused, or angry?

She found herself amazed to incredulity because she could not, for all her knowledge of him, foresee what Andy would do or say, think or feel.

If I can work here, she told herself, and not mind—that is, I don't *think* I'll mind—so can he.

She tried to forget him but it wasn't possible. There was Kate, Andy's pleasant secretary, with whom Carol lunched one day and who talked of him a good deal. She had a fund of amusing stories that concerned him. From these Carol gathered that he was well liked by all the office staff and the majority of the writers. 'Funny,' Kate said thoughtfully, 'that he doesn't marry—he's extremely attractive, as you'll discover.'

Carol said, 'He must be,' and regarded her salad. She could hardly say, I discovered that long before any of you existed for him—much to my sorrow—

Peter Tarrant, Elsie Norris, everyone, talked about Andy. Casual bits of conversation … 'I wonder what Andy will say to that?' … and at the end of the first week when the Watterly matter came up someone—perhaps it was Steve Hall, said, 'Well, Andy will be pleased with your management of that situation, Carol.'

It was Carol, easily, to everyone.

The Watterly situation hadn't been very difficult. Mrs Watterly was one of the oldest of the M. and H. stable of authors. She was a desiccated, acidulous female who wrote charming, fanciful romances of young married life and whose books, two a year, year in and year out, sold some thirty thousand copies annually. She lived alone in a staid hotel-club for women, dressed execrably, was reported to be miserly in the extreme and descended upon the office regularly to demand more advertising and publicity. Upon this occasion she had reminded Steve that her contract would expire with the publication of the next book and that she had half a mind not to renew it, having, as she primly confided, received tempting offers of larger advances and a really wide-awake publicity campaign.

Poor John Hogan and, of course, Elsie had struggled with her for years. She was a person whom it was almost impossible to publicize.

Carol took her to lunch. It was by sheer luck, she afterwards said, that she had discovered Mrs Watterly's passion for old fans. She had a collection of them in her suite and Carol went up to see them.

Sheer luck indeed. Desperately endeavoring to find something in which the Watterly was interested, Carol had tried everything from American glass to theater programs and at last,

37

grudgingly, Mrs Watterly had admitted the fans.

They were on the walls of her bedroom and living room, beautifully framed, superb ... priceless lace, delicate paintings, gem-inset handles, mother-of-pearl, tortoise shell. They were worth a fortune.

Pleased by Carol's interest, Mrs Watterly thawed. She said that many years ago her husband had given her the first fan ... she exhibited it. Carol thought, Husband? ... but that's impossible! She had paid little attention to the Mrs. After all, Laura Thurston was still Miss. But it appeared that Watterly had once existed in the flesh. His name had been Horace and he had been a banker, 'in the days when that meant something,' added his relict. It also appeared that Mrs Watterly's royalties went into fan collecting ... as Horace had left her 'more than adequately provided for, as my needs are modest.'

The fans might make good copy. Carol talked of photographers and of an exhibition ... there would be a Hobby Exhibition soon. Would Mrs Watterly lend her fans—they were of course insured? And other exhibitions could be arranged.

Mrs Watterly was coy. The fans were so— personal, she demurred. But Carol persuaded her. She owed it to her public, Carol said firmly; most people collected something and fellow collectors felt a great, warm, human bond. Readers would be thrilled to learn of Mrs Watterly's devotion to her hobby. Newspapers, women's pages, home magazines, and those devoted to collections and hobbies would be grateful for stories about Mrs Watterly's exciting interest ... 'delicate,' said Carol, wondering how far she could go in hyperbole, 'exquisite, fragile and lovely—like your books.'

When she was leaving the hotel Mrs Watterly said, 'Do call me Gwendolyn, my dear. As we are going to work together—'

It was her astonishing name. And the Watterly contract was saved.

Others popped up during that week, notably a gentleman named Banner whose explorations of the most unlikely parts of the world made news, lecture contracts, and books brimful of vitality and oomph. Banner could describe a new kind of fever as if it were a new brand of whisky and make his readers feel that they must go out immediately and get a case. Club-women worshiped him and little boys, after reading Banner on their schools' selected list, went forth equipped with a hunting knife, a flint, two bars of chocolate and a can of fruit juice and promptly lost themselves in the nearest woods, necessitating a great turnout of the neighbors and Boy Scouts and the complete collapse of their parents.

Banner was tall and lank, with burning eyes and a stentorian voice. He used them both with great effect. He always dressed for dinner in the jungle or desert, and he had been worshiped as a god by all manner of susceptible natives. Natives, thought Carol, upon encountering this hero, must be subnormal in intelligence. Mr Banner suffered from the my-God-I-haven't-seen-a-white-woman-in-months complex. He quite forgot that in order to return from wherever he had been he had eventually journeyed by civilized means ... boats, trains, airplanes ... and it was doubtful that all his traveling companions had been male or, if female, black.

He was a knee-presser. Carol, learning this at luncheon, was not at all surprised.

He wasn't, of course, difficult to publicize. He did it himself, every waking moment. But it would be interesting, she thought, to get a new angle on the gentleman. She had read a number of his clippings, and knew that upon his every return to Manhattan tired reporters had gone dutifully to his hotel to learn of the latest exploits. She could imagine them saying, 'Strike up the band, Banner's back.'

He took the war as a personal affront as it had narrowed his field of action. But there were still places in South America ... yes, next time he'd be off to South America. For the moment he was content to remain at home with Mrs Banner, long enough to become acquainted with the newest of his five children—born since his departure—and then to tour the tolerant

United States in his latest lecture series.

'It's a great bore,' he told Carol sadly and a wisp of curling black hair fell over his high bronzed brow, 'but people seem to like it.'

He spoke with animation of a tiger cub he had reared from infancy but had been forced to sell to a dealer. 'Followed me like a dog,' he said sentimentally. 'Tigers are so satisfactory, don't you think so, Miss Reid?'

Carol replied faintly that she preferred the domestic cat.

'How sweet,' he cried, 'how feminine.' His knee pressed hers emotionally. 'I adore cats.'

Well, here was a new angle. Cats. Cat shows. Siamese cats, alley cats. Great explorer loves cats...

When her first week ended she felt a little less anxious, a little less pushed, less breathless in her mind. Laura Thurston had approved. Gwendolyn Watterly would sign a new contract. Mr Banner and his cats would make the front page if Carol had to rent every cat in every pet-shop window in town. The staff had been more than helpful: Elsie Norris was definitely thawing and Miss Harris, Richard's secretary, had given her the accolade. She had said, 'You're doing all right.' Kate, who had been present, had smiled, in agreement. 'Andy will be delighted,' she said, 'I can't wait for him to get back.'

Andy, the fly in the amber; Andy, the unknown quantity. Although she had thought

41

about him so much since that day she had lunched at the Waldorf, she had been too busy and, at night too tired, to worry much. But as the time for his arrival drew uncomfortably near she became anxious. How would he look, what would he say, how would she feel when, for the first time in a decade, their eyes met and she heard his voice again?

She did not know and she was definitely afraid.

CHAPTER FOUR

Andrew Morgan returned from his cruise on the morning of May twenty-fifth. He felt more like himself than he had in a year, or certainly than he had since his bout of pneumonia which had pulled him down, left him thin, overtired and irascible, early in the winter. He had regained the lost weight, he was brown and ruddy and had had a very good time ... He had not wanted to take this six weeks, he had been more than willing to wait until summer. But his doctor had urged him, and so had Steve and Richard. They had reminded him that since he had come to the firm he had never taken a real vacation, a long weekend here, a week there, but nothing that amounted to anything. He could afford this time and so could they. 'Don't be so damned egotistic,' Steve had argued, 'we won't collapse without you.'

He was anxious to return to work. The last few days on the boat had bored him, he'd been restless. But the cruise had been fine, he'd enjoyed it. A good ship, excellent service, calm seas varied now and then by a sudden storm which was all right too. He was a good sailor and he had liked wave and wind, the brave staggering of the ship and her stout heart beating. He had made a friend or two and some pleasant acquaintances. He had seen some odd little places, palm trees, moonlight, old houses and wharves, strange people. He'd kissed a pretty girl, and they had both enjoyed it. He'd danced a good deal and the ship's pool was attractive. He'd played golf in Cuba and met an old college friend who was on a sugar plantation down there.

True to their pledged word, the occasional letters or cables which had reached him from his associates had not spoken of business except the cable about John Hogan. He'd felt badly at that. Hogan was a good fellow, and amiable. But inwardly Andrew was a little relieved by the way things had turned out. He'd been dissatisfied with the publicity department for a long time. Steve had agreed with him privately but Richard was slower, it took him longer to be won to newer methods and besides he had a strong sense of loyalty. This way, no one was hurt and Hogan, on his legacy, could retire to his little place on Long Island, raise ducks and collect first editions and phonograph records. He had never married, there was no one to be upset, after the novelty had worn off, at having him underfoot. With reasonable care, the doctors said he would live for years.

In the ordinary way of things Andrew would have looked for Hogan's successor, and having found a likely candidate, would have consulted his associates. But that had been taken out of his hands, and he was perfectly satisfied. He stood on the deck watching all the activity of docking and when he put his hand in his pocket for his pipe he encountered the crumpled flimsy paper of the cable. He took it out and read it over. The new head of publicity had been hired. A woman. He frowned a little, he wondered why a woman—? But that was nonsense, it was just being used to John for so long. He was glad that no one had suggested Elsie Norris. She'd been there years, long before Andrew himself. Possibly Richard had suggested her ... but if so, Steve would have vetoed the idea. Elsie was loyal, hard-working, excellent in routine matters. But her tongue was sharp, her patience thin, and she often antagonized people, authors, reporters ... also she lacked imagination and surely imagination was a quality greatly needed in a promotion job.

Richard had his pet economies. He could give lavish dinners, send lavish orchids, but when it came to telegrams and cables he grew increasingly stenographic. After reporting Hogan's resignation he had added, 'Hired young woman late Facts Hogan's job.'

'Late facts...' It had taken Andrew half a day to figure out what that meant. His reply must have startled Richard too. 'Better fact than fancy' he had cabled, with a light heart.

He was supposed to return to the office on the following Monday. Monday was a long way off. He'd go home, get himself straightened around, and turn up after luncheon. He grinned, remembering that Thursday afternoons were sacred to the weekly editorial meetings.

Sacred! With people popping in or dashing out and smoke ascending in clouds and Peter Tarrant bringing a new puzzle. Peter was practically puzzle crazy. Andrew's experience with Remsen and Company before coming to Maynard and Hall had been of large solemn sessions in the directors' room with everyone sitting rigid on high-backed chairs and the whole business of editorial conference conducted with pomp and circumstance and no room for pleasantries. But M. and H. was different. Everyone in the organization was welcome if they had anything to suggest. So the advertising department—plus puzzles—was apt to come along now and then, or someone from production or John Hogan...

He cabled that he'd be docking today and

45

would ring up when he reached home. No one would meet him, he wasn't a visiting author, ready for reporters, cameramen, a lecture trip. He was just Andrew Morgan, back from a holiday.

Millicent met him, however. Millicent Allen. She was there on the dock, under the letter M. Nice girl, Millicent, his heart warmed when he saw her.

She greeted him with a smile, and both hands. She said, 'It's been a long time. I've missed you, Andrew. Did you bring me my perfume?'

Yes, he had brought her that. The customs inspector pawed through the battered luggage. Cigars for the lads at M. and H., perfume for the gals, perfume for Millicent, and some curious costume jewelry. He couldn't run to the type of stuff Millicent wore, carelessly, but she liked junk, she would widen her eyes and say, 'Andrew, how amusing!'

It was hot today, very hot on the docks, people rushing around, women gasping with indignation as their small dishonesties were exposed, one by one, men arguing about liquor, taxis hooting...

Millicent looked cool, as always. A small girl, twenty-six, twenty-eight. He didn't know her age.

He had known her for over a year. Maynard and Hall had published her first book. Andrew was first to read it and he'd gone overboard

46

about it, delicate, brilliant, worldly ... without sentimentality, without tenderness, very honest. Rather like Millicent herself, her book.

She was writing her second. She had had some success with short stories. She'd be in Who's Who presently but for the moment the Social Register claimed her and Dun and Bradstreet listed Mr Allen.

Money, lots of it. The best schools, those which wore the tall chapeau with an air ... schools which taught you to pour tea, ride horseback and be kind to your inferiors. The best places, the right places, in town and out. The right clothes.

Millicent had made her debut properly, plenty of stags, not too much champagne, and even the most invincible gate crashers hadn't been able to make that grade. A tea for the older people, all very correct. A dinner dance for the younger fry. Not a splurge, it wasn't considered correct to splurge at that time. The words 'glamour' and 'girl' hadn't been teamed. Millicent had never sung in a night club, or hired a publicity man, or collected cards from night spots. But she had written a book which had horrified her parents no end.

Standing there, watching the customs man, Andrew remembered meeting Millicent. At a party—not an M. and H. party, just a party. He'd run into a man he hadn't seen for years, they'd lunched and had somehow collected several other people and someone had asked them to cocktails on the following day, he'd gone and there she'd been, ash-blond, arresting rather than pretty. Over the clamor, clink and chatter, she'd asked, lazily, 'Didn't someone tell me that you had something to do with publishing?' and he admitted it. Then she had said, 'Don't look now but, like everyone else, I've written a book.'

Two drinks and he had committed himself to read it.

Today he said:

'Nice of you to meet me . . . I didn't expect it.'

'If you had, I wouldn't. I've the car here. Looks as if you were through. Let's go.'

On the way uptown he talked about the trip, he asked her how the new book was coming, he deplored the fact that he had not heard from her.

'I cabled—twice, three times.'

'But you didn't write. I looked for mail at each stop.'

'I loathe writing,' she said with finality, 'even to you.'

She turned and smiled at him and he was aware of her self-contained charm. During the last decade he had met a number of women who had attracted him briefly . . . not seriously. Millicent Allen was not quite like any woman he had ever known. She had a considered brutality . . . well, perhaps brutality was not the word; she used a scalpel rather than a bludgeon.

She said:

'You are really very good-looking. Have I told you that before?'

'No. Thanks very much.'

'How old are you, Andrew? I don't believe I've ever asked.'

'Thirty-four, nearly thirty-five.'

She said, 'When I first met you I thought you were older.'

He said ruefully:

'I don't know why all the gray hair. Mine is not a family to turn gray young.'

'Have you a family?' she inquired. 'I don't know that, either. It's odd how little we know of each other.'

'A father,' he told her, 'a country doctor, upstate. A very grand person. You'd like him.'

'Would he like me?' she inquired, her hands deft on the wheel, her eyes alert.

He said slowly:

'Perhaps not at first. Later he'd fall in love with you.'

She had an air of waiting, as if he had not completed his sentence. Should he finish it, should he say, 'as I have'? But he was not in love with her. He liked her, she disturbed him. But as for that head-over-heels, that lunatic enchantment ... he laughed inwardly and shook his head. Was that why he hadn't married during these last nine years, had he expected the same crazy business, the curious loss of identity? Romantic love. Perhaps the

49

cliché was right, perhaps it happened only once. Possibly he wasn't ready for it yet, possibly that's what occurs to the men you know who at forty or forty-five, at fifty, at sixty even, suddenly go off the deep end ... looking for, thinking they had regained, the ecstasy which properly belongs to youth.

'Why are you smiling?' Millicent asked him.

'I like being home.'

'We're nearly there. Will you lunch, later?'

'Usual place,' he agreed. 'Can you make it twelve-thirty? I'm going to the office.'

'I thought you weren't due till next week.'

'I'm not. When Richard says six weeks, he means six weeks. But I'm anxious to get back.'

She said carelessly:

'There are changes. I dropped in yesterday to talk over the new masterpiece with Steve. I'll need your help, by the way, Andrew. I seem to have come to a full stop.'

'I'll help if I can. I don't promise.'

'You were invaluable last time. Why not this? I'm still grateful. Andrew, why don't you write?'

'There was a time when I thought I could. Now I don't want to, I've found what I want to do. What did you mean, changes?'

'But you must know ... I mean the girl who has taken John Hogan's place,' she said.

'Everything happened while I was away. Did you meet her?' he asked curiously.

She said, 'Briefly. We are lunching together

tomorrow. She has ideas for publicity releases, and wants to talk them over with me. She seems very keen on her job.' She looked at him sidelong as the car slid to a stop. She added, 'She's very attractive, by the way.'

'Good,' said Andrew heartily. 'I'm rather proud of the fact that none of the women in the organization would frighten little children.'

The doorman came out, with words of welcome. Andrew's bags were seized. He promised, standing at the curb, 'See you later.'

Millicent smiled and drove away and Andrew followed his luggage into the house.

An old apartment on Riverside Drive. He liked it there, the sweep of the river, he liked his rooms, uncompromisingly masculine in atmosphere. He had lived here for eight years, looked after by the same servant, an elderly, capable man who cleaned, cooked and valeted.

Howie opened the door, beaming, a lean shambling Negro with a shock of curly white hair, and less accent than Andrew's southern cousins.

'Hi,' said Andrew. 'Glad to see me, Howie?'

Howie was very glad and said so. Coffee would be ready in a moment. He'd ordered cream and the morning paper. He'd procured a supply of Andrew's pipe tobacco. There was mail, a lot of it. He added that Andrew looked just fine.

Andrew drank his coffee and glanced at the paper. Howie was unpacking. The telephone

51

rang and it was Richard Maynard calling from his home in Connecticut.

'So you're back. How do you feel?'

'The way I ought to feel. How are you, Richard?'

'One foot still in the grave. I want you to have a checkup before you return to the office, Andrew.'

'Do you insist?'

'I do. Unless you have something else on your mind, I'll pick you up tomorrow afternoon and bring you out here for the weekend. We'll talk. Steve will be up. I'm not going in today,' Maynard told him, 'I've had a touch of sinus ... Better let Steve know you're back.'

Andrew hung up, smiling. He thought, stretching his long legs, that few men were as content in their job as he. Ten years ago he would have laughed aloud at the thought of the salary Maynard and Hall paid him. Chicken feed, he would have said. Ten years ago he had thought in terms of hundreds of thousands. Ten years ago he had been a rich young man, on paper. Funny how your ideas change, and what you believed necessities, what you considered luxuries.

On his way to meet Millicent he dropped into his doctor's office and found that earnest, hard-working gentleman free. When, a little later, he was leaving, Dr Bridges whacked him soundly on the shoulder.

'That did the trick,' he said; 'you're in good shape. I congratulate myself. You see, I spend part of each day telling patients they must get away, go south, take a trip, take a cruise. Those who say they can't afford time or money or both, are the ones who need it. Those who jump at the chance generally don't need it at all.'

'Then why give them the prescription?' inquired Andrew.

'Oh, in such cases I am baffled and don't know what else to prescribe,' Bridges admitted.

Andrew waited five minutes for Millicent in the small French restaurant, in the Fifties. When she came, it was with her unhurried air. He had the perfume for her, and some beautifully embroidered handkerchiefs. She put them in her enormous soft handbag and they sat on the bright red bar stools to drink their cocktails. Afterwards, they lunched.

He said, sighing:

'Someday I wish you'd astonish me.'

'Perhaps I will—someday. But in this case, how?'

'By ordering a large steak, a lamb stew or a whole turkey. I yearn to meet a woman with an appetite.'

'Have you ever known one? We speak, of course, of an appetite for food.'

He said, regarding Millicent's small, unadorned order of broiled sweetbreads:

'I once knew a girl who could wrap herself around a T bone steak, a chocolate cake, a quarter of an apple pie alamode, and love it.'

She said, laughing:

'She probably weighs one hundred and eighty on the hoof—'

'Her weight never changed, while I knew her.' He laughed, remembering. 'She was as greedy as a good child.'

'How long did you know her?' asked Millicent.

'Less than three years.'

'Recently?'

'Long ago.'

'Look her up now,' advised Millicent. 'She will be very fat, she will have a hearty husband and six children.'

'I wonder,' said Andrew.

Millicent wasn't interested in girls with appetites for chocolate cake. She was saying:

'Miss Reid wants me to have new photographs taken, she doesn't like the ones she has on file. I think she's right, Andrew. I didn't like them either ... you did, if you remember.'

He asked, 'Miss who?'

'Reid. Why?'

He asked, 'That the new publicity gal ... what's the rest of her name?'

'I don't know,' said Millicent. 'I didn't ask. I saw her for only a moment.'

He hadn't thought of Carol for years. Yes,

now and then he thought of her as he had when he'd listened to Millicent's order. He knew always what Millicent would order, what most of the women with whom he dined and lunched would order. Chops, or a sweetbread, a salad, compote of fruit. Some seemed to live on black coffee and melba toast. He recalled a writer he had known when he was with Remsen and Company. A big lush woman who wrote big lush novels. Then she began to worry about her figure ... a clear case of locking the barn door too late. She went into retreat, she dieted, steam-bathed, paraffin-packed and emerged like a sword from its scabbard. Since then, melba toast and coffee. Her disposition had suffered and also her writing. Her books were now as thin, as acidulous, as empty as herself.

He didn't think often of Carol. When he visited his father he did, because Dr Morgan always spoke of her, he had been very fond of her. On the cruise she had crossed his mind fleetly. Once when he saw a girl with dark hair and a pure, strong line from brow to chin, once when he was buying Millicent's perfume and remembered that Carol's preference had been white lilac, and again when standing alone at the rail of the ship on a quiet moonlight night, watching the water break away, white and hissing, watching the silver indifference of stars, he had remembered that Carol planned that they would travel together someday. Well, that hadn't happened ... a lot of things hadn't happened.

When he thought of her it was without rancor or regret, as if the time they had known, and been important to each other belonged in another era, as indeed it had, belonged, almost in a past incarnation, a different dimension.

'You look sober, suddenly,' Millicent remarked. '*Weltschmerz?*'

Reid. But she wouldn't be Miss Reid. She'd be Mrs Something-or-other. He wondered if she had children. You'd expect the supposition to affect him emotionally, to afford him at least one pang. It didn't. She could have the six Millicent had suggested and he not care. He wondered why he hadn't looked her up in recent years. There'd be someone who'd know where she was. The last time they had been in touch was when her father died. He had written her and sent flowers and had had a restrained note in return. He had not seen her in all these years, which was odd considering that sooner or later you meet everyone you know in New York. Perhaps she wasn't in New York. At first, he had looked for her consciously, in order to avoid her ... at parties, in theaters, in restaurants. He had succeeded in dodging most of the people they had mutually known. It wasn't hard, the conditions preceding the crash had brought them together, the conditions subsequent to October, 1929, had separated them. That particular little group, he reflected, was probably scattered all over Manhattan by now, if not over the United States.

Millicent was frowning. Her thin curving lips, which she painted very brightly, were drawn. She was growing impatient. He came back to her with a start.

'Sorry,' he said.

She removed her superfluous sables and laid them on a chair. She said:

'That's all right. What were you thinking about? You looked rather different.'

'I was thinking about myself, of what I was like when I graduated from college and went into a broker's office to make my fortune.'

'You must have been rather sweet,' she said softly, 'I wish I'd known you.'

'I was a simple-minded young ass,' he said; 'you wouldn't have liked me. And it was before your time.'

'Did you make your fortune?' she inquired.

'Certainly.' He smiled at her. 'Tell me about the book,' he said, 'and what's wrong?'

Animation, color transformed her, her eyes shone. She leaned forward, her elbows on the table.

'I can't get it right,' she said; 'it breaks down in the middle, I can't seem to define the relationship between Katharine and her husband or get into words the shock, the impact of Paul's personality on the entire household.'

He listened as her light, unemphasized voice ran on, halting her at one point or another to

57

ask a question, to make a suggestion. He had forgotten Carol. He was back where he belonged, at work. He had almost forgotten Millicent.

CHAPTER FIVE

It was rather late when he reached the office. The editorial conference was in full swing. Jessie, the girl at the switchboard, greeted him with rapture. Tarrant, coming out of the conference room, whooped like an Indian. Everyone he met stopped him to wring his hand as he made his way to his office, between Richard's and Steve's. His secretary was there, glaring at some mail.

'Hello, Kate.'

She looked at him open-mouthed. She said feebly:

'You're not back till Monday.'

'Yet here I am. What goes on, where's everyone?'

'In the library,' she said. 'Mr Maynard's not here today but—'

He asked:

'Been having a good time with me away? No work...'

She said, 'There's always work in this shop,' without resentment, and he laughed. They understood each other. Kate Byrd was a good-looking, capable girl, with a husband who worked in an advertising agency. Andrew liked her. He liked all the M. and H. secretaries, they pinch-hit for one another on vacations, and every one of them had been there longer than he had. He drew a deep breath, went to the window and looked out on Madison Avenue below him. He liked being back. He liked this place, its efficiency, the congenial atmosphere, the lack of office politics. Less here than in most organizations, much less than at Remsen and Company. He liked the informality, which was part of Steve Hall's contribution to the firm. First names and no nonsense. Damned few annoyances, in the actual working of the machine itself and, oddly enough, practically no office romance. One of the boys in the accounting department had married one of the typists and one of the production men had married Jessie's predecessor at the switchboard. But most of the youngsters looked for their romance out of working hours and there was none of this secretary-boss business. He grinned, reflecting that Kate would have laughed in his face if he'd ever started anything with her and that Steve's wife and Richard's were plenty able to hold their own with any office siren. For that matter, M. and H. didn't go in for sirens although they enjoyed, visually, what the gods provided and were grateful that none of the feminine staff would give a clock repairer any work.

Kate was talking about letters. She had saved some, she said, which required his personal attention. She'd answered them. 'I said you were away, would be back next week. The rest is finished business.'

He broke in, idly, sitting on the edge of his desk:

'I'm not here till next week,' he reminded her. 'What about the new member of the staff?'

'Miss Reid?'

'That's right. What's she like?'

Kate said:

'She hasn't been here very long, but everyone likes her. She's begun to make things hum. Mrs Watterly—remember how she and John used to battle? Well, she's delighted. I mean it. She's purring, like a kitten in cream.'

'Kitten!' repeated Andrew. 'You amaze me.'

'You wouldn't want me to say cat, would you? Miss Reid discovered that hobby of hers—you know, old fans. I think everyone here has known about it for a thousand years but no one paid any attention...'

'It's a good thing Sally Rand didn't yearn to write.'

Kate giggled. She went on, 'Anyway, Miss Reid found out and she's managed to wangle a syndicated feature story out of it, so Mrs Watterly's thrilled.'

'Good for Miss Reid.' He asked, 'By the way, what's her—'

The telephone rang on his desk and he

60

waved Kate over. He said, going to the door, 'I'll be in Monday. Use your own judgment.'

He walked into the library. Steve, Tarrant, Elsie Norris, Olga James, Heckman, some of the younger fry—and Carol.

She was sitting there, facing the door. Her dark hair curled softly about her temples and ears. The last time he had seen her it had been shingled, flat to her head, the prevalent boyish bob. She wore a black linen suit with a tailored shirt of an odd green-blue. She wore lipstick, but not as much as he remembered. No rouge, no eye stuff.

She saw him standing there, at the door. Tall, as she remembered, a little heavier. His hair was quite gray. His face was startlingly brown, there were lines she had never seen before.

She thought, It's funny, I don't feel a thing. This might have been any man I'd once known. I recognize him, that's all. I don't feel sorry, I don't feel glad...

He thought, You read about these things... haven't I read about them a million times? They always talk about shock. I don't experience shock. She's grown up, she's more attractive than she was, in a way.

The others were on their feet, crowding around him. Steve was whacking him on the back, everyone was talking at once. Carol rose, and stood over by the window watching. She was smiling faintly. He saw, it irritated him, he

61

wanted to slap her. Where had she learned to smile like that? When he knew her she hadn't learned. She'd smiled all over her face like a kid, laughed from the bottom of her flat little stomach, cried, when she cried, uproariously, with sniffles and sobs and gulps, like a child.

Steve was apologizing, dragging him over to the window, saying their names . . . Carol Reid. Andrew Morgan. Explaining Carol, looking at her as if he had created her, saying something about her work, and that she was sitting in on this conference because—

Andrew wasn't listening. He held out his hand and Carol put hers in it. Carol said:

'We know each other. Hello, Andy.'

'Hello, Carol,' he said. He released her hand and stood away, his hands in his pockets. He commented:

'Lord, this is funny.'

'Isn't it?' said Carol. 'When they told me about you . . . I wasn't sure it *was* you, you know.'

'Same here,' said Andrew. 'You're looking very well.'

Steve interrupted, looking from one to the other. He asked:

'What's this . . . reunion in Manhattan . . . how long since you've seen each other?'

'Between nine and ten years,' said Carol; 'silly, isn't it?'

Tarrant, the irrepressible, asked, offering Andrew a cigarette, 'Do we witness the ghost

62

of an old romance? You know me, inveterate reader of mysteries, even those we publish. Or am I wrong?'

'Elementary, my dear Watson,' said Andrew absently; 'old romance, of course.'

'Very old,' agreed Carol sedately.

'Those things do happen,' said Steve; 'we just don't publish them all. Well, now that you're here, Andrew, put your feet under the table and listen to our current griping. I shudder at the thought of what the production department's going to have on its mind at its next meeting.'

Andrew sat down opposite Carol. He thought, This isn't really happening. It struck him as immeasurably comic. He laughed aloud, in the wrong place. Carol's eyes encountered his and he knew that she was thinking along much the same lines.

The conference ended, people went back to their offices, but Steve detained Andrew and Peter Tarrant. There was something on his mind, he said, an advertising problem, not editorial. 'Stay here, Andrew, and give us the benefit of your sea-swept opinion.'

Later, Andrew walked back to Steve's office with him. Steve asked:

'Going to Greenwich tomorrow?'

'Yes ... and you?'

'Tude and I will be up Saturday. Some sort of doing tomorrow night which we can't duck. Funny your knowing Carol Reid.'

63

Well, Carol had given him his cue. If she'd wanted to be explicit, she could have been. It wasn't up to him. Andrew said, with genuine indifference:

'Yes, wasn't it?'

'What sort of girl is she?' asked Steve.

'I wouldn't know,' Andrew answered honestly; 'ten years, or damned near it, is a long time. I imagine she's changed.'

'People don't change. Or do they?' asked Steve. 'I must think that out. Basically, I mean.'

They had reached his office, they went in and Mitty Lenard hailed Andrew. She said she was glad to see him back.

'We all are,' said Steve. 'About Carol Reid, what was she like—was she working when you knew her?'

'No,' said Andrew. 'Her people had a lot of money. Some of it survived the crackup. More of it went with the Kreuger incident. Her father died of that. I lost track of her then—before, really,' he added.

'She's held several responsible jobs,' said Steve. 'Wait a minute. I've got it all down here somewhere ... where the hell is it?'

He found it, in the welter of a desk which his secretary was pledged to let alone. Andrew took the sheet of paper and ran his eye down the items. 'I wouldn't have believed it,' he murmured. He put the paper aside. 'You never know.'

64

'Seems capable and likable,' said Steve. 'Poor old Elsie had the fur the wrong way. That's understandable. In ten days she's smoothed down. Reid has the magic touch. Of course, Elsie is still waiting for her to pull a boner. Recently she saved the new Watterly contract—'

Andrew grinned.

'I know. Kate told me.'

'A good job,' said Steve fervently. 'God knows that as far as I'm concerned, L. Gwendolyn Watterly is a pain in the...' he looked at Mitty and ended meekly, 'neck. But she turns out three a year and we sell 'em. How we sell 'em! She always threatens, we don't believe her, but this time it looked like the McCoy. Along comes Reid, finds out about the fans and we're set. L. Gwendolyn told me yesterday it was the first time in twenty years she had obtained the type of publicity she thought suitable, dignified and interesting.'

'I lunched with Millicent Allen,' said Andrew.

Steve whistled.

'A fast worker,' he said ambiguously.

'Which of us? Don't answer without advice of counsel. She seemed quite happy about Carol. Something about pictures.'

'Carol,' said Steve, 'can handle the ladies. Because of her work with the charity outfit, I suppose. I wouldn't know. She's all right when it comes to men. Banner is back from Tibet.'

'My God.'

'I thought you'd feel that way. He blew in, full of lamas, Yogi, mystery, and what not. He has a list of the new fevers which he's acquired. And a manuscript ... I haven't read it yet, Richard took it home with him. God's gift to clubwomen is with us once more and his poor wife is in for another half year of waiting on him and then bidding him farewell when he goes elsewhere and she stays home to have the current baby. Did you know that he is crazy about cats?'

'I knew he was crazy.'

'Your friend Carol discovered that too. She has him judging some sort of amateur show, for charity, next week. She's also coaxed a Siamese kitten from some big dealer, as a welcome-home present. Lord knows what Mrs Banner will do with the brute when he departs. He's having his picture taken with it, a skull and a couple of dinosaur eggs...'

'Steve, you ass.'

'Something like that, ask Carol. Anyway, he took her to lunch and has since confided in me that if it weren't for Mrs Banner...'

They both laughed.

Half an hour later Andy went back to his office. He regarded Kate in her cubicle. He asked, 'Mind ringing Miss Reid and asking her if she'd come here for a minute?'

He was standing by the window when Carol came in. Kate had gone off somewhere.

He said:

'I don't mean to take advantage of you—sending for you, like a higher-up. But I didn't want to talk to you with Elsie looking at us from her desk. And we should talk, don't you think?'

'I do,' she said calmly.

'Would you rather talk over a dinner table?'

She smiled. 'I'm sorry,' she told him, 'but I have an engagement tonight. I'd like a rain check, if I may.'

He said, 'Thanks—and I mean it, Carol.'

Carol asked frankly:

'Did you expect another attitude? That would be stupid of us. We're here, we're working together. Is there any valid reason why we can't?'

'None that I know of, none at all.'

'When Mr Maynard spoke to me about you,' she said, 'and I wondered if it *was* you, I thought perhaps I'd better not take the job. But I wanted it, Andy.'

Her eyes were direct. She looked as if she expected him to understand. There was no appeal in them.

He nodded. 'Sure,' he agreed, 'why not?'

She said, 'It's been a long time, we've changed. At least I know I have and I assume you have . . . or I wouldn't find you here, would I?'

'No,' he replied, 'you wouldn't.'

She smiled at him.

'I thought that it might be very awkward. I was frightened. When Peter Tarrant came barging into the library to say you were back and he expected you'd be right along, I was so scared I felt sick at my stomach. The minute you walked in I—I felt nothing.'

He said, 'That's the way I felt. Or didn't.'

'You see?' she said. 'It sounds stupid and conventional, but I mean it—I have nothing but the most friendly—'

'Skip it,' he suggested. 'We'll get along all right. I'm going up to the Maynards' tomorrow for the weekend. Back Monday. We'll have dinner. Okay?'

'Okay,' she agreed.

He said, 'We'll have to catch up on a lot of things: your mother—'

'Mother died, Andy,' she told him, 'over a year ago.'

His face was grave. He said:

'I'm sorry, Carol. I didn't know. I missed seeing it in the papers. You would have heard from me if I had.'

'I'm sure of that,' she said.

'Carol, wait a minute. You gave me my cue a little while ago. I'm not arguing, I'm just curious. Why didn't you tell them—Steve, Richard, anyone—the truth about us?'

'I don't know, Andy. It just happened that way. I wasn't sure it was you. I said I'd known someone of that name ... Do you want me to tell them?'

He shrugged.

'Makes no difference to me. I didn't know you'd kept your maiden name.'

'The court let me resume it,' she said. She turned, with her hand on the door. 'It would be difficult to tell them, Andy, that we were married once upon a time. You see, I can't believe it myself. Because now we meet again, we're two different people.'

CHAPTER SIX

Carol reached home a little late, and looking at her watch shrugged, resigned. She'd be late, she would keep Kim Anderson waiting—well, it didn't matter, Kim was a pleasant, unimpatient person. She had known him for something over a year and they had seen each other with moderate frequency ever since.

She ran a tub, creamed her face, hopped in, and lay soaking in the hot, scented water. She must remember to ask Bess where she'd bought the bath salts. They'd come from Bess, hadn't they? Bess had a way of turning up with small surprises ... 'an *un*birthday present,' she'd say gravely, 'many happy returns of nothing very much.'

Nice salts, smelling, when released in the hot water, like a spring garden. Carol hadn't been able to find them in any shop. Maybe she rolls her own, she thought, laughing at the idea of Bess solemnly concocting bath salts in her spare time.

Reluctantly, she reached for tissue, wiped the cream from her face and rose to stand bravely under a tepid shower which gradually turned to liquid ice. You're lucky, my girl, she informed herself, toweling vigorously, a job you like, a place of your own, hot and cold water laid on...

Dressing, in a navy print frock, a thin wool navy coat lined with the print, a silly little sailor, she remembered with amazement that she hadn't thought of Andy for hours. Of course, after she left his office she had thought about him. She had thought, How strange to feel so little; she had thought, How wonderful. If further, belated evidence had been needed to show her the wisdom of her decision nearly ten years ago she had it now. How incredibly stupid of her to have worried. She looked back upon her uncertainty, her agony and embarrassment of mind which had almost decided her to give up the Maynard and Hall offer, with astonishment.

Andy, she had decided, was nice. He would be pleasant to work with, he would be fun as a friend. She had reflected, brushing her hair, that she and Andy had never been friends. That was an interesting thought. They had fallen in love so promptly, so 'all out,' that they hadn't had time for friendship and they had not lived

70

together long enough to grow into it as, she supposed, good marriages do. No. Their entire relationship had been one of *Sturm und Drang* ... all emotion, excitement, passionate loving, violent quarreling, tears, misery, unhappiness, earthquakes. They had fought, sworn a truce, kissed under the white flag and been reconciled, until next time. They hadn't had a moment for friendship, really. Now they had all the time in the world. It would be interesting, she thought, turning an ex-lover, an ex-husband into a friend.

Or, perhaps you couldn't. Perhaps the old relationship would stand there as a barrier?

Why should it?

She was almost ready when Kim rang the bell and she went to answer it. He stood there smiling at her, a personable young man, with sleek blond hair, battered down until its natural wave was disciplined, nice blue eyes, and a stocky, athletic build. He wore clothes as well as any man she knew and had a much better job than any of those who also rang her doorbell. At thirty-three, he was an executive in one of the big broadcasting corporations.

She cried, 'Come in, Kim, I'll just get my hat—'

Kim obeyed and stood turning over the pages of a magazine while she vanished into the bedroom for the final touches. When she reappeared he looked at her with pleasure.

'You're prettier than ever—the job must

71

agree with you.'

'I bet you say that to all the girls. Let's go, shall we?'

'I don't say it to all the girls,' he said reproachfully, 'only to ten per cent ... and they don't rate it, really. Just you. I thought, the old place?'

Not very old, as their friendship was hardly aged in the wood, but this restaurant was one they both liked, and one which few of Carol's friends could afford. Very upper drawer. No prices on the menu. Movie stars, radio highlights, Broadway fashionables, deftly sprinkled among the purely social names, like stars among planets. Mr Anderson received a welcome which placed him halfway between the malefactors of great wealth and the currently celebrated. He and Carol had their cocktails sitting on the slippery round red stools at the little crowded bar and were afterwards conducted to a table in the corner. It was small and a little cramped but definitely a table to be coveted.

'I thought we'd be quieter here,' said Kim, 'but perhaps you're tired of it ... we might have gone to Twenty-One.'

'I like this. How have you been, Kim?' she asked him. 'I haven't seen you for a week.'

'Two,' he corrected her, 'and I'm anxious to hear about the job. Let's order, shall we?'

After they had ordered Carol leaned back and sighed. She felt relaxed and comfortable.

Pretty women, attractive men, hurrying waiters, the sounds of laughter and conversation. All very pleasant.

'Now, about that job?'

'It's good,' she told him; 'I like it. The people are swell, and the setup—I don't know, it has a special flavor, informal, hard working, congenial. I'll be very happy there, I think.'

He said, 'That's bad news.'

'Why, Kim—' She broke off, looking at a blond woman advancing toward them, followed by a much older, rather grim-looking gentleman who, without lifting a finger, exuded an aura of economic royalty. One could almost hear the sharp clash of scissors severing coupons. And his progress was attended by a retinue of captains and waiters that was almost overpowering.

Kim Anderson said, low, 'That's Ollin Jones,' but Carol was concerned with Mr Jones's companion. She said, 'And that's Millicent Allen,' just as Millicent turned, slightly, and saw her.

Millicent was wearing a dinner suit, black, superbly tailored, and fitted. Pearls in her ears and around her throat, a yellow orchid at her lapel, a blouse of cascading lace, very Cavalier. She smiled at Carol and said, 'Miss Reid—how nice—'

She stopped, waving Mr Jones forward imperiously. Kim rose, impressed, and Millicent sat down.

73

'Just for a moment. How pleasant to see you,' she told Carol after the introductions had been effected. 'I was talking about you today at luncheon.'

'You were? To whom?'

'Andrew Morgan ... just back from his cruise. Possibly you've met him, by now.'

Carol said, 'Yes, today,' and waited.

So Millicent had lunched with Andy. Right off the boat, she reflected. And they had talked of her. Evidently Andy had offered no confidences ... perhaps, she thought, he hadn't known at the time that his new publicity woman was his ex-wife. Possibly Millicent hadn't even mentioned her name. Or, if she had ... She could imagine Millicent's light voice running on, 'that new girl in the office, Miss Reid ...' Well, there were lots of Reids. 'A bruised reed shall he not break,' she thought absurdly, and 'Man is but a thinking reed.' Wasn't that the title of a Rebecca West?

Millicent Allen was saying:

'I gave you an excellent build-up.' She turned to Kim Anderson, smiling. 'Andrew Morgan,' she explained, 'is managing editor of the firm of publishers which recently—and very brilliantly—employed Miss Reid and which—not so brilliantly—publishes me. I have missed Andrew,' she told Carol, 'he has been the greatest help imaginable, ever since I first signed with Maynard and Hall. Seeing him today, talking shop, was a direct answer to

74

prayer.' She added, 'I'm very new at this game,' and rose. 'I mustn't keep you from your dinner,' she said, 'and I'm being very rude to my host. Don't forget, lunch tomorrow,' she reminded Carol, smiled at Kim who had leaped automatically to his feet, and departed.

'Quite a girl,' said Carol; 'I noticed you were practically spellbound.'

Kim sat down. He said, ignoring that:

'Andrew Morgan? Good Lord, Carol, isn't that the—?'

She interrupted mildly:

'Exactly.'

'The man you were married to,' he finished. 'I can't believe it.'

She said, laughing, 'How flattering of you to remember. I had forgotten that I ever told you his name.'

He said, 'Once early in our acquaintance we sat up half the night growing confidential over our pasts.'

Carol poked at her jellied soup. It quivered but she did not. She said:

'I remember. At the Baryons' studio party. I drank one of the famous Baryon rum specials. Only one, I beg you to remember. And afterwards...'

'We sat together on a couch,' he said, 'and watched two incredible people executing a rhumba and you told me that no, you weren't married, but that you had been and I said I would like to wring his damned neck, and what

75

was his damned name and you said Morgan and I said, Not the banker and you said, No, Andrew, and I said, wasn't there a pirate—?'

They looked at each other and laughed and Carol said, 'I remember. You told me all about the dark girl, half Spanish or something, who had done you wrong and how you hated all women and how you thought maybe radio was here to stay.'

He said, 'We've had fun together, haven't we?' Then he scowled at her, 'But I don't like it.'

'Fun?'

'Your working in the same office with Morgan.'

'Oh, hush,' she said, 'don't be absurd. He's nothing to me, nor I to him.'

'But how you could deliberately—'

'Kim, I didn't. He was away when I first went to work—you heard what Millicent Allen said. He just reached home today. I didn't know when I took the job that—'

'That's crazy!'

'Well, not at the very first. Then when I did find out … it seemed very stupid,' she said defensively, 'to pass up a chance like that just because a man to whom I had once been married…'

'You saw him today for the first time then?'

'I did.'

'And what—?'

'Oh, good heavens,' she said, exasperated,

76

'he was as astonished as I had been when first I knew. But we didn't swoon or knock each other down or call out the National Guard. Do be sensible, Kim. We're not in Victoria's reign, you know. This is a new era. All Billy Rose and Orson Welles. Victoria is dead, so is Mrs Grundy, and instead we have *My Day*.'

Kim grinned sheepishly.

'Sorry,' he said, 'I was jealous.'

'Well, that's a frank admission,' said Carol, 'if a little on the lunatic side.'

'That's what you think. Maybe you'll change your mind. Tell me about the blond iceberg who lingered at our table for a moment. I have a slight case of pneumonia coming on. Mind if I have a Scotch?'

'Have two,' she said cordially, 'and drink them both. She's a Maynard and Hall author. Not the type who plaintively wires for a slight advance against royalties. She's practically rolling in the ill-gotten wealth of her ancestors. Seems unfair, doesn't it?' she added thoughtfully. 'Money, looks, charm, and a gift ... because she has one definitely. Writes very well. Did you read her first book ... *Without an Echo*?'

'Oh, that! For Pete's sake ... decidedly a woman's book,' he said uneasily.

'You'd like to think so,' she said. 'It isn't, of course. Too frank for the average man,' she added, 'shows 'em up.'

'If men are like—' He looked across the

room and saw Mr Jones studying the wine list.

'Is she married?'

'No. Pleased?'

'I was thinking of Jones. He has as much reputation as money—the money's good but the reputation's bad.'

'I fancy,' said Carol, smiling, 'that Miss Allen can take care of herself—and Mr Jones too.'

He said soberly:

'He collects jades.'

Carol laughed. She liked Kim. He was immensely entertaining. She liked his quick mind, his humor, his occasional audacity, and the pleasant, not too obvious, confidence his success had given him. She was not in the least in love with him nor could he provide her with any of the various substitutes for love ... the quick lunches which temporarily still normal hunger. He had kissed her a time or two, lightly enough, but still with sufficient emotion to prove to her that he was not for her.

She enjoyed being with him, he was a most agreeable companion. Once or twice she had believed him on the verge of a serious declaration and had managed to avoid it deftly. She hoped it would never come to that.

She said, 'Tell me what you've been doing.'

She was a good and intelligent listener and she knew something about his work. He was still talking when the coffee arrived. They had lingered over dinner and many of the diners were already departing, bound for the theater. Others were coming in, for late dinner. And Carol said idly:

'Thursday. Do you believe it's ever maid's night out for the habitués of this place?'

He said, 'I meant to ask you if you wanted to go to a show—I can always get seats.'

'How too arrogant,' she murmured. 'No, let's sit and talk and then take a bus ride or something. It's a lovely evening.'

'Any desire to drop in to a broadcast?'

'None whatever, thank you. You've taken me to a good many and I've been hopelessly disillusioned by most of them.'

'A bus ride it is,' he said cheerfully, and called for the check. Signing it, leaving the not quite exorbitant tip, he said, 'I'm still worried about this job of yours.'

'Why?' She thought, I hope to heaven he doesn't introduce the topic of Andy again.

'You'll be so damned busy,' he said.

'My dear man,' said Carol, 'I hope I shall be. Otherwise, the ax. Maynard and Hall didn't hire me as window dressing.'

'It would have been a good idea. I wish you could sing or act or something.'

She said soothingly, 'Well, I can't. What's the matter, do you find me dull? Should I break into an aria over coffee or perhaps declaim a little Browning with the salad?'

He said crossly, 'Idiot! I meant, if you could, I'd get you a radio job and keep you under my eye all the time.'

'It would be dreadful,' she said serenely, 'being under anyone's eye. Sounds creepy.'

They went out and walked for a time down Park, over to Madison, looking in the windows. And finally over to Fifth where they hailed a bus. Climbing upstairs, finding a seat, he was grumbling.

'A hansom would be more romantic,' he said.

'I'm always so sorry for the horses ... they must all be half dead, of old age and carbon monoxide.'

Riding along, Carol looked from the window, never tired of the spectacle of Fifth Avenue at night. She had almost forgotten Kim when she realized he was still talking—

'I know what publicity work entails ... running here and there, most of your evenings not your own any more ... I—'

'You are very old-hen tonight,' she said, amused. 'Am I to consider myself a chicken at my age?'

'That's just it.'

'What?'

'Your age. Carol, you're only thirty, you're wasting your life, you—'

'Grandma!'

He said, low, 'I don't suppose a bus is the most perfect setting, but here goes. I've been trying to muster my courage all evening. You know I'm in love with you, so—will you marry me, Carol?'

She was sorry, and genuinely touched. She liked Kim. She shook her head and looked at him gravely.

'No, Kim.'

'But...'

She said, 'I'm not in love with you.'

'I love you enough for two.'

'It's never enough for two,' she told him.

He said disconsolately:

'It took me eight years to get over the last time I was in love. I've had a lot of fun in that time. I thought I'd never want to marry. I believed I'd grow into one of those amiable, paunchy old bachelors who are asked everywhere, for whom people are sorry. But I'd never be sorry for myself. I'd like my life. Weekends in other people's houses, a place of my own and a garden. Florida, the Bahamas, in the winter, after I retired, and footloose summers. The right sort of flat, the right sort of servants ... I command an excellent salary and earn every bit of it. I've even saved ... I have a backlog of bonds which my father left me. I've one sister, and you'd like her.'

'I know, the one who lives in England.'

'I hope to take her kids for the duration,' he said abstractedly. 'Carol, look ... we could be happy together, I swear it. We talk the same language. And I'm crazy about you. This isn't one of those sober, suitable things. I've missed you damnably these last weeks—'

81

She said slowly, 'I'm sorry, Kim, it's no good.'

'You can't be so definite.'

'I can,' she said, 'I mean it.'

He said angrily, 'If you hadn't seen Morgan again—'

'Don't be silly,' she said sharply. 'Andy has nothing to do with it ... or with me.'

She turned and looked at him, and added, after a moment:

'Please, Kim, we won't discuss it any more. I'm touched, I'm flattered—what woman wouldn't be?—but that's all.'

He said, 'This won't be the last time.'

'I'm afraid it must,' she said.

'What on earth do you mean?' he demanded.

'Don't shout,' she said; 'people are looking at us. Let's get out, Kim, and take a taxi back to the apartment.'

CHAPTER SEVEN

In the taxi—

'Do you mean to tell me,' he asked her incredulously, 'that I'm not going to see you again?'

She said regretfully:

'Not if I can help it, Kim.'

'But why?' He was almost speechless with misery and rage. '*Why?* It doesn't make sense.'

She said, 'If you care for me as much as you say you do . . .'

'You doubt it?'

'No, my dear. If you do,' she went on, 'it wouldn't be fair to you . . . and I don't like being unfair.'

He said, 'You might change your mind.'

'No,' she said, 'I won't change my mind. I'm afraid I know that, definitely.'

'I—don't attract you at all?'

'No,' she said gently. 'No, Kim, you don't.'

When he left her she said good-bye with the knowledge that they would not meet again unless by accident. She would miss him. She did not know many eligible men. She was thinking of this when she went upstairs to allot the remainder of the evening to newspapers and the page proofs of a new book which looked more than hopeful.

She was reading in bed when the telephone rang and she thought impatiently, Who on earth, at this hour?

'Yes?' she said.

'It's Bess. Can you put me up for the night? We've had a fire.'

'Good Lord,' said Carol, 'in your apartment?'

'In the house. Started in the flat over mine.'

'Where are you . . . you're all right?'

'I'm fine, and in the corner drugstore. I'll buy a toothbrush. They won't let me go back and collect anything. The place is a shambles, what

83

with water, axes and general confusion.'

'Take a taxi and come galloping,' advised Carol.

She employed the time before Bess's arrival by making up the comfortable living-room day bed, supplementing towels and face cloths, selecting a nightgown. Bess would be engulfed in Carol's extra slippers but that would amuse her. She found a brilliant kimono, the purchase of which she had long since regretted, but Bess would love it, and then wandered into the kitchen to start coffee under the vague impression that coffee followed fires as religiously as the insurance adjuster. There were crackers and cheese and fruit. She set these out and went to the door to admit her friend.

Bess looked disheveled but not much more so than usual. She said:

'I could have gone to a hotel. I look respectable, even without luggage, but I am wide awake and full of conversation. Mind awfully?'

'On the contrary, I'm delighted,' said Carol. 'Coffee's perking ... and you may wear my most alluring nightgown. Bess, what happened?'

'I never held with going to bed early,' said Bess dourly, casting her new toothbrush on the table, 'and now I'm justified. The teacher who lives overhead did just that. She retired. She also fell asleep and that was unfortunate as she was smoking her erudite head off at the time. The bed took wings of flame, she leaped up, screamed and seized the handiest liquid. She thought it was distilled water. Don't ask me why she had a gallon of distilled water, it has something to do with eyewash.'

'You're making that up!'

'I'm not. Anyway, it wasn't distilled water, it was cleaning fluid. The poor woman's in the hospital. Meantime, all hell to pay. Alarms and excursions, large men in shiny black raincoats, as it's raining—or didn't you know that?— loud shouts and stupendous goings-on. The woman in the next flat meant to save her jewelry, but she reached the street with a bottle of Scotch and a bicycle lamp.'

'How about your place?'

'The windows are shattered, there's water all over the shop,' Bess reported.

Carol said:

'Wish you'd stay here while things are being settled.'

Bess grinned. She said:

'Thanks, I'd like to, but I have other plans. Jerry has a comfortable place. When he returns from Akron tomorrow, I'll inform him that I'm moving in.'

'But...'

'Oh,' said Bess carelessly, 'we'll attend to the technicalities. Why wait till the New Year? We'll get ourselves married presently, with you and Jerry's pet bar fly for disapproving witnesses.'

'I don't disapprove, I like Jerry. I don't know why you've postponed this so long.'

'Once bitten, twice neurotic. After I left Sam I decided that it might be possible to fall in love again and, if so, I'd enjoy it to my fullest capacity but I'd be damned if I'd ever remarry. Jerry and I have been arguing about that for years. Also, he doesn't want me to work and I thought that I'd the work habit to such a degree that I couldn't quit. Hence the tentative New Year's Eve arrangement. I said, I *might* quit after that. Lately I've been wondering. I'm not in what you might call the first bloom of youth and it might be fun to go parasitic. And just between us, the idea of marrying a traveling salesman affronted me ... I had a vision of Jerry, in later years, producing my picture in the smoking car and fondly referring to the Little Woman.'

Carol shouted.

'He isn't a traveling salesman. You make him sound as if he traveled in underwear or corsets or—'

'Well, he travels, doesn't he?' asked Bess gloomily. 'That was another argument against my quitting work. What would I do? I'd look elegant on a charity board, wouldn't I? I'd probably abscond with the funds for the starving Hottentots. I don't play bridge. I hate the movies. I can't sew on a button...'

They went into the kitchenette and Carol

poured the coffee and sliced the cheese. She asked:

'You're tired, aren't you?'

'I'm dead,' said Bess frankly. 'I've been out on my feet for about six years. That's smart of you, Carol. It took a fire to bring me to it, I would have gone on arguing and postponing, sheer stubbornness, old phonograph needle stuck in the same place, the same refrain over and over again. So what? So a school-teacher falls asleep and I'll marry Jerry, settle down, and be glad of it, if you must know the truth. I won't resign immediately, I'll hang on another couple of months and sort of ease into the domestic life. Jerry will take himself a vacation during August and we'll go off on a trip.' She grinned. 'I don't expect any emotional fireworks, Carol, I'm forty ... and Jerry's forty-five. But we'll get along. We like each other pretty well ... and he makes enough money to take care of us both.'

Later she asked:

'I haven't seen you since you took the new job. Our telephone conversations haven't been very satisfactory. What about Andy, have you seen him?'

'This afternoon. He blew in from his cruise looking very fit and fine.'

'Is that all you have to say?' Bess seized the knife and cut another piece of cheese. She mourned, 'I'll regret this. Go on, say something.'

'Nothing to say,' Carol told her. 'I was scared. Then I saw him. It was like seeing any other man you'd known once upon a time.'

'You're crazy,' said Bess. 'You think you don't and won't remember, but you will. A year after our divorce I ran into Sam at a party. We were modern and lively and backslapping. It was hell.'

'You were still in love with him,' Carol reminded her.

'Maybe that was it,' Bess agreed. 'But even so—you can't dismiss your ex-relationship.'

'I can,' said Carol. 'You were married to Sam, how long?'

'Sixteen years.'

'Andy and I were married a little over two,' Carol said. 'I was eighteen when we married, he was twenty-two. I tell you, Bess, I hardly remember that girl now, much less the boy. It was so long ago ... not so much in time as in events. The things which have happened since make it fifty years ago, a generation, a lifetime.'

'Did he say anything?'

'We talked for a moment,' said Carol. 'We agreed that there was no reason why we couldn't work together. We're having dinner Monday.'

'You're nuts,' said Bess flatly. 'If I ever had dinner with Sam, I'd bring along the arsenic.'

'Now?'

'No,' said Bess slowly, 'of course not. Not now.'

'You see?'

'Has Andy changed?'

'He's quite gray,' Carol answered, 'and has put on weight. He has lines I've never seen before, around his eyes and mouth. His eyes are the same ... no, not exactly,' she said thoughtfully, 'but I can't explain that. His voice, of course. He's better looking than he ever was. Only I suppose my taste has changed.'

'What do you mean by that?'

Carol laughed. She said:

'The first time I saw Andy I thought he was the answer to any maiden's prayer. Of course, I was a little in love with the public heroes: I'd switched from the Prince of Wales to Lindbergh ... but along came Andy, and since then ...'

'Name one.'

'I met a man some years ago,' said Carol. 'You don't know him. He was married, and he had, I may add, not the slightest interest in me. Nor was I turning on the gas because of that,' she added. 'Still he was very attractive, the type I suppose which had become my type. He was about as much like Andy as I'm like Garbo!'

'Well,' said Bess, yawning, 'it's your own funeral. I think you're a dope though.'

'Why?'

'You know why.'

Carol said vigorously:

'We'll see each other every day from

now on.'

'Let it rest there.'

'That's silly,' Carol told her. 'I'm interested in learning a lot of things about him; perhaps he feels the same way about me. I wouldn't know. But we might as well be friendly.'

'I wonder,' asked Bess, 'what the current boy friend will have to say about this?'

'There isn't a current boy friend.'

'I refer, my pet, to Kim Anderson.'

'Kim and I parted tonight,' said Carol, 'and I made it plain, if without diagram, that I'd be awfully busy from now on.'

'Why,' asked Bess, 'are you crazy? Nice guy, good job, dotes on you, dearie.'

'He wants to marry me.'

'What's wrong about that,' inquired Bess, 'or am I being old-fashioned? You don't have to marry him, out of kindness, do you? And as long as his heart remains in its present molten state he is good for many an elegant meal, to say nothing of opera, theater, hockey, football and concert tickets, plus a spin in the new car come next Sunday.'

Carol said frankly:

'I don't like it; it isn't fair. As long as he wasn't hell bent on matrimony, it was all right to run around with him. But not now.'

'My girl, your scruples slay me.'

'He'll recover,' Carol prophesied, 'and faster, this way.'

Bess said presently:

'Well, it's too bad. He's all right; there aren't many unclaimed like Kim.'

'There are lots,' said Carol, 'only we don't meet 'em.' She laughed. 'I'm always amused by career-girl fiction in which, during the course of the story, the heroine meets, knows, and fascinates at least a dozen or maybe two dozen men. Sometimes one is married, of course, and generally there's a heel for contrast. But what tickles me is the idea that every working-gal has such unlimited opportunity for man hunting. It's the bunk.'

'You've got something there,' Bess agreed.

'I've met plenty of men,' Carol said, 'in the last decade. Ninety per cent of them were married. About nine per cent were ineligible. They were out of jobs or nor interested in marriage, unattractive or were carrying a torch, stupid or just free feeling. You know as well as I ... Kim belongs to the lone one per cent.'

'Maybe you're right,' Bess said. 'I imagine that finding Jerry in a bar on Sixth Avenue was sheer good luck as far as I'm concerned.' She yawned again. 'Lend me some cold cream and skin tonic,' she suggested. 'Also an aspirin. My head aches, excitement and smoke most likely, and I must be as fresh as a daisy when I meet Jerry for lunch tomorrow to break the news that he's as good as married. Not a daisy,' she added, trailing into the living room and beginning to shed her clothes absent-mindedly;

91

'I forgot he's allergic to daisies. Something to do with vernal grasses, a part of rose cold and hay fever, daisy intolerance. It's a damned good thing he wasn't a Vassar girl!'

Carol was nearly asleep when Bess spoke hollowly from the living room.

'Awake?'

'I am now.'

'Sorry . . . I was just thinking. I remembered something I once saw in Winchell's column. Maybe I spoke about it at the time. It was about Andy being seen frequently with Millicent Allen. You know. The lady out of the top drawer who wrote *Without an Echo*. Good book, silly title.'

'You did speak to me about it,' said Carol, 'and I said, "More power to him." So what?'

'So she's published by Maynard and Hall and so you watch your step, or she'll have your back teeth and most of your hair.'

'I've seen her,' said Carol. 'I'm lunching with her soon. She's an ash-blonde, well brought up in a frigidaire; therefore, if I know Andy . . .'

'But,' cried Bess in triumph, 'you don't, you've admitted it, and if your tastes have changed, how about his?'

Carol giggled. She said:

'Nice going. In that case I'll knit ear muffs and a pair of mittens and wish him luck.'

'Do the higher-ups know that you and Andy once enjoyed a divorce?'

'No. It just happened that way . . . besides,

it's none of their business.'

'Wait till Authoress Allen learns,' said Bess, with a cheerful chuckle.

'By that time,' said Carol, 'she'll be eating out of my hand—'

'Keep the iodine handy—'

'I mean,' said Carol, 'I'll put Miss Allen on the map. She has the map for it, by the way. I have at least seven good publicity ideas for her. She has a new book coming along. The first one sold almost eight thousand, which is pretty good. The next will do better. I'll make the public Allen-conscious if it's the last thing I do. Therefore, she'll forgive me my past.'

'Trusting little woman, ain't you?' asked Bess.

'Shut up,' said Carol firmly, 'and go to sleep or I'll set fire to *this* flat.'

CHAPTER EIGHT

On Friday Carol spent the morning with Elsie Norris, revamping some of the biographical material and planning a publicity campaign for several of the novels on the fall book list, Millicent Allen's among them. Miss Allen's script was overdue, and there seemed to be considerable hair tearing in the office because of it. Elsie was of invaluable help as, once the blow had fallen and she knew that she could not step into Hogan's shoes, she was far too loyal a member of the organization to hinder the efficiency of her department. Also she found that she could not justly harbor resentment against Carol. She liked her as a person. Carol's attitude was not apologetic, nor did it come under the masked head of diplomacy. She was perfectly frank about the extent of her ignorance, she asked for Elsie's help and made it plain that she expected and would be grateful for it. She did not gush. She tried no winning tactics. She was merely herself, trying to get her teeth into things, working hard, endeavoring to assimilate as much as possible every day and perfectly aware that there was a great deal to learn. Basically she had a good working knowledge of general promotion. It was a question of adapting that knowledge to the particular job, of amplifying it, and of methods. She toiled cheerfully over lists, clippings and galley proofs, she investigated the files with their photographs and other material, and listened attentively while Elsie lectured on routine in general, the sending out of review copies, of proofs, and the assembling of jackets and catalogues, and basic copy written by the editorial department.

Her telephone rang constantly. Someone wanted a copy of something or other. The production manager of a radio program would like Laura Thurston next Tuesday. She talked to the production managers of two other programs, surely Mrs Watterly's interest in fans would enliven this program and Mr Banner's passion for cats could be used to advantage on the program featuring *Pets I have Loved*?

She saw Andy during the morning. He put his head in the door at about eleven and grinned. He asked:

'How are you coming?'

'Slowly,' she admitted, 'but I'll get there.' She remembered Bess's comments in the night and a spark of amiable malice informed her. She added sedately:

'There seems to be a general opinion that Miss Allen's manuscript had better come in—or else ... I've been plotting a campaign for the book—a little difficult until I know what it's about.'

He came in, filched a carnation from a vase on Elsie's desk, broke the stem, inserted it in his lapel. He said, 'Hi, Dottie,' cheerfully to Miss Owen and then walked over to Carol.

'It's about an unhappy marriage,' he said solemnly, 'with overtones of undercurrents.'

'Thanks,' said Carol, 'I can use that.' She laughed. 'Seriously,' she said, 'everyone's worried.'

'We always worry. I'm seeing Millicent in a few minutes. We're going over the book together. It's finished, you know. But she's editing and has come to something of a full stop.'

'I'm sure you'll be an inspiration,' said Carol.

Elsie Norris giggled and then turned the giggle into an unconvincing cough.

'That sounds female,' Andy said critically.

'I meant it. Although I can't believe...' She broke off. This was neither the time nor the place to reorganize her beliefs.

Andy said:

'Late afternoon I'm going to Greenwich and I'll take the manuscript with me so Richard and I can have a session with it—also Steve will be along tomorrow.'

She said absently:

'Miss Allen's lunching with me next week.' Her telephone rang and she picked it up. The editor of a high-school paper wanted a picture of Miss Mary Diston. Miss Diston's career books for girls were at the height of their popularity.

While she was talking Andy went out. He shaped some words silently. 'Monday night,' he said.

Carol lunched with an out-of-town book critic who was enchanted that John Hogan had been magically transformed into a good-looking young woman with curly dark hair and fine eyes.

Carol spent the weekend reading galleys, page proofs, and printed volumes. She was to continue this for many weekends and to devote numerous evenings to it. She had to catch up,

96

she must become acquainted with the M. and H. writers. They were scattered all over the United States, two of them lived in Paris and one in London, quite aside from the writers they published in translation or whose American editions they published. Some of them she might never meet personally. Those who lived in or near New York she was likely to see with relative frequency, those who lived out of town would be sure to descend upon M. and H. at intervals, annual, biannual, for conferences, cocktail and theater parties. One was coming in from San Francisco the middle of June. There would be interviews to obtain and a party to plan for which Miss Norris would suggest the list of invitations.

On Monday morning when the arrangements for the visiting fireman were already under way, Carol asked Stephen Hall solemnly:

'Do you ever tuck them in bed and run errands to the drugstore for them?'

He had stopped in her office to ask a question. At hers he grinned amiably.

'All but. We've seen several through their divorces and more through their marriages or remarriages. We've bought railroad tickets and in one instance a baby carriage. Of course, agents double in brass as nursemaids too. But every so often the publisher is called upon to officiate in an emergency. It's fun. I like it.'

Andy did not come to the office Monday or,

if he did, she did not see him. He called her Monday afternoon.

He asked:

'Any preference ... I mean as to where we'll eat?'

'None whatever.'

He suggested a place in the Fifties. 'Seven o'clock?' he asked.

'Seven it shall be.'

She found herself dressing with unusual care. She had an excellent taste in clothes. She could not afford to be one of the ten best dressed women in the world, or even one of the ten thousand. But she bought with a regard for line and material. She selected accessories cleverly. She did not spend much money on clothes, less than Bess, who always looked as if she had emerged from a grab bag, but she made her money count. She was careful about gloves and stocking seams, hair and skin.

She said to herself:

Well, off to the races with the ex-husband. How absurd, how utterly ridiculous.

She kept him waiting a little while, not by design but from habit. It was unwise to arrive at an appointment in advance of your host, although it sometimes happened by accident. You looked pretty silly sitting there with your mouth, figuratively, open. Sillier still hopping to your feet and crying, 'I just arrived, this minute!' in order to put him at his ease, or to erase from his mind any impression that you couldn't wait to see him. She never kept her men waiting very long—three minutes, five, ten at the most—and was always on time when the occasion was business and not social.

The restaurant was small and quiet. The tiny lounge was filled. The bar was just beyond. There was a faint, pleasant odor of good French cooking. A radio was playing piped-in music, not distracting, very pleasant.

Andy rose and advanced upon her. She asked:

'Been waiting?'

'Of course. How about a drink?'

'I'd like one.'

They sat at the bar and he looked at her questioningly:

'Pink Lady, Jack Rose, White Lady—Sidecar ... what shall it be?'

'An old-fashioned.'

'Two of the same.' He added, 'Your tastes have changed.'

He laughed, remembering the girl he had married, who had liked her drinks sweet. She drank very little, one cocktail was sufficient to redden her cheeks and loosen her tongue. Now he watched Carol drink her old-fashioned without haste and spear the cherry. She said, 'That was very nice.'

'Another?'

'No, thanks.'

'Still a one-cocktail girl?'

'As a rule. I prefer one. I don't always drink

99

that,' she said frankly. 'Now and then, yes. But I've seen too many women skip to two and then acquire the three and four habit. It isn't pretty and it all adds up.'

They went into the dining room. The captain knew Andy, took them to a table and removed the 'Reserved' sign with a flourish.

They were in a corner, the lights were flattering, and the music unobtrusive.

He admitted, picking up the menu:

'I'm afraid to ask you what you want.'

'Why?'

'Are you dieting?' he asked. 'Tell me so, at once, if you are. I like my illusions shattered with one smashing blow.'

She laughed.

'I've never dieted,' she said.

'Thank God! Do you still like roast beef rare, baked potatoes, mixed green salad, artichokes and ...'

'I do. And oysters, only this is May. Shrimps would be very nice.'

When he had ordered he sat back and looked at her. 'I forgot,' he said. 'What to drink?'

'Nothing.'

'Mind if I have a long one?'

'Not at all.'

He beckoned the captain. Presently he said:

'Begin at the beginning. How did you get into this racket?'

'Originally, by mistake,' she told him.

'How come?'

'Time hung on my hands, and friends of Mother's became interested in a charity campaign. I volunteered and worked on the publicity, no pay, a lot of work and plenty of hair-pulling females to handle. I was green as crème de menthe. I went around and talked to people, at the Junior League some of my friends were helpful, gave me all sorts of tips. Anyway, it was fun while it lasted. The next time something came along I volunteered again. I did everything, ran errands, badgered editors, wangled advertisements for programs. That was all right too. I knew a lot of people and I became conscious of the fact that there is certain publicity beyond evaluation, which can't be paid for, and matters greatly ... society column mentions, for instance. After that I took a business course and then my father died.'

He said soberly:

'I felt pretty rotten about that, Carol. I liked him so much.'

'He liked you, Andy. It was hard. He'd kept his chin up, the autumn of 'twenty-nine. The Kreuger fiasco finished him though. No fight left. When he got pneumonia, he didn't fight at all.'

Andy said:

'Doesn't seem like him.' He thought of his father-in-law. He hadn't known him long or well. A big, confident, generous man, with a hot temper and a tremendous fund of

101

kindliness. They'd had a fishing trip together once. Andy had never enjoyed anything more. Carol and her mother had stayed at the hotel, on the lake, but the two men had taken guides and supplies and gone off, back of beyond, for four grand fly-bitten days. He'd grown to know Jake Reid then, they'd talked around campfires. Andy remembered Reid's picturesque profanity, his fund of entertaining stories, his hard, common sense.

She said, 'I know. Well, after that, I found jobs which paid a little. I tried for newspaper work at first. No good, nothing doing. They didn't want me at any price. I free-lanced around, mostly charity campaigns, political campaigns, all publicity work, short, sweet, hard. But I was learning all the time, being kicked around a little, not minding much. There was a good deal of that. Finally the big organization job.'

Andy nodded, he remembered it in her dossier.

'Work with women,' she said thoughtfully. 'The volunteers were the most difficult. The women who gave the money and wanted to keep track of it, the women who gave the money and wanted a mention in the society pages every other day. I had an underling's job, of course, first as a sort of assistant and typist and then as a secretary assistant and finally assistant. My boss was swell. She was fifty, shaped like a broom handle, and she was a cynic. But she knew her stuff. She was paid a good salary to know it and she made short shrift of problem patrons. She liked me, so she trained me and, when she retired, recommended me for the job. There was a dither about that. I was too young, they said. But she had a good time playing up my connections.' Carol laughed.

He grinned. Carol's Aunt Minnie was the widow of a knight. She lived in England, more English than the English. She was county. She opened bazaars and owned a cottage with antediluvian plumbing outside of London. Andy had met her once, shortly after his and Carol's wedding. Lady Carruthers had not approved of the marriage. 'Too young,' she said, sniffing. She had come over on a brief trip, the purpose of which was to persuade Carol's father to persuade certain corporations that they should increase their dividends. Otherwise she would have to cut down on her annual contribution to the vicar and to the cricket fund.

'Only time Aunt Minnie ever helped me,' said Carol, eating her good, rare, thick roast beef with enjoyment. 'But there it was. I did all right in the job. Then when *Facts* was about to be launched, a friend of mine, Bess Manners, persuaded me that I needed a change of scene. You know the rest.'

'It's incredible,' he commented, 'but you still hate fat.'

'Some kinds.' She was cutting off the fat of the beef carefully. 'Why?'

'Nothing. It used to irritate me. You'd sit down to eat and suddenly you'd have a sheep and goats sort of business, fat and lean.'

She said calmly:

'Well, it can't irritate you now. I notice you still strangle yourself.'

'Meaning what?'

'Yank at your tie. It's under your ear now. That always irritated *me* and the portentous way you opened your egg at breakfast and your silly habit of pouring the remains of a demitasse on a dish of vanilla cream.'

They looked at each other and laughed. He said, 'I still do that.'

'No doubt. Tell me about yourself. How did you ever get into publishing?'

'Have you forgotten that I once wanted to write,' he asked, 'and that I told you that after I had made my first million I'd have my own publishing business?'

She said, 'I'm afraid I have.' She frowned, her slender brows drawn. 'Yes—I remember the writing part,' she said.

The house party at New Haven. Andy and herself, and a fireplace. The boy who was her host sulking in a corner. The girl Andy had brought fit to be tied. She could see it clearly, she hadn't thought of it for years. Her funny dress, the last word, straight, just below the knees and the waist almost at the knees. The

104

pinkish stockings and the high heels. The shingled bob...

Talking around the fire about what he wanted to do when he graduated.

'My dad wanted me to be a doctor, but I couldn't stick that stuff—I'd hate it. I want to write ... I know I can...'

She was sure of it.

The first house party. The next time it was a dance and she'd come up to go with him ... she was in her sophomore year at Smith then. After that, the weekend meetings in town, the cut classes and presently Andy graduating and their marriage, less than a month later. For Andy had been persuaded that he could write on the side. His roommate was Jigs Hobarts. Jig's father was something Very Big on the Street. So Andy went into the Hobarts office, one of a myriad customers' men, with the right attitude, the right clothes, the right friends, the right score at golf. Andy, who could ride a horse or whack a tennis ball, who could dance and swim and hold his liquor, Andy who had the right way with the right prospects, uncles and fathers and family friends of his classmates ... uncles and fathers and family friends of her friends. The Reids had a large, very correct acquaintance.

He said:

'After you-know-what, customers' men were a dime a dozen. I had a little dough, damned little, but I ate and slept. You wouldn't take a cent, you little goop, and, boy, was I glad!'

She said, 'I was a fool. I should have taken something if only to annoy you. It wouldn't have hurt you. But I was full of pride and prejudice. Also I had a family which, at the time, could still support me.'

He shook his head. He said:

'We were crazy, both of us.'

She said, rather coolly:

'I thought we were rather sane.'

'I didn't mean the divorce,' he said honestly. He looked at her gravely. 'I don't know you but I think I like you,' he said. 'You seem a forthright, interesting critter. That other girl, well, she isn't you—or wasn't. Discount my confusion of tenses. In any case, the divorce was the sanest thing that ever happened to either of us, and the best.'

Carol nodded.

'I can agree with you there, Andy,' she said. 'The very best.'

'I meant merely that we were crazy,' he explained, 'before our own personal private crash and after. No, it wouldn't have hurt me if you had nicked me for a little alimony. I might have earned it sooner. As it was I drifted around until I got myself settled. I tried writing. My manuscripts returned to me like homing pigeons, with their feathers on the bedraggled side. But I met a man I had known slightly in college, whose father was editor of a magazine—I won't tell you which one, you'd laugh your head off—and I got me a job finally, as a sort of super office boy. It worked into something better and by that time I'd met the editor in chief of Remsen and Company, and to Remsen and Company I went. And stayed until I came to M. and H.'

She said, 'We've come a long way, haven't we?'

He lifted his glass and toasted her.

'Good luck,' he said. 'I mean it. And now, do you still like chocolate cake?'

CHAPTER NINE

After dinner Andy had a suggestion to make. He asked:

'Seen the picture at the Music Hall?'

She hadn't, as it happened. And Andy said:

'How about going along and seeing if we like it?'

They walked to Radio City, through the sultry evening, the air felt sticky and thick. On Sixth Avenue hatless girls skipped along, in thin, short-sleeved dresses, walking solidly on their platform heels, their figures, high-breasted, small-waisted, perfectly apparent. Andy asked suddenly:

'Remember the girls a dozen years ago?'

'Why wouldn't I?' inquired Carol. 'I was

one of 'em.'

'Women are amazing,' Andy stated. 'In those days every girl looked like a squirt of Vichy ... not a curve in a carload. Look at 'em now.'

Carol laughed.

'These youngsters were in kindergarten or grammar school then.'

He looked at her, smiling.

'That doesn't solve the mystery. You haven't reached the sere and yellow. What I'm getting at is how it happens ... what becomes of the planklike figures? ... you don't see 'em any more. Yet the little splinters grew up and are still around, all in the prevailing mode.'

She asked, 'Am I to believe that you are coaxing me to betray trade secrets?'

They entered the Music Hall and Andy bought mezzanine tickets. The stage show was ending, the picture hadn't started. He said:

'I like this place.'

'So do I,' said Carol.

His voice reached her, necessarily intimate in order not to disturb other people.

'Carol, do you come here often?'

'Relatively ... why?'

'Doesn't it seem funny to you—it does to me—that we've never been here together? That, back in the dark ages, this place wasn't even built.'

'That's so,' she said, 'nor the Empire State nor the Planetarium—lots of—'

Someone hissed at them like an angry goose.

When they left the Music Hall they were arguing over the picture.

'But you used to like happy endings,' he said; 'you were all washed up with a picture or a book which didn't portray the final clinch.'

'I've outgrown that, I suppose. I've found it isn't so simple. I like a little realism with my romance.'

'You don't cry at pictures any more,' he accused.

Carol laughed.

'Did I, ever?' she inquired.

'Quarts. And never had a handkerchief. I kept sneaking glances at you all through the tragic episodes ... you were calm, dry-eyed, mildly interested. I was disappointed.'

She said:

'When we went to the movies together I hadn't known grief. An unbecoming dress, a broken date, a bad mark in English, the death of a dog to which I was attached ... that about summed it up, Andy. So I took it out vicariously, wept over books, howled at movies, theaters, operas, even sunsets. Football games too. I'd get a lump in my throat as big as the football itself, just because of crowds, music, excitement. But since then...'

He said hastily:

'I get it. What you're trying to tell me is that you've grown up.'

'Perhaps.'

109

'Carol, think before you answer. I don't want to be let down too often. Could you eat again?'

He thought, there was never a time when she didn't want to eat—that was one of the funny, exasperating, lovable things about her.

She said gravely:

'I could do with a snack.'

'Sandwich and a glass of beer?'

'Will you be horrified if I tell you I could manage a chocolate soda nicely?'

They walked to Fifth Avenue and to Hicks'. Perched on a high stool Carol absorbed a soda. Andy drinking a fruit mixture with feelings as mixed, watched her. He said finally:

'Well, you haven't changed in one way. You're as greedy as ever.'

She said serenely:

'And I don't get fat. Nice, isn't it? Matter of metabolism. I would be definitely sunk if I had to renounce the pleasures of the table.'

When they were leaving she said:

'My bus will be along presently.' She held out her hand. 'It's been fun, Andy.'

'I'll take you home.'

'No, don't bother. You can see me across the street.' She added, 'I haven't asked you where you live.'

He told her and she nodded. She added thoughtfully:

'I wonder why I took it for granted that you wouldn't be married!'

110

'That deserve discussion,' he responded.

'We'll save it,' she decided.

'There's a lot of ground we haven't covered,' he reminded her.

'That's right. But it will keep.'

A little later he watched the bus drive off and then started to walk aimlessly uptown. Tramping along he thought, I wouldn't believe that anyone could change so much...

Sitting beside her in the theater he had let his mind drift from the screen. He had thought with the utmost astonishment, But this woman beside me has been my wife. I have kissed her a thousand times, I have held her in my arms. I have watched her brush her hair before the mirror, I have an intimate knowledge of her body, the shape of flesh and bone, the feel of her skin under my hands. I have seen her with a cold in her head, and prostrate with a bilious attack. I have known a hundred of her little habits, personal to herself. In the dark night she has lain beside me, with her head on my breast and talked to me as she might talk to herself. All this is true, yet I cannot believe it. It never happened. It is a life we lived together in some mutual dream. I keep telling myself, It is true, it existed. But the words don't make sense. I still can't believe them.

He could not think of her as having been his wife. He could think of her far more clearly as a girl he had once known, whom he had re-encountered ... almost a stranger, yes, entirely a stranger in many ways. She interested him, it was fascinating to see the changes which had taken place in her, some trivial, some important ... changes in her way of thinking, even in mannerisms. Now and then he could recognize a gesture, an expression, but for the most part he was seeing her as someone quite new. He thought, stopping at a corner to hail a cab, I like her, she's all right.

It came with something of a shock to realize that during the brief time before their marriage and after he had not stopped to consider whether or not he liked her. He had been in love with her and that was all that seemed to matter.

Reaching home, Carol glanced at her watch. Not too late, she could do some reading before she slept. She had brought home a manuscript, one upon which Steve Hall had asked her opinion. It occurred to her that she hadn't asked Andy about Millicent Allen's book. She thought, Well, the strangeness will wear off, we'll shake down, ask all the questions, get all the answers, and then go on like any two people in business together. In her brief case she had some figures she wanted to study before the night was over. She was trying to orientate herself in the profession of publishing. It would take a long time. Meantime she must acquire as much knowledge as possible, from the ground up, not only about her own department but on every phase of the business. The figures she had brought home dealt with manufacturing and selling costs, with overhead, office expenses, advertising...

She was not sleepy. She had never been more wide awake. She found herself oddly keyed up. She told herself, That's only natural, my girl; there is a certain awkwardness about this situation ... which will pass. Tonight you were tense, on your guard against—a lot of things. It all comes under the head of thin ice.

She had put on the wine-red pajamas and was just about to heap her pillows high, lie on her bed and read when her doorbell rang stormily. She swore mildly, and padded to the door. Arm in arm, Bess and Jerry. Bess's hat was on the back of her head and Jerry's long lank form looked as usual, as if he had been sleeping in his clothes.

'Let us in,' begged Bess, 'this is practically Jerry's bachelor dinner.'

'Elucidate,' said Carol. She closed the door after them and bade a mute farewell to good resolutions.

Bess said, 'We won't keep you up longer than it will take to give us a drink. We're calling on all our pals. What are you doing at noon tomorrow?'

'No dates,' said Carol. 'Why?'

'You're invited to City Hall,' said Bess, 'to witness a wedding.'

Jerry grinned.

113

He said, in his slow, deep voice:

'I think she set fire to the place herself. She's been angling for me long enough, poor girl. She deserves her catch.'

'What about your license?' asked Carol practically.

'We've had one,' Jerry said, 'for three months. Don't you remember? That was the last time Bess went domestic. She repented the next day.'

They had their drink, and Carol looked at them smiling. Bess looked happier than she had ever seen her, as if her mind was at rest, had achieved some sort of peace. She regarded Jerry proudly. She said:

'He's no Gable, but I'm not choosy.'

Jerry Barnett looked something like a pleasant horse ... he had a long bony face, a long upper lip. His scant pepper-and-salt hair was unexpectedly curly. He had the biggest hands and feet imaginable and a contagious smile. Carol liked him very much. She was happy for him, he had been in love with Bess for a long time.

When they were leaving, 'Noon,' Bess reminded her. 'And a party after.'

'I'll have to duck that,' Carol said regretfully. 'I must get back to the office.'

'New broom,' said Bess. 'Maybe we should postpone the wedding until you slacken up. What's the rush?'

'Sales conference,' said Carol, 'and other

114

things.'

The door closed behind them and Carol went back to bed. She picked up the manuscript, she read the first chapter. Her eyes felt heavy. She gave up finally, substituted a nightgown for her pajamas, opened her windows and turned out the light.

She was tired, she was sleepy, she couldn't concentrate properly on manuscripts, yet she couldn't get to sleep. She thought, It's late, I'll look a wreck in the morning.

Sitting there in the Music Hall beside Andy had disturbed her. She faced it squarely, saw it in part for what it was, a strange remembering of her senses. Her heart hadn't accelerated, her pulse had been normal, she had experienced no excitement. Yet the disturbance was there, it went deeper, and she could not define it wholly nor dismiss it. It was, she thought, the pull of the old attraction that had brought them together ... the ghost of that attraction perhaps, a dim carbon copy. She and Andy had not separated because they had felt sharp revulsion, but because, as they had put it, they were no longer compatible, they did not 'get along.' She had left him because they quarreled incessantly, because he drank too much, because they had taken to saying unkind, bitter things to each other, because the pull of their attraction was no longer sufficient. In the beginning of their estrangement it had brought them together, with remorse, self-recrimination, tears, promises, reconciliations. But not for long. The things on which they differed, about which they had quarreled, had been stronger. When they finally separated it was without any sense of physical loathing, of hatred even ... but with a hot, burning anger, a wild, impatient desire to be rid of this unpleasant business once and for all, free of quarrels and scenes and the shouting of hard, brutal truths.

He's a very attractive man, she told herself, lying there. You were once in love with him. She thought of herself with a faint smile, with unemotional pity, as if that bewildered girl were someone else. Too much in love to have any sense, she reminded herself firmly. And it didn't last, for you or for him.

After a while you got over it. Tonight you were just remembering things against your will. This will lessen as time goes on, in six months your new relationship will be so established that you won't give the old one another thought, why should you?

She remembered the months after she had left Andy. Her mother had been querulous. She was shocked, mainly because she didn't believe in divorce, especially for someone who belonged to her. She hated thinking of her child as a failure. Her father had been more gentle than she had ever known him. He had been sorry, he was fond of Andy. They had had a long talk, he and Andy, before Carol and her mother left for Reno. Her father never told her what had been said, or left unsaid, between them.

Reno was something of a nightmare; she disliked thinking about it even now. Her mother hadn't helped. And on their return home everything had seemed flat and stale and unhappy, and Carol had done her share of weeping in the night, of missing Andy, of wondering how much of a mistake she had made. Yet loneliness had not been able to convince her that it had been a mistake. She had recovered, nicely. Before the year was up she could tell herself without fear of contradiction that the mistake had lain in her marriage, at eighteen, and not in her divorce at twenty.

She thought, before she slept, I wonder what happened to Andy that year. I'll be able to ask him someday.

CHAPTER TEN

Bess and Jerry were safely married, the office of M. and H. struggled with autumn catalogues and general routine, Elsie Norris was home ill with a heavy cold, the fifteenth of June came around and the visiting author blew in from San Francisco. The date marked activity for Carol's office and also the conclusion of her first month with M. and H.

Mr Hardwick Reynolds was the author of that stupendous best seller *Leave It to Youth*. He was a shy, quiet man of fifty-odd with a very pretty wife, some years his junior. Carol attended to flowers, and theater tickets, and directed the interviews which she had obtained, easily enough in this instance, as Reynolds was known to be a recluse and seldom gave interviews. He asked Carol in premonitory horror if she wouldn't be present when the reporters came.

So for several days she was busy, sitting in the Reynolds suite guiding conversation as best she could, away from the things which troubled Reynolds and which she had been warned he did not like discussed. One was his divorce from the first Mrs Reynolds, who was a motion-picture actress of considerable renown.

She took the second Mrs Reynolds—who had been Reynolds's secretary, who had typed *Leave It to Youth*, that extraordinarily vital novel of the American Revolution—about the city, taking her more or less under her wing. Reynolds was busy with his agent, with editors, with all the things Carol had planned for him to do, as well as with Richard and Steve and Andy. He had to attend two luncheons and speak at one important dinner. Mrs Reynolds kept in the background; she preferred it, she said. But she liked to shop and Carol spent two afternoons shopping with her.

When the Reynoldses had taken the Century out on their way home, Carol returned to her less spectacular muttons with a sigh of relief. But not for long. M. and H.'s new prestige writer, the gentleman who had the proletariat at heart and who had made a fortune out of it during the last year, flew in from some strange place and turned the office upside down. The trouble was not in getting publicity of the right kind, but in avoiding publicity of the wrong kind. By the time he was poured on a train, prattling of tumbrils and barricades, and laid out in an unproletarian drawing room, Carol was ready for a straitjacket.

Elsie said unsympathetically:

'Wait until the horde of lecturers hits us, come next autumn. I hear that three of our English writers are coming over, as well as one French and one Chinese.'

'Fun,' said Carol, brightening. 'As a matter of fact, I haven't minded the recent merry-go-round at all. I just enjoy griping now and then.'

She went along to Andy's office. The year was now nearing July and uncompromisingly warm. He demanded, as she went in:

'How you manage to look as cool as endive on ice ...?'

He was coatless, his hair ruffled. He raised his voice for Kate and she came with some neatly typed notes. He told Carol to sit down. He wanted to talk about library lists and book clubs and one thing or another. He also had some reprint figures on Laura Thurston which would interest her. He asked presently:

'You've read the new Allen Novel?'

Carol nodded.

'Like it?'

Carol hesitated.

'Speak your mind,' he said, 'everyone else has, the place is divided into two camps, two and a half, let's say. The lads are very keen...'

The lads were the younger members of the editorial staff, nice enthusiastic boys.

'What about you?' asked Carol.

'That's not fair. But I'll answer. I like it, so does Steve; Richard doesn't, especially.'

Carol said slowly:

'It seems to me to be a better book than the first, less dependent on tricks. She has a lovely economical style. She writes with a knife, I think. I don't believe in the validity of her argument, but that's neither here nor there. It's of no significance, whether it's true or not. It may be true, for her.'

'You mean, of course, her contention that physical infidelity is unimportant, that a man or woman surrenders less actual integrity through temporary philandering than in daily mental hostilities—'

'Yes.'

He said:

'Most of the women readers will agree with you.'

Carol said definitely:

'I'm no prophet; if I were, money wouldn't be able to repay my value to a publishing house. If I knew what people were going to think, want, read, discuss a month from today, six months, a year, I could name my own price.' She smiled briefly. 'But I do feel that this book will have a tremendous sale because it's provocative, controversial. People will eat it up, it won't matter whether or not they agree with it or whether they like it, even ... or am I wrong?'

'You're right. You lunched with Millicent some weeks ago,' he said, 'she took quite a fancy to you.'

'She's a very clever woman,' began Carol and Andy shouted with laughter. She continued serenely:

'Not because of that, you idiot. But she is clever, and also very attractive. Did you like her new picture?'

It was framed, it was signed, it hung back of his desk. He answered, 'Very much.'

She said thoughtfully:

'I think we can direct prospective readers' attention to the book through its controversial angle ... it shouldn't be hard.'

He said, after a moment:

'Millicent has a place in Connecticut. Her people stick to Newport but, since she more or less emancipated herself some years ago, she spends weekends, long holidays up there, near Bethel.'

Carol said, expressionless:

'Where do you think I have been for the last six weeks? We have pictures of Miss Allen's pre-Revolutionary farmhouse, her cocker spaniels, her horses, her herb garden, her roses...'

'That's so,' he said. 'Forgive me. What I was getting at—I think she'd like you up for a weekend. She mentioned it to me—' he looked at her, with curiosity—'or doesn't it appeal to you?'

She said frankly:

'It would be fun. But she hasn't spoken of it to me, Andy, perhaps you're mistaken.'

'No,' he said; 'you'll hear from her.'

A few days later Millicent Allen called her. She said, in her light voice, sweet and frosted as frozen strawberries:

'Miss Reid? ... I wonder if I could coax you up here next weekend? Andy's coming, and some other rather amusing people. It would be a great pleasure, if you'd come.'

'I'd love to,' said Carol. 'Thanks very much.'

'Andy will drive you up,' said Millicent. 'Any allergies ... feathers, shellfood, cats, horses?'

Carol laughed.

'None, expect, at the moment and in this heat, I'm allergic to work.

'I don't blame you,' said Millicent cordially. 'I had to ask, however; so many of my friends

122

come lugging their own pillows or what not.'

On Friday Carol left the office a little early, to pack her bag... Andy had told her there was a swimming pool and she could ride if she wished. She hadn't ridden since she was a child. She packed slacks and a linen dress, a bathing suit, a cotton dinner gown, and was ready when by arrangement he called for her.

He came upstairs and looked around appreciatively. He asked:

'Don't I recognize the chair?'

'*And* the love seat, the water colors, and the desk.'

They were silent a moment. Then he said quickly:

'You've made an attractive place of this.'

'I like it. The rent's a little higher than I should pay but I'm not very extravagant otherwise. My reading's taken care of nicely, now.' She laughed. 'And I find myself being asked out to dinner rather frequently. So I manage.'

Driving out of the city through the dusty country they talked, mostly of the office, of a new find in biography, of the jacket for Millicent's book, of a dozen other things. Carol asked idly:

'Doesn't Miss Allen's family object to her having her own establishments, here and in town?'

'They did at first, I understand. To appease them she has a sort of nominal duenna, an elderly cousin of the genteel-poor variety, who lends considerable tone to the proceedings but doesn't interfere. Millicent has her own money, by the way.'

Carol took off her hat and slung it in the back of Andy's small car. She said:

'Golly, it's hot ... I envy her ... talent, money, independence...' she said vaguely.

'You're independent,' he reminded her.

'Yes, and perfectly comfortable.' She explained briefly about the bonds, and added, 'I drew a ridiculous salary while I was on *Facts*, and could save. I put the savings into annuities.'

He said, 'I can't believe it. I remember when you couldn't add up your checkbook.'

'I still can't,' she admitted.

'I think,' he said quietly, 'that you're happier than Millicent. She's an odd girl—'

She asked casually:

'Andy, did you ever think of marrying again?'

'Any connection—?'

'None, really. I have wondered often.'

'Once or twice, never seriously. What about you?'

'Once,' she said, 'some time ago, quite seriously. But it didn't come to anything.'

'I see ... This is lovely country,' he said, drawing a deep breath.

'Isn't it?' She added, 'Sometime I'd like to drive around Ridgefield and see the house. I used to think I couldn't bear it. I don't know if the people who bought it still live there. I wouldn't mind seeing it now. That's over and done with so long ago. It's stupid to live in the past. I'm over that. I've quite recovered from the pang which assailed me every time anyone even mentioned Connecticut.'

He said, 'It was a grand old place. I hope whoever lives there loves it as much as your father did.'

Millicent's farmhouse was in the standard tradition, long, low, white, with wide shingles, the original hardware, and squat chimneys. There was a lovely flower garden, fine old trees, and a wide green lawn, but the rest of the property rolled away in meadows and little hills, in fields bounded by stone walls. The modernization had included heating, plumbing, the raising of ceilings, the preservation of old paneling and fireplaces ... and the swimming pool.

Millicent met them at the door, in tailored slacks and a bright thin shirt, her heavy uncut hair coiled at the nape of her neck. A red cocker spaniel leaped about her knees. Her face held the pallor which will not tan, her lipstick was very red, a freckle or two lay across the thin bridge of her nose.

'So glad,' she said, and gave them her hands. 'You'll want a swim before cocktails.'

Carol's room was on a corner, big and quiet, filled with flowers, blinds drawn against the

125

sun. She put on her bathing suit and robe and went downstairs to meet Millicent's cousin, Miss Parker, and the other guests, a married couple, the Talbots, a dark young man, James Greene. Millicent explained that there was a back door and stairs which they could use to their bedrooms after swimming. 'Drip all you want,' she said.

She was a pleasant hostess, apparently quite unconcerned. Her servants were good, the house operated smoothly, she had but to give her orders and relax.

A swim in the green-painted pool, cocktails on the pool terrace, a rest, a walk in the gardens before dinner, contract afterward and people dropping in. Saturday, Andy, Millicent and the Talbots rode, and young Mr Greene, who was something or other in banking, made himself agreeable to Carol. In the early evening they had a picnic, taking steaks, and a man to cook them, to the picnic oven built near a brook on the property and afterward when they had returned to the house someone rolled up the rugs and they danced to the radio. Carol, drifting around in Andy's arms, commented, 'You dance better than ever.'

'Thanks,' he said. 'I've been practicing all these years.'

Millicent watched them, standing by the mantelpiece, her curious gray-green eyes thoughtful. When they stopped, she said:

'You didn't tell me you had known each

other before.'

'Didn't I?' asked Andy, astonished. 'I thought I had ... yes, indeed, once, long ago.'

'How did you know?' asked Carol. She was conscious of uneasiness. This woman saw a little too much.

Millicent shrugged.

'I've no idea. I watched you dancing. It came to me that you had danced together hundreds of times.'

'We might have,' he said, smiling, 'since Carol came to the office. As it happens, we haven't. But how were you to know that?'

Talbot came up and said:

'It's too hot to dance. But I can't resist. How about it, Miss Reid?'

Much later Carol stood, with a glass in her hand, on the terrace which overlooked the garden. Andy was beside her. There was a silver paring of a moon and the sky was thick-sown with stars. Something grew near by, very sweet, raspberry shrub, lilies, nicotiana, petunias. He said:

'Always wanted a place like this.'

'Andy, you loathed the country except for holidays. You used to wonder how Mother and Father stood it.'

'Getting old,' he apologized, 'beginning to hanker after peace and quiet and a swatch of ground under my feet which is mine, mortgage and all. Not this sort of place, that's out of my reach, too rich for my blood. Simplicity like this costs like hell. But some place, somewhere ... books, and another go at writing perhaps—a different type this time—lots of music and a couple of good dogs, not too well bred. A horse maybe, if it would run to that. But it wouldn't. I'd have to win a lottery to get even that much.'

She said, 'You'll have it someday if you want it enough. I know you will.'

'You're a good kid.' He put his arm around her shoulder, casually, and she did not move. It seemed right and comfortable to have it there, the arm of a good friend. She felt no awkwardness, no excitement. They stood there for a moment without speaking until Millicent called from the lighted doorway.

Andy took his arm away, gave her a friendly pat on the shoulder. He said, 'Contract, poker, something—or maybe someone's dropped in. That's the drawback to the country. Droppers-in.'

It was late when Carol was ready for bed. She stood at the windows in her nightgown, and looked out over the dreaming garden. She was sleepy, sun and wind and water had contributed to her drowsiness, her sense of well-being.

Someone knocked and she called 'Come in' and turned to face the opening door. Millicent stood there, a cigarette between her fingers, her child's body in pale-green pajamas, her bare feet in mules. She asked, 'Mind if I come in? I saw your light.'

'Do. It's been such a marvelous day,' said Carol; 'such a good time.'

Millicent brushed that aside. She asked abruptly:

'Why didn't Andy tell me that you and he had been married?'

CHAPTER ELEVEN

Carol's face burned. She touched it with her hand. She thought, The wind, the sun ...? in utter confusion. But it wasn't wind or sun. It was Millicent's cool eyes. Carol felt awkward and guilty. She felt young. This angered her. She wasn't a child, she was some years older than Millicent Allen.

She answered:

'I suppose he didn't think it mattered.'

Millicent crossed the room, with her light, unhurried step. She sat down on the edge of the chaise longue and put one slim knee over the other. A mule slid from a slender foot. The toenails were painted to match her lips.

'I don't suppose it does,' she said. 'Mind if I smoke? And do sit down. You make me nervous, standing there—glowering.'

Carol tried to laugh. She asked:

'Was I? I didn't mean to—I don't glower very well.'

129

Millicent's regard was the color of stormy water, of winter skies. Carol sat down in a low soft chair, near the window, and waited.

Millicent fished in a pocket for a slim gold case, offered it to Carol, picked up the matches from a little table.

Smoking, she remarked reflectively:

'I still don't see why you wanted to make a mystery of it.'

'I didn't,' Carol denied. 'When I applied for the position I hadn't the remotest idea that Andy was in the firm. I hadn't heard from, or of, him for years. When I was leaving the office after my interview with Mr Maynard, he spoke of Andy, casually. I couldn't be sure—the name is not uncommon. Please remember that when Andy and I were married he was in a brokerage office...'

'I can't remember anything I didn't know,' said Millicent evenly. 'All yesterday and today I have been puzzled. Seeing you dance together, coming upon you out there on the terrace ... So, when the opportunity arose, I asked Andrew. You had gone up to bed.'

'You asked him?'

'Why not? I said merely, "You've known Carol Reid before—I realized that this evening. How well did you know her?" He laughed, seemingly quite amused. Then he said, "I thought I knew her very well, as she was once my wife. I was probably mistaken."'

Carol said slowly:

'It was a shock to him to walk in after his holiday and find me there.'

'But not to you?'

She moved uneasily.

'No. The name worried me. I made inquiries, before—'

Millicent lifted her eyebrows.

'You knew, then, when you went to work? It didn't make any difference?'

Carol said, her confusion dying, clear anger burning in her:

'Why should it? I wanted the position. In this day and age it would have been pretty silly to relinquish it because of a relationship which no longer exists. Or don't you think so?'

'I should think,' said Millicent, 'that it would be awkward ... but then I have never been married to Andy or'—she permitted herself a bright-lipped smile—'to anyone else.'

Carol said evenly:

'I suppose any explanation seems stupid, and far-fetched. When we saw each other that first day it was in the midst of a conference. Naturally everyone present realized that we— knew each other. But it didn't seem indicated to shout we'd been married. Once you haven't said a thing you can't come out with it, afterward, can you? Or at least, so it seemed to me.'

'I have no interest,' said Millicent, 'in the office side of it. I am interested solely—from my own viewpoint.'

Carol asked carefully:

'What is that?'

Millicent put her cigarette in the ash tray. She said:

'I like Andrew. I think I'm in love with him. He isn't in love with me, however; but up until yesterday I was certain that he liked me better than any woman he knew. We—complement each other,' she went on steadily, 'and he has been exceedingly useful to me in my work. Necessary, I believe ... I was content to go on, this way ... for as long as ...' She broke off and shrugged. She added, 'You constitute an unexpected complication.'

Carol was silent. Then she asked:

'Why?'

'My dear Carol,' said Millicent, 'are you as insensitive as you appear? I think not. You and Andy were in love once, or so I assume. You were married. You lived together for a number of years ... how many?'

'Two,' said Carol. Her lips felt stiff. She resented this conversation bitterly. It was indecent. It should never have taken place.

'Two years,' said Millicent. 'Assuming further that you quarreled, fell out of love, began to dislike each other ...'

'Assume what you please,' said Carol shortly.

'I shall. You were divorced. Now, after a long time, you find yourselves in the same office, continually in contact, day after day.

132

Can you sit there and tell me it means nothing to you?'

'I don't know what it means,' said Carol.

'That's what I was afraid of, you see,' Millicent told her.

Carol said:

'Look here. We're fencing. We're not getting anywhere. What are you trying to tell me?'

'I think you know.'

'That you are in love with Andy and that, if possible, you intend to marry him?'

Millicent shrugged. She said thoughtfully:

'I don't know. I've never wanted to marry ... intimacy, day in day out ... possessiveness ... the everyday things...' Her face expressed a faint, fastidious contempt. 'No, I've never wished to marry. Not even Andy.'

Carol looked at her, appalled.

'You're in love with him,' she said slowly, 'you find him necessary—to your work, to yourself as a woman—but you don't want to marry him. But what, exactly, do you want from me?'

'You have an advantage,' said Millicent coolly; 'you see him every day. You have memories in common. You no longer dislike each other, if ever you did.'

'In other words,' said Carol, 'you want me to keep my hands off?' She found herself laughing with genuine amusement. 'You're afraid Andy and I will fall in love again?'

'Why not?' asked Millicent. 'It would be up

133

to you, naturally. It's always up to the woman. In your shoes I'd know just how to manage.'

'If you were writing this,' Carol said, 'you'd know how to manage because you could make your characters do as you please. But we aren't characters in a novel. We aren't, I must remind you, the same people who married ten years or so ago. We've grown up, we're adult, and I may add, civilized.'

'Of course,' said Millicent, smiling.

Carol went on hotly:

'And not only that ... we're different people.'

'Which is dangerous,' said Millicent; 'with the appeal and interest of strangers to each other and yet, people who remember—'

'Please,' said Carol, 'you have no right.'

Millicent's eyes widened. She said:

'That distresses you? I thought you were—adult and—what was your word?—civilized.'

She rose and went to stand by Carol's chair. She touched her on the shoulder. She said quietly:

'Don't misunderstand me. It's a matter of indifference to me whether or not Andrew tells Stephen and Richard, or anyone at all about your former relationship. I was angry, I suppose, and even hurt, because he didn't tell *me*. I shan't tell anyone if you'd rather not, although you must realize that it will get out, as, after all, people who knew you when you were married will see you together now and the grapevine will take up the story. My advice would be for one of you, preferably Andrew, to mention it to Steve or Richard before someone else does. It shouldn't make any difference to you.'

'It wouldn't,' said Carol.

Millicent said:

'I can see your mind work. It's amusing. You're wondering if I am planning to get you out of the office. I'm not, I couldn't. I'm not so important to Maynard and Hall, my dear. I've written one book which sold well enough and another which will sell better, but I'm not in a position to dictate interoffice decisions. If I said, "Let Miss Reid go or I'll find another publisher," they'd probably reply, "All right, find one then." It wouldn't be too difficult. But unfortunately if I went elsewhere I couldn't take Andrew with me.' She laughed. 'No, much as I wish someone else would offer you a better job . . .' She paused and stood looking down, thinking. Then she said suddenly:

'I wonder if that isn't the solution?'

'What?' asked Carol, startled.

'But, of course, you wouldn't.'

Carol demanded impatiently:

'Wouldn't what?'

Millicent spoke slowly. She said:

'I know many important people . . . it might be that I would, by chance, hear of an opening for someone like yourself, in public relations. More scope, more money. If that should occur, would you be interested?'

'No,' said Carol, 'I wouldn't be.'

'I thought not,' said Millicent. She added lightly, 'You can't give me a logical reason. You're a clever woman, and ambitious, or I'm no judge. So, if there isn't a logical reason there must be an illogical one. Could it be—Andrew?'

Carol was scarlet. She said:

'No.'

'Then, for the sake of argument—why?'

Carol shook her head. She said:

'If you don't know, then I couldn't possibly explain.'

Millicent's smile was disarming. She said:

'I do know. I don't blame you. And I like you, Carol, as a person, very much. If I didn't I wouldn't bother to warn you that it isn't wise to try to revive old embers . . . or shall we say an old influence? Because I'd combat it, for better or worse.'

'Worse, most likely,' said Carol. Her anger had passed. She was entertained. This whole conversation was too fantastic to be taken seriously.

'That,' said Millicent serenely, 'is not your affair . . . unless you have taken a maternal interest in Andrew's welfare.'

'I have,' said Carol, 'no interest in him whatsoever. I like him. He's nice. I hope we're friends and will continue to be so—I hope we can go on working together.' She looked at

Millicent with laughter in her eyes and added, 'Of course, I don't pretend to know anything about him now but, unless he has changed very much basically, I might issue a warning too.'

'For instance?' asked Millicent cautiously.

Carol answered lightly:

'Andy's rather conventional, at heart, I believe. So perhaps you'd best reconsider your plan and make it for better, instead of for worse.'

If it was a challenge, Millicent accepted it. She said:

'I might, at that.'

She walked to the door, her mules clicking, turned, smiling, with her hand on the knob. She said:

'We could be friends, you know.'

'Could we?' asked Carol.

'I think so. We'll find out. Let's go along on that premise at all events. You're comfortable here?'

'Very—it's a charming room.'

Millicent said:

'I hope you'll occupy it often.' She opened the door. 'I've kept you up very late. But Sunday breakfast is a movable feast. Good night, Carol.'

'Good night,' Carol said mechanically.

Presently she snapped off the lights and went to bed. The sheets were cool and smelled of lavender. Fine linen sheets, beautifully monogrammed. Millicent did herself well and

137

why not? She gave a fleeting thought to the negligible cousin or whatever she was, living on this tolerant bounty, mouselike, grateful for crumbs. Millicent's family, Carol reflected, must be quite old school, for nowadays there was nothing even slightly unusual in a young woman making her home apart from her parents.

She could not sleep. She found herself reliving this extraordinary encounter, and hot with anger because she feared she hadn't come out very well. But after a while she relaxed and the humor of the situation again appealed to her. What did it amount to, anyway?

Millicent, young, talented, attractive, with more money than she needed, was in love with Andrew—and uncertain of him. She didn't want to marry him. She simply wanted him around, in a dual capacity of lover and editor. That was, thought Carol, extremely funny.

Why should she be afraid of me? Carol wondered. The fact that she was afraid was flattering.

She's clever, Carol thought, but not clever enough. She shouldn't put ideas in my head.

But they'd only be—ideas. She had no claim on Andy, no right to interfere with his life ... if she could. And she didn't think that she could.

Millicent lived, Carol decided, in a fictional world. Situations became plots, people became characters. As if, thought Carol, I'd have any real influence over Andy—or he, over me, for that matter—merely because we were once married.

Influence. That wasn't exactly what Millicent had meant or what she was afraid of, Carol thought. She was afraid of the pull, the power of senses, once in tune with, and responsive to, each other. She was afraid of old sentimentalities, of shared memories softened, perhaps, even englamored, by the passing of time. Well, she needn't be, thought Carol.

Just before falling asleep it occurred to her that she would have to walk softly in the office where Millicent was concerned. She must see to it that she obtained her meed of publicity and more. Otherwise, thought Carol sleepily, she will think I'm holding out on her for personal reasons. Her mind works that way, poor girl.

Her final thought was of Andy. She wondered exactly how embarrassed he'd been, earlier in the evening, with Millicent prying and prodding. Perhaps he hadn't been embarrassed at all.

Poor Andy, she couldn't contemplate him embarking upon an affair with Millicent ... Millicent seemed a figment of her own imagination, with ink in her veins, thought Carol, falling asleep.

139

CHAPTER TWELVE

She woke late and by the time she was dressed and ready for breakfast it was after ten o'clock. Millicent was nowhere to be seen, nor Andy nor the Talbots. Young Greene was serving himself from the sideboard as she came into the big sunny dining room.

'Good morning,' Carol said; 'or is it noon?'

'Not quite. I slept my head off.' He looked at her in frank admiration. 'You're looking in the pink,' he said.

'Must be the English influence.' She poured herself a cup of coffee. 'That smells good,' she said.

'Broiled kidneys,' he suggested, 'scrambled eggs, lots of toast. There's a pitcher of fruit juice.'

She asked:

'Where are the others?'

'The Talbots are playing golf. I never knew such energetic people,' he complained; 'it tires me to think about them. Golf, tennis, swimming ... do they never sit down and relax? Morgan and Millicent are riding. That leaves us. Shall we go out on the terrace and steep in the sun?' he inquired. 'I can't imagine a better way of spending the morning.'

Something after noon the others came back. Carol, lying lazily under the shade of a vast

140

umbrella, heard Andy's laughter. He was saying:

'You'll never make a passionate lover of horseflesh out of me, Millicent. I regard horses with too much reverence. That brute you assigned me...'

'Gentlest old hack in the world,' said Millicent, 'wouldn't hurt a baby.'

'I'm not a baby,' said Andy gloomily.

They came up on the terrace to contemplate Carol and Greene.

'Sloths,' said Millicent firmly, 'you've missed the best part of the day.'

She wore a white shirt, beautifully tailored breeches, superb boots, and a sleeveless leather jacket. Her hair, braided and clubbed at the back of her neck, was tied with a narrow black ribbon. She looked very young but not in the least defenseless.

Andy, thought Carol, looked well in riding clothes. She regarded him until he laughed and turned away. He said:

'Glad you didn't see me. I spent most of my time yanking the beast to a walk. Practically sat on his neck saying "Good old horsie" in unconvincing tones. Once he looked at me, and I realized he had no respect for me whatever.'

They went away to change, the Talbots came in, the mouselike cousin crept timidly into the sunlight, and after a while it was time for luncheon.

In the afternoon they lazed about, and

141

swam. Tea was served at the pool's edge. Supper was late, served on the terrace while tall candles in hurricane shades flickered under the sky. Carol, thinking absently that Millicent was fortunate in her cook, reflected that she had not had a moment alone with Andy. Not that she had tried—only now and then when they had been standing or sitting together, Millicent had always appeared. Nothing obvious about it ... nothing at all.

She smiled.

Andy, sitting beside her, between her and Mrs Talbot, asked quickly:

'What's funny?'

He'd always said that, she remembered. Just 'What's funny?'

'Nothing. Myself perhaps. Or maybe you,' she answered cheerfully.

They left about ten o'clock. Millicent asked:

'You don't mind taking a passenger?' She explained that the Talbots had driven Greene up but were not returning to the city as they were going on to Stockbridge.

'Not at all,' said Andy heartily.

'I'll curl up in the back seat,' promised young Greene, 'and sleep. Dormouse, that's me.'

So there he was in the back seat, and Carol in the front. Millicent stood in the lighted doorway, waving good-bye. The Talbots had already departed in sound and fury.

This couldn't have been calculated, thought Carol; Millicent could not have wangled an invitation to Stockbridge for the Talbots since last night! No, of course not. But that Millicent was pleased with the present arrangement Carol had no doubt.

The absurd thing was that young Greene did fall asleep. Carol looked back at him anxiously.

'He's lopping about, his head bobs up and down,' she reported. 'Do you think he'll break his neck or anything?'

'He'll be all right,' said Andy. He added, 'Have a good time?'

'Grand, it's a lovely place.' She added politely, 'Millicent's a delightful hostess.'

'It isn't hard,' he argued, to her astonishment, 'when she has everything to do with—money oils the machinery.'

'She'd still not be a good hostess,' said Carol, 'unless it was in her.'

'Maybe not. But it isn't Millicent who looks after your comfort,' he said; 'things run for her. She pays for that type of service. She herself is completely casual.'

'Maybe that's being a good hostess,' said Carol feebly, astonished to find herself defending Millicent.

Andy lowered his voice. He said:

'She knows about us.'

'Don't be so conspiratorial,' said Carol, laughing. 'You'd think we had a deep dark mutual past.'

He chuckled.

'Well, haven't we?'

'Not so deep,' she said, 'nor dark. Merely briefly mutual.'

He said:

'She asked me about us. I had to tell her, of course.'

Carol felt slightly impatient. She said:

'My good creature, why shouldn't you? There's nothing disgraceful or even secret about it. At least we didn't mean it to be secret, it just happened that way.'

He said:

'I'll speak to Steve and Richard. It's bound to come to light, sooner or later.'

'So Millicent said.'

She saw him turn and look at her.

'She spoke to you too?'

'Last night, in my room.' Carol laughed. 'It seemed to trouble her. I assured her I was no longer your wife and certainly not your guardian.'

She heard him swallow. He felt uneasy, as a man, the subject of intimate discussion between two women, one of whom had been his wife. It was a situation he didn't like. She could sense that, and with complete understanding.

He said:

'I don't know why she did that.'

'Oh, come,' Carol said, 'you're not stupid, Andy. She's in love with you, she regards me as what the movies call a menace.'

144

'Good God!' said Andy blankly.

'I told her,' said Carol blithely, 'in effect, that she needn't worry. I have no designs on you. You have my blessing, both of you.'

'A little prematurely,' said Andy, 'and I must say, Carol, I don't like the idea.'

She said gently:

'Neither did I. But since we were twenty, Andy, certain situations have altered. Modern ex-wives and ex-husbands dine together, with their current spouses. Everything is very ducky, cozy and *gemütlich*. So there's nothing out of the way in your present heart interest—'

'She isn't!' he interrupted angrily.

'My mistake,' said Carol cheerfully. 'Anyway, she's interested in you. You'll have to admit that. And I think she's afraid that I might be too. A sort of emotional hangover. For auld lang syne, and all that sort of thing.'

'It's indecent,' he said hotly.

'I thought so,' said Carol, 'but Millicent doesn't. She's very'—she laughed—'civilized.'

'Women!' said Andy profoundly, after a considerable silence.

He took a bump without slackening his speed. It woke up Mr Greene, who spent most of the remainder of the trip leaning forward and talking about nothing very entertainingly in Carol's ear.

They dropped him at his apartment and went on uptown. While the doorman was taking Carol's bag from the trunk, Andy stood

145

on the pavement talking. He said:

'It was fun, we'll do it again.'

Carol grinned infuriatingly. She said:

'I'll be amazed if I rate another invitation, Andy.'

'Nonsense.'

She said, not too dramatically because of the doorman's presence:

'Old evil creeps back into your flawless life, disconcerting new fine influence.'

'Shut up!' said Andy. He wanted to smack her. He remembered other times when he had wanted to smack her, he remembered that particular grin—it hadn't grown up at all—and the tone of voice. She'd always been able to get under his skin. He remembered a blond girl who had had too much to drink, he remembered going home afterward and wrenching off his collar to the tune of Carol's taunts ... 'Oh, Mr Morgan,' Carol had chanted, 'you're so big and strong!'

She subsided obediently.

'Sorry,' she murmured.

Suddenly he laughed. He said:

'You haven't changed after all.'

'Lord, I hope so,' she said, sincerely shocked.

As he was getting back into the car, she halted him with a hand on his arm.

'Won't it be difficult,' she asked, 'to explain things at the office?'

'Less,' he assured her, 'than if it comes to the

146

office from outside channels. I hadn't thought of that.'

'Neither had I. Thanks for driving me down, Andy, and good night.'

The car pulled away from the curb and she followed the doorman and her luggage inside.

She did not see Andy the next morning. She did not see anyone to talk to except Elsie Norris, Dorothy Owen, and a few million people who kept popping in. No one important. She was lunching at the St Regis in order to witness a fashion show, the reason being a tie-up between the show and one of their new authors, a designer who had turned her hand to writing, and doing it very well. She did not return to the office until three; when she did, Dorothy, reporting six telephone calls, two telegrams and a stack of mail, added that Mr Maynard wanted to see her.

Carol, picking up the telephone to see if he was free, felt distinct misgiving. When, in ten minutes the bell rang and Jessie at the switchboard told her that she could go in now, she went down the corridor, aware that her knees shook slightly. For all the world like a schoolgirl about to be put upon the carpet. She lifted her chin and took a deep breath. He couldn't eat her, she reminded herself defiantly, the worst he could do would be fire her. Although for what, she couldn't imagine.

Maynard laughed when she came in and waved her to a chair.

'Don't look so guilty,' he advised.

'I feel guilty,' she told him, 'although I don't know why. You may remember that I boggled rather when you told me that your absent general manager was one Andrew Morgan. You asked, did I know him? And I said I knew someone by that name once. I didn't dream it was Andy,' she defended herself; 'last time I saw him he was still in a broker's office ... although there wasn't any business.'

He said:

'My dear child, I'm not blaming you. I understand perfectly.'

She said, after a moment:

'I haven't been quite honest. I went home that day wondering if he was Andy, thinking I shouldn't take the position if there was a chance of it ... and then, I made sure ... a friend of mine knew a friend of his ... you know. Roundabouts. So, it was Andy. So what? I did want the job very much.'

'Andy says he was struck all of a rubbish heap when he saw you sitting at the conference table,' Maynard told her, 'but I understand why you didn't make an announcement in the circumstances. Once you've been silent on a subject, every day that passes makes it increasingly harder to break that silence. I just wanted to tell you that we can take it in our stride. It will get around the office, we'll see to that ... but I doubt if anyone will be more than mildly amazed.'

'Thanks,' said Carol. 'The whole business was pretty silly. But after all these years—'

'You and Andy get on all right?' Maynard asked casually.

'Beautifully.' Carol laughed. 'Better than we ever did. Well, not quite that. Better than we did during the last months of our marriage, anyway,' she conceded.

He said:

'It's difficult to think that you and Andy...' He shrugged and smiled. 'You may come in for a little interoffice kidding. Steve, for one, finds it an amusing situation.'

'Well, it is, I suppose,' she said.

'Don't go,' said Maynard, as she rose. 'There are some things I want to discuss with you.'

He pulled a letter from a folder, and tossed it to her. A little later he said, 'I think we'll have Pete in on this.'

Peter Tarrant came in, a long, lean, redheaded young man with considerable charm. He was momentarily busily engaged in pursuing one of last year's most enchanting debutantes. Once when Maynard had to speak twice to make himself understood, Pete grinned disarmingly.

'Don't mind me,' he said, 'I'm sheep herding.'

'Why?' asked Carol.

'Wool gathering,' Peter explained and Maynard explained further, kindly:

149

'He's in love, Carol.'

'Carol,' said Pete, 'wouldn't know about that. An aloof, efficient female. When she first joined our little family I tried to interest her in my extraordinary personality. She'd have none of me. She's in love with her job.'

'A woman dedicated,' admitted Carol modestly.

The door opened and Andy burst in. He grinned at them impartially, said raptly:

'I've almost nailed the Dawson child ... her father's coming to see you tomorrow, Richard ... I've been talking to him most of the morning.'

'Banzai!' cried Peter, while Carol exclaimed:

'Andy! You're sure?'

'He's still uncertain,' said Andy, throwing himself into a chair, 'but I think you'll persuade him. Carol, you'll have to handle this job very carefully. One of the things Dawson worries about is publicity.'

'Wait a minute,' said Maynard, 'let's get Steve in.'

The Dawson child had been a subject of office conversation for several months, ever since Andy, dining one night at his club, had met her father and through him had discovered a little girl who might become the Marjorie Fleming of her generation.

There have been a good many child prodigies, down through the years, but Marjorie Fleming's brief life still shed its

150

special luster. There had been no one like her ... but now there was Lydia Dawson.

Dawson and Andy had been at the university together, as freshman and senior. Dawson had married soon after graduation, and Lydia's mother had died in childbirth. Andy hadn't seen Dawson since their college days, until their chance meeting at the club. They had been very friendly at college, had worked together on the college paper. Now, they renewed their friendship, over dinner, and during the course of the evening Dawson had spoken about Lydia.

Andy had groaned inwardly. He knew too many proud parents who wanted him to read Junior's essay or Elmira's English theme or tiny Betty's poem to Santa Claus. Yet things which her father had said of Lydia interested him and a week or so later he had dined at the Dawson apartment, met the child herself, and after she had gone to bed, read some of the poems which Dawson produced from a desk drawer. He had been, quite literally, speechless, for this was not the poetry of a child prodigy but of a prodigy. You couldn't, you shouldn't, judge it on the incidental factor of age.

It was simple verse, lyrical, lovely. It sang of the things Lydia knew best, the sun warm on her skin, the wind in her hair, the clouds overhead, the fleet shapes of birds. Cool, sexless, perfect. There was emotion, but

151

emotion of the spirit, an admitted kinship with earth, yet an effortless winging upward to things not of earth.

Ever since then Andy had been imploring Dawson to let Maynard and Hall publish a book of Lydia's poetry ... but Dawson was reluctant. He feared to expose the child to publicity, excitement, furor. It would harm her, he said; she was a perfectly natural, happy youngster, with a normal love of fun, companionship, play. He didn't want her spoiled.

He had, however, been prevailed upon to let Richard Maynard and others on their staff read some of the verse. Recently, not more than a week or so ago, Carol had heard of the Dawson poetry and had seen the few examples which Lydia's father had permitted Andy to take. Now she cried:

'If only we could do it!'

Maynard said:

'After I talk to Mr Dawson perhaps you'll come in, Carol. If it's just the publicity that worries him, I'm sure that you can handle it.'

He looked at her and smiled. Steve grinned and Andy said, 'All is forgiven.' A statement which was obscure, at least to Peter Tarrant, who looked at them in bewilderment.

Carol said:

'I'm sure I could. I think I know what Mr Dawson wants to avoid. It's more a question of what we avoid, for the child's sake, than what we do, isn't it?'

'Dawson will be here tomorrow,' said Andy, 'at eleven.'

CHAPTER THIRTEEN

Leaving Maynard's office Andy drew Carol aside. 'Come talk to me a moment,' he urged.

She followed him in, spoke to Kate, busy at her typewriter and they went into his room. Standing by the windows she said:

'Can't stay. I'm busy.'

'So am I. Lord, if you'd seen Richard's face when I told him!' He chuckled. 'You didn't find it—disagreeable, did you?'

'No, why should I?' she said honestly. 'I felt a little small, that's all. It all seemed pretty trivial.'

'I suppose so.'

'What is Dawson like, Andy?' she asked.

'Big guy,' said Andy, 'quiet. I've always liked him. He's a little alarmed by all this. By the child, I mean. She's not at all terrifying to meet—no airs, no graces, no poses, no big eyes and languid lily business. Just a regular little kid with freckles on her nose and some teeth missing. But it's a terrific talent, Carol. Talent? It's damned near genius. It would scare the hell out of me if I were her father. It scares him. It's a responsibility. And he honestly doesn't know

153

what's best for her. He's believed all along that the better way is to encourage her, let her write all she wants, but not force it, not make it public until she's grown. Until I came along. I've been persuading him that it can't hurt her to be published, that nothing can hurt her, provided she isn't shoved into the limelight plus a lot of interviewers and photographers and all that. Now he's sort of swinging over my way and I am wondering if I'm wrong. You'll understand better when you talk to him.'

'What does he do?' she asked.

'He inherited a chain of restaurants, believe it or not.'

'Oh, that Dawson! Is his father dead?'

'Some years ago. Bill runs the chain. He's a notable businessman. He doesn't understand why this happened to him. From all I can learn his wife wasn't unusual . . . I mean, she had no special gift. A nice, pretty girl whom he'd known ever since prep-school days. No talent in the family so far as anyone can discover.'

'Odd,' she commented, 'how it strikes. Not the usual run-of-the-mill talent, that can crop up in any family. But something like this. Do you believe it, Andy?'

'Believe what?'

'Believe that it is the child. Couldn't it be— her father?'

'Bill?' He laughed. 'I doubt it. Wait till you see him.'

She was conscious of more than usual

curiosity when she went to Maynard's office toward noon of the next day. The big man who rose as she entered did not, she admitted to herself, look like the father of a prodigy. He was good-looking, heavy through the shoulders, with a square, dogged chin and dark hair. His eyes were light, a clear gray, and he had a pleasant smile. She was immediately aware that he was shy.

She said, after the introductions:

'I understand how you feel about your little girl, Mr Dawson.'

'Don't think me rude,' he said hesitantly, 'if I say, I doubt it. You see, it's all so inexplicable. And frightening. And I want to do only what's best for her.'

Carol glanced at Maynard, who nodded slightly. It was as if he said, 'Take over.'

She said:

'Well, I understand that, at least.'

'Of course,' he agreed gravely. 'I—I've been interested enough to follow the—shall we say?—careers of other gifted children. Most of them—' he shrugged—'a flash in the pan. Nothing valuable after they were grown. A lot of press clippings, ballyhoo, controversy, and then—silence. It must be hard on a youngster to be dragged into the spotlight and then pushed back into normal living. In some cases, the controversy raged about the authenticity of the child's gift—or production. In several instances I would swear there had been adult

155

help—if only a matter of polishing, the right word, the right place ... parents perhaps, or teachers. In Lydia's case ... well, no one has anything to do with this, except Lydia. I—wouldn't know how, for one thing; I don't even, Andy tells me, wholly appreciate the scope of her talent.'

Carol said:

'If it is a gift that is going to endure, going to grow, you can't harm it—or her—by sharing it with other people, Mr Dawson. If it is, as you say, a flash in the pan, there's no harm in letting people know about it either. The harm would be if she were exploited, if it would separate her from, say, her schoolmates, set her too far apart. But surely they realize her gift at school?'

'They do. Her teachers sent for me ... she was only six, and was already writing verse. It's a very modern school,' he added; 'sometimes I wonder if it isn't a little too modern. Anyway they believe in permitting their pupils full self-expression. But they seem to think there that this is much more than the effort made by the average articulate child.'

Carol said after a moment:

'You could count on me to help ... in so far as my jurisdiction goes. I am sure Mr Maynard and everyone will agree that it would be wise to show you every publicity item before it goes out. There will be, of course, a question of newspapers, interviews, and the like. I think we can eliminate a lot of that without offending the press, and make it as easy as possible for both you and Lydia.'

The telephone on Maynard's desk rang and he spoke into it. He said, 'Ask him to wait a moment.'

He looked from Carol to Dawson. He said:

'Appointment's coming up. Perhaps you'd like to take Mr Dawson to your office, Carol, and go on with your conversation?'

He rose to shake hands with Dawson. He said pleasantly:

'I needn't tell you that I hope you'll decide our way.'

As they left the office Dawson looked at his watch. He said, in dismay, 'I had no idea it was as late. I wonder ... would you lunch with me? We could talk things over then. And before I decide anything I—' he looked at her with an expression that was almost appeal—'I would like you to meet Lydia. I have a feeling that if you talked with her, you'd understand better, and so help me to a decision.'

She said, startled:

'That's very kind of you, Mr Dawson, very flattering.'

He was groping for words. He said:

'I didn't mean it that way. I meant ...' He broke off to ask:

'You aren't married, are you?'

'Not now,' she told him. She added, 'You didn't know ... that Andy and I—?'

157

He flushed. He said hurriedly:

'I'm sorry. I lost track of Andy over the years. I remember now, hearing that he was married and divorced.'

'We were,' she corrected him. 'Does it seem curious to you, our turning up in the same office?'

'A little,' he admitted.

They had reached her office. She said, 'Come in, and find yourself a chair while I get my hat and powder my nose.'

The office was empty. He stood there, waiting, looking at all the outward signs of her activity, wondering about her, Andy Morgan's wife. His ex-wife.

Crazy idea thinking that if she met Lydia she'd understand his problem. For it was a problem—

Just because she was dark and tall, and had direct eyes and a sudden smile which reminded him of Lydia's mother ...

They went out together and Carol found that she had to take the lead. He asked, 'Where shall we lunch?' and she said, smiling, 'There's a Dawson's on Madison, you know, several of them,' but he shook his head.

'Come,' she said, as they went out to the hot dusty street, 'don't tell me you never eat in your own restaurants.'

'Very frequently,' he admitted, 'but let's not today. Where do you like to go?'

She told him of the small French place, not

far off on Park. He had never been there. She said, 'It isn't where I take visiting authors. They like it livelier.'

When they had found a corner table and had ordered, she said:

'Tell me about Lydia.'

'She's just a kid,' he told her gravely, 'she's short and fat—puppy fat, Lorna says.'

'Lorna?'

'Her nurse. She's been with her since she was born. She was with Lydia's mother.' He stopped. 'She's a graduate nurse, and wonderful with children. Of course, Lydia's in school but Lorna stayed on, to run the house, to look after her. She's a strong little thing really, Lydia, I mean, but—'

'I see,' said Carol, understanding. She thought, He's besotted about the child. If she's in a draft, he sneezes. I can see that. She asked casually:

'Is Lorna old?'

'Oh, no,' he said instantly, 'quite young. About thirty, I'd say. I've never asked her.'

Carol thought, And she wants to marry you, naturally. She felt sorry for him. Big man, big business, a financial expert, at least an expert at organization, completely helpless before the child he's produced, completely at her mercy.

She asked:

'Is Lydia in town?'

'No, I've a place on the Island,' he told her. 'I thought perhaps if you'd care to drive down for a weekend ... to see Lydia, to talk with her ...'

'I'd like to, very much. Tell me more about her.'

'But there *isn't* anything,' he said, 'that's the odd part. She's just like other little girls her age. At least she seems so to me. In one way, she's older. Old-fashioned, Lorna calls it. That's from being with me so much and with Lorna. Not that she hasn't playmates, Lorna's seen to that. But she's interested in the things a child of her age likes—the pony I bought her recently, her cat, her dogs. She likes clothes, she loves to go to the movies. She's just like anyone else,' he said imploringly.

Carol thought, He's afraid.

She asked thoughtfully:

'She's always written?'

'Since she could form letters. Before that she used to—sing.'

'Sing?' asked Carol.

'Make up songs,' he said painfully, 'sing them. A sort of tuneless little singing. We didn't think anything of it at first. Then Lorna began writing them down and we realized that they weren't just songs Lydia had heard—they weren't anything either of us had heard. They were hers.'

'I haven't seen much,' said Carol after a pause; 'just the little Andy had at the office. It's breathtaking that a child ...' She paused and frowned. 'That's the error we mustn't commit, Mr Dawson. We mustn't judge what she writes

160

by her age, mustn't say, "This is remarkable because a ten-year-old child produced it." We must judge it on its own merits. We must look on a poem as just that, a poem. As if anyone had written it, you, I, a woman of forty-five, a man of sixty. If this gift,' she said slowly, 'is going to matter it must be divorced from the child, it must stand alone.'

He said:

'I can see that. No one has ever said that to me before except one of Lydia's teachers. Everyone else, everyone who knows Lydia, looks at the whole business from the standpoint of her age.'

'They mustn't,' said Carol.

After a moment he asked her:

'You and Andy—you had no children?' He flushed again as he said it, looked at her as if he regretted speaking.

'No,' said Carol. 'We were very young, you know, when we married.'

'We—were too,' he said.

'We thought we would wait,' she admitted. 'We knew we wanted children, or thought so, but we believed we'd have plenty of time for that. So—well, we didn't have the time, we were divorced so soon. And therefore it was just as well.'

'Why?' he asked soberly.

She said, after a moment:

'Perhaps a child would have kept us together. If we hadn't wanted to be together,

161

the compulsion would have been wrong. And if we'd had a baby and hadn't stayed together, well, that would have made things difficult, especially for me, going home as I did to my people and afterward having to earn a living.'

'Yes, of course.' He added, 'You mustn't think me rude, Miss Reid; I didn't mean to be. I was interested, that's all. I've always liked Andy.' He said directly, 'I like you.'

It was a simple statement of fact. She accepted it and smiled.

'Thank you,' she said.

When they parted it was with the understanding that she would drive down to the Island with him the following Friday afternoon.

He said:

'It's a household that doesn't need a man around, really.'

'What do you mean by that?'

'Lorna runs things,' he explained, 'and my wife's mother lives with us. She is an old lady, an invalid. Lydia—my wife, it was her name too—was her only child, born after Mrs Wales was forty.'

Carol thought, Poor dear. A hagridden household. Yet he was shy with women. He shouldn't be, she told herself. It was hard to visualize him in that household. She could see him in all sorts of situations, on the deck of a ship, in a lumber camp, riding herd, on a baseball diamond ... anywhere masculine, anywhere free. But not cooped up with a lot of women!

Returning to the office she reported that Mr Dawson had not come to any conclusion but that he had asked her to visit him, meet the child and talk with her.

'I don't know why or how,' she ended, 'but I have the feeling that my reaction to the child—or hers to me—will determine this matter. Yes, probably hers to me.'

'It's a step in the right direction,' Maynard said approvingly and Andy, who had been with Maynard when she entered, grinned. He said:

'You're a fast worker.'

He left Maynard's office with her. He said, in the corridor:

'Be careful. He may fall in love with you.'

'Why not?' she asked tartly. 'Is there a law against it?'

Andy shouted. He said:

'No, but you needn't go to that extreme to bring a new author into the fold.' He looked at her and grinned. 'But that's all right,' he said, with sweeping generosity, 'as long as you don't fall in love with him.'

'Why shouldn't I?' she retorted.

Andy shrugged. 'No reason, of course. The Dawson chain is not to be sneezed at unless you're allergic to white tiles and good food. But you won't.'

'Won't what—sneeze?'

'Fall in love with him.'

163

'Why not?' she demanded.

'Because,' explained Andy kindly, 'he isn't in the least like me.'

CHAPTER FOURTEEN

She was laughing, as she returned to her office, amused by the casual effrontery, the touch of pseudo arrogance. It reminded her of the Andy she had known long ago.

Toward the end of the week Millicent Allen dropped in at the office and came to sit by Carol's crowded desk, smoking innumerable cigarettes and talking of the publicity campaign which would launch the new book in September. Advance copies would be in the office by August, if all went well.

Millicent had a hard business head. Before seeing Carol she had been in conference with Maynard, Andy, and Peter Tarrant on the matter of advertising. She spoke of that now, and of some concessions she had won. Carol looked at her in astonishment. She looked rather otherworldly, in a cool, delicate, blond way. Despite the blazing heat, she was like curly lettuce in green linen with jade buttons at her ear lobes. It seemed absurd that she could discourse knowingly of advertising figures. However, Carol reflected, there must have been other hard business heads in the family or

the Allen fortune wouldn't be where it was ...
and if Millicent has inherited a love of figures,
all the better for her.

Millicent asked casually:

'You saw the dedication?'

'No.'

'That's right, you read the book in manuscript, I didn't send the dedication in until afterward.'

'You've dedicated it to Andy?' asked Carol directly, tiring of Millicent's fancy for fencing.

'How did you guess?' inquired Millicent blandly.

'Elementary, my dear Watson,' said Carol, smiling.

The gray-green eyes flickered. Millicent murmured:

'We are not amused?'

'Why should I be?' inquired Carol with Girl Scout bluntness. 'I think it's fine, Andy will be flattered ...' Her eyes added, Which was, I take it, your design.

Millicent said, rising:

'I hope so. I won't take up any more of your time now, Carol. Are you free this weekend?'

'I'm afraid not.'

'I'm sorry,' said Millicent. 'I hoped you'd come up to Longfields—no one else will be there. We'd have a pleasant, lazy sort of time. I'd like very much to know you better.'

Carol, entirely off guard, could only gape at her. She said feebly:

'That's nice of you. But I'm going to Long Island ... it's business really.'

'Oh, of course. The Dawson child. I'd forgotten.'

'How did you know about it?' Carol asked.

'They were discussing her today, Andy and Richard,' Millicent told her. 'Personally I think child prodigies are dreadful. They should be drowned at birth. They frighten me if they are genuine, and disgust me if they aren't. I'll be interested in your report. Promise me that you'll come to Longfields. If you say next week, I'll clear the decks. No other guests...'

Carol hesitated and Millicent said quickly:

'If you don't, I'll believe that you don't want to be—friendly.'

Helplessly, Carol nodded. She agreed, 'Next week then.'

'Good.'

Millicent gathered her gloves ... how can she bear them in this weather? Carol thought—and went to the door. There was a faint tracery of amusement about her lips. Hardly a smile; a shadow perhaps; and perhaps not so much amusement as triumph.

'Damn,' said Carol crossly, when the door had closed behind her.

Dorothy Owen poked her head around the opening into her little room.

'Call me?'

'I was swearing,' said Carol, 'and with very good reason.'

166

'It's hot enough,' Dorothy said sympathetically.

Why did I let her bait me into that? thought Carol angrily, waiting to talk to a radio production manager. What in the world is up her sleeve, why should she want me there for a weekend alone? What's the matter with her? Is she being obvious or subtle? Damned if I know. 'Oh, hello, Mr Anderson,' she said aloud, finding the transition difficult, 'this is Carol Reid.'

She had dinner with Bess and Jerry on Thursday night. Jerry had to go off on one of his innumerable business engagements. 'He sells things at the oddest times and in the oddest places,' said Bess, lamenting.

The apartment—Jerry's—was perfectly masculine. Bess looked around it with satisfaction. 'I haven't even attempted the woman's touch,' she said, pleased with herself. 'Isn't the result wonderful? All books and leather shabbiness, smoke and superb disorder. I'm sick of living in a woman's world. This is easier, and lots more fun.'

'Happy, I take it?'

'Very.' Bess sobered. 'Different from before,' she said, lighting a cigarette. 'More—laughter. More silences. Companionship, that's what they call it. None of this seesaw business, the blue sky one minute and—wham! Flat on your rear elevation the next.'

'Sounds satisfactory,' Carol admitted.

'It is. Haven't seen you for ages. What have you been doing?'

Carol told her.

'Millicent Allen,' exclaimed Bess, 'the gal in the columns ... Andy interested?'

'I think so,' said Carol carefully, 'I don't know.'

'Oops,' said Bess, 'does she know about you and Andy?'

'No, when we went up there together. Yes, before we left.'

It was good to have someone with whom she could talk, about herself, about Andy. Bess was comforting. You tossed your confidence at her as you might throw a pebble into a well. It sank. That was all there was to it.

Bess said, 'Tell me some more. Don't look so continued-in-our-next.'

'She's in love with him,' said Carol, 'she warned me off.'

Bess looked astonished.

'With cause?'

'Without,' answered Carol, laughing. 'Furthermore, she invited me for another weekend.' She explained and Bess said:

'Wants you up there alone, does she? Why?'

'Why?' repeated Carol. 'You tell me.'

'Pump,' said Bess, 'nice pleasant pump, accompanied by hospitality. What was Andy like? Why did you quarrel? She's interested in learning your mistakes in order to avoid them.'

'That's silly,' said Carol, 'seeing that she's

involved with a different man.'

'What, another? Who—do you know him?'

'I mean Andy ... as he is now.'

'Of course,' said Bess, annoyed at her own stupidity, 'but she doesn't know that. So far as she is concerned, Andy was born the way he is now, she can't picture him as ever having been otherwise. Will you Tell All?'

'Within reason,' Carol said, laughing. She added, 'How Andy would hate it.'

'Naturally. But he won't know. You won't tell and certainly Millicent won't, if she has any brains. Well, it's a nice situation. What's this Long Island jaunt tomorrow?'

Carol explained briefly ... A new author, she said. She did not go into details. It was office business and not even Bess was entitled to it. If Dawson signed a contract on behalf of his little girl she'd be free to give Bess chapter and verse. Not now.

'But who is it?' demanded Bess.

'William Dawson,' said Carol. 'You know, the restaurants.'

'Lord,' said Bess, 'I've increased that man's income a thousandfold. Don't tell me he's taken to writing fiction!'

Carol smiled. 'Now it's your turn. What have you and Jerry been doing with yourselves since you didn't return from a honeymoon?'

*   *   *

169

Friday, about half past five, William Dawson called for her at her apartment. The long, chauffeur-driven car was sleek and shining in the hot yellow sunlight, and Dawson waited for her in the lobby. He regarded her with quiet appreciation as she came from the elevator.

'You look so cool.'

'I'm not,' she denied. 'It's marvelous to escape to the country.'

He said, 'You'll like it, I think ... an old house, on the dunes ... the bathing is very good. I hope you brought a suit.'

She had, she said, just in case.

He helped her in, sat beside her. The car pulled away and headed for the Fifty-ninth Street bridge. He said diffidently:

'This is very kind of you. You must have had other things to do.'

'Of course not. I am most anxious to meet Lydia.'

He said hesitantly:

'She doesn't know why you are coming, of course.'

He rolled a window farther down.

'It's hot,' he added, 'for this time of year. But then we always say that in late June, don't we? With the new highways we'll be there in about two hours and a half. If you think you'd mind a late dinner, we can dine on the road.'

'I can't bear to think of eating,' she assured him seriously.

'That's all right then,' he told her. 'I ordered

a cold supper ... and you'll have time to change. Lydia won't be up, of course. But you'll see her tomorrow.'

On the way he made conversation, courteously. It was, she realized, an effort. She said after a while, 'Look here, Mr Dawson, you mustn't try to—to amuse me. You don't have to, honestly. You must be tired ... after a week in town. Don't make the effort.'

He said:

'Funny, isn't it? I'm always surrounded by women yet I'm not much on small talk.'

She said lightly:

'That's why, perhaps. You hear so much.'

He was silent for a while. Then he said suddenly:

'But I like talking to you. Tell me about yourself, won't you? If you don't mind, of course; if you do—'

She thought impatiently, What in the world is the matter with the man? Aloud she said:

'But I don't mind.'

In a sense, she had already discussed her marriage with this stranger. Now, she did not speak of Andy ... but of herself, in more recent years, amusing incidents of her first jobs and of how she came to be with Maynard and Hall. He listened, she felt as if he were interested. She said presently:

'Enough of me. Your turn.'

'There isn't much,' he said; 'college and then I married, and when Lydia was born, her

171

mother died. I'd gone right into my father's business, and have been there ever since. I took it over, on his death. There's an uncle still in the firm but he's not well, he's away much of the time. His son, my cousin Charles, and I carry on ... I expect you'd think it a very dull sort of life.'

She said frankly:

'It sounds that way. Yet I don't believe it is.'

'No, I like business,' he said seriously. 'I like organization and dealing with people. I haven't had much reason to take time off, to any extent. When Lydia is older I shall. I want her to have everything ... necessary to her. Perhaps travel will be an essential. If it is, I shall take her abroad, we'll spend two years, three, any amount of time—providing that one can travel then,' he added, 'providing the world is at peace.'

She said, 'It never is, is it? We think of life as peace with interludes of war but it's really war with interludes of peace, or partial peace.'

He said, with a sudden emotion:

'I loathe thinking that Lydia must grow up in this kind of world.'

After a moment Carol said, 'I understand. I'd feel that way too if I had a child.'

It was not wholly dark when they reached the house, the dusk was misty blue over the ocean, the sky still flushed with sunset, illuminated by a single star.

A big frame house, old lawns, old gardens

172

and the singing sea. It was very peaceful. Servants met them and presently Lorna Sheffield, a tall woman, with a lovely figure and braided black hair. Her quiet face was oval and her eyes were blue.

She did not wear a uniform, but a tailored dinner frock of linen with a little jacket. She gave Carol a firm hand and a pleasant smile and took her to a room overlooking the marching dunes and the sea. She said, lingering, 'Plenty of time to shower and change.'

'Thank you.' Drawn to her, Carol smiled. She asked:

'You know why I'm here?'

'Yes,' said Lorna.

'You approve . . . or perhaps you don't?'

'I don't know,' Lorna said after a moment. 'It's hard to detach myself. You may understand when you see Lydia.'

Later they dined in a cool paneled room smelling of salt and roses. Dinner was hot soup, superb coffee, and a procession of cold dishes between. They talked, the three of them, out on the terrace after, for a little while. And then Lorna said, rising:

'I'm sure Miss Reid must be tired.'

Gratefully, Carol went up to bed, so sleepy that she had little time for thinking. It seemed a very short while before she woke, to morning. She saw the sunlight on the polished floor, she heard a child laughing in the corridor.

Rousing, she bathed and dressed and went downstairs. Hesitating for a moment at the door of the dining room, she saw Dawson rise, saw Lorna hurry forward, but looked beyond them to the child, Lydia, unaware how important this encounter would be, how in a sense it was to alter her life.

CHAPTER FIFTEEN

Dawson was saying, 'But we didn't think you'd be down ... this is an unexpected pleasure,' Lorna was moving forward to tell Carol earnestly, 'I hoped you'd get a good sleep and ring ... when you were ready for your breakfast...' and Carol was apologizing, 'But I *forgot!*'

She had forgotten completely that Lorna had told her, the night before, 'You'll want to sleep, I know ... when you wake and are ready for your breakfast—if you'll just ring...' and had then consulted her on orange juice, cereal, eggs...

'I'm so sorry,' Carol told them, smiling.

'We aren't,' said Dawson promptly, 'we're delighted.' He turned to his little girl who was standing, regarding Carol with wide, friendly eyes. 'This is Lydia,' he said. 'Lydia, weren't you saying just now that you wished Miss Reid would hurry and wake up so that you might meet her?'

Carol moved forward and held out her hand. Lydia gave a firm, plump little hand and smiled. She was much as her father and Andy had described her ... a fat little girl, freckles on her short nose, brown straight hair cut close to her head like a boy's. When she smiled there were gaps. Her eyes were gray as her father's, but long and narrow, tilted at the corners. She had a cordial grin. She wore shorts and a thin cotton pullover. She was all curves, like a puppy. She said, in a clear direct way:

'We really were talking about you.'

Carol's place was set, beside Lydia's. Orange juice arrived. Smiling, Lorna Sheffield poured the coffee. In the bright streaming light Carol regarded her and thought, She's even handsomer by daylight than I thought her last night.

She said:

'I feel as if I had intruded upon a leisurely family breakfast. That's the worst of guests, they never stay in their proper places.'

Lorna said briskly:

'I'm glad when they don't. But we like to give them an opportunity to escape us.'

Lydia said confidentially:

'Last summer a lady came to stay with us'— she widened her eyes at Carol—'and she *never got up until lunchtime*! We had to tiptoe past her door, even Daddy.'

Lorna shook her head slightly, but her eyes

smiled. She said:

'Mustn't tattle.'

'I didn't say her name,' Lydia expostulated. Her eyes shone. The forbidden name was imminent but she put her finger across her lips and twinkled at Carol.

Her father asked:

'Well, what about today? What shall we plan?'

'Does Miss Reid like picnics?' Lydia inquired.

'Ask her,' suggested Dawson.

'Do you?' Lydia asked hopefully. 'We do—a lot.'

'I love them,' said Carol.

'Daddy—Lorna, can—I mean, may we?' asked Lydia, bouncing slightly, like a rubber ball.

Dawson looked doubtfully at Carol but Lorna answered. Carol could see with what ease she ran the household ... whatever she had planned, a change of plans would not disturb her. Carol thought, She's a coper if ever I saw one ... and wondered a little ruefully if 'coping' were not a special talent. I don't believe I possess it, she speculated. I manage, that's about all.

Lorna said, speaking to Bill Dawson across the table, her untroubled regard on him:

'If Miss Reid isn't just being polite ...?' She turned to Carol, in explanation. 'Unfortunately,' she added, 'I have to be away today. My sister is in the Southampton hospital and I must spend the day with her. I'd like to go on a picnic today too. If you would, really, it's easily arranged.'

Lydia bounced more than ever.

'Please,' said Carol, adding her plea to the unspoken one and was immediately rewarded by a wide, delighted grin from the child.

'A beach picnic,' Lydia stipulated, 'in bathing suits.'

So it was agreed. After breakfast Lydia lingered beside Carol, regarding her with frank interest. But Lorna shooed her brightly upstairs. She said, 'Lots of things to do, you know ... then, the rest of the day, you'll be as free as air.'

She disappeared with the reluctant Lydia, who argued feebly, as if argument were part of their personal game, a habit of opposition you were in duty bound to offer but in which you really didn't believe. Dawson, offering Carol a cigarette, asked:

'Would you like to see the garden? It's a rather nice one, although we wage a constant battle with the wind, and sand blowing...'

They walked along in the bright-bordered paths ... an old-fashioned garden ... annuals, perennials, and roses. The sky was a flawless blue and the ocean, which lay almost at the foot of the garden, cobalt.

'This is a lovely place,' said Carol, sighing, 'no wonder Lydia looks so healthy.'

'Doesn't she?' he agreed eagerly. 'Of course, we owe that to Lorna ... she watches her like a hawk.'

'But not too obviously,' said Carol. 'I could see that in the short time I saw them together, at breakfast.'

'Lydia loves her dearly,' he said. 'They are devoted to each other.'

'She—Lydia—' Carol commented, 'has charming natural manners ... she makes one feel truly at home. Few children convey that impression to strangers.'

'She's inherently friendly,' said Lydia's father, 'but there again Lorna's training has a lot to do with it.'

They turned and began walking back. He said, after a moment, 'Here comes the other member of our household—Mrs Wales, my mother-in-law ...'

The old lady was in a wheel chair, propelled by a pleasant fresh-faced young woman in uniform. Despite the early morning heat, tempered by the ocean wind, she was bundled up in various coverings, a rug over her knees, a shawl over her shoulders. Carol and Dawson walked toward her and the wheel chair halted. 'Mother,' said Dawson, bending close and raising his voice, 'this is Miss Reid ...' He smiled at the nurse, 'Miss Reid—Miss Leaming.'

He added to Carol, 'Mother's quite deaf ... so, if you'd speak clearly?'

Obediently Carol shouted in a subdued fashion. The old lady was extraordinarily thin. Her face was a network of lines but her eyes were black, young, and watchful. She did not hold out the hand. She merely nodded, casually. She spoke to her son-in-law in the uninflected tone of the elderly deaf. She said:

'Looks nice. And very pretty.'

Carol flushed and found herself laughing. Yet of the two Dawson was the more embarrassed. He said, 'You mustn't mind her—she says what she thinks ... she calls it the privilege of age.'

'Of course,' said Mrs Wales, who could hear on occasion—when she wished. 'It's about all that's left me, isn't it? I can't walk. I don't hear very well. I don't relish my meals and I never sleep. Books bore me. But my sight's still good, and people forgive me when I talk too much and speak my mind. They think I haven't any mind.' She chuckled. 'That's where they're wrong.' Her tone changed. She said petulantly, 'I haven't seen Lydia all morning. Where's Lorna keeping her?'

Miss Leaming shouted soothingly:

'They'll be along presently.'

'Likes to keep her away from me,' said the old lady, annoyed, 'never could stand the woman.'

Miss Leaming raised her eyebrows at her employer and began to move the wheel chair slowly down the path. Mrs Wales turned her

179

head on its skinny neck. The protecting shawl fell back a little and Carol saw an astonishing head of thick, short, white curls. Mrs Wales shouted:

'Come talk to me, Miss What's-your-name. Like to see a new face for a change. Hope you spend the summer with us.' As the chair moved away Carol heard her say hopefully to her nurse, 'Maybe she'll get Lorna out. High time someone did.'

In silence Carol and Dawson moved back toward the house. He said presently:

'In all justice to Lorna I think I should explain...'

Carol said quickly:

'Please, Mr Dawson, you owe me no explanation.'

'I feel that I do. Besides, I can't look on you as a stranger. Andy's wife—and all.' He stopped, embarrassed again. Carol waited. After a moment he went on.

'She—my mother-in-law—is old ... I told you that, didn't I? Over forty when my wife was born. Had she lived, Lydia would have been just my age. She was an only child and her father died when she was six. Her mother adored her, spoiled her, did not wish her to marry. After Lydia's death she—was very bitter. She blamed me for it, of course,' he said heavily, 'and would not even see the baby. She lived alone in a town outside Chicago, where Lydia was born ... she had a considerable

180

income from her husband's estate.'

He paused to offer Carol his cigarette case, to light a cigarette himself.

'Five years ago,' he went on, 'she had a stroke. I went out—her doctor notified me, of course. Lydia is her only close relative. I found her in very bad shape and her affairs exceptionally tangled. The doctor and her neighbors told me that she had been growing— odd ... for a number of years. She had sold excellent investments against the advice of her lawyers and bankers and reinvested in crazy, fly-by-night schemes ... growing, it appears, susceptible to plausible young salesmen. Well, there you have it. When we could move her, I brought her home with me, and with her her nurse, Jane Leaming. We could make her comfortable in her own quarters in town, and down here. She has become reconciled to me and devoted to Lydia. Her mind, as you have seen, is not always clear. She confuses Lydia with Lydia's mother at times and has taken an absurd dislike to Lorna. Lorna understands. She's wonderful with the old lady really ... it's hard on her, of course.'

'What about Lydia?' asked Carol.

'Lydia accepts things,' said Dawson. 'It's one of her most endearing qualities. But it sometimes alarms me—for her sake. She seems to have an instinctive understanding of unhappiness, the dark places in people's lives. She is fond of her grandmother, I think. She's never been in the least afraid of her. Of course,' he added quickly, 'there's nothing to fear. A helpless old woman, with a sharp tongue ... that's all. Her mind wanders occasionally and she has certain fixed ideas, but if there were anything further I would, of course, for Lydia's sake make other arrangements.'

They had reached the house. He asked: 'Play tennis?'

'Not very well, but I like it.'

He looked with approval at her sleeveless white frock, its full skirt and tailored blouse. He suggested, 'If you care to take me on ... We won't go off on our picnic for a while yet. By the way, does it really appeal to you? You mustn't give in to Lydia just from politeness.'

Carol said, laughing, 'I don't know when I've had a picnic and I adore them. Suppose I run upstairs and change my shoes ... I won't be a minute.'

Lorna came in as she was changing. She said: 'I'm so sorry not to be here today.'

'I am too,' said Carol sincerely. 'Is your sister very ill?'

'She had an operation,' Lorna said, 'last week. She's doing very well. But I promised that I'd drive over today. Her husband has to be away. She's a good deal younger than I, and depends on me,' she added.

Carol said, 'I can see that people would depend on you.'

'Do I give that impression?' Lorna asked

ruefully. 'I suppose so—it's my training, I suppose. I was the oldest of five children. They're scattered now, east, south, west—except Betty, my youngest sister, the one in Southampton.'

She added:

'Sure the picnic won't bore you? Lydia is picnic crazy, as are most children.'

'It will be a treat,' Carol assured her, 'and a relaxation.'

Lorna asked practically:

'Have you an adequate beach robe? No? I'll put one in your room, and slippers and a bottle of oil. You'll burn, you know, out on the sand half the day, and a bad burn can be very dangerous. Don't lie around unprotected in your suit—it isn't wise, especially so early in the season. We're all black already,' she added, 'as we've been coming down weekends since April. But we have to keep an eye on our guests.'

'There you go again,' said Carol, laughing.

Presently she went down to play tennis with Dawson. Lydia appeared and sat on the side lines, watching. Now and then she rose and chased balls. She did so without much conviction. Her father commented, laughing, 'She gets lazier all the time.'

'I like being lazy,' said Lydia firmly.

Once Mrs Wales appeared in her chair to demand:

'Who's that girl playing with William? Is she

183

going to marry him?'

Her voice carried, and Dawson missed a shot. Lydia went over and stood by her grandmother's chair. She said, in a clear, penetrating voice:

'She's a friend, grandma. Her name's Miss Reid. She's nice.'

'Don't call me grandma,' said her grandmother crossly. 'Who do you think I am?'

The wheel chair moved away.

When Dawson and Carol came off the tennis court Lydia put her hand in Carol's and trotted along to the house with her. She said:

'You mustn't mind Grandma. She doesn't think like us. She gets things mixed up.' Lydia sighed. 'I do too, often,' she admitted, 'but not her way. Sometimes she thinks I'm me, sometimes she thinks I'm my mother.'

Carol said, 'I didn't mind.'

'Daddy did,' said Lydia. She laughed. 'He missed a shot. An easy one.'

Dawson had stopped to speak to a gardener. Lydia lowered her voice, she said wisely:

'Grandma's always thinking Daddy will marry someone. Sometimes she forgets he was married to Mother. She thinks I'm Mother. Oh, I told you that before, didn't I? I don't know who she thinks Daddy is,' she added, her straight brows drawn. She looked up at Carol, her eyes earnest, the short thick black lashes giving them depth. She said, 'Grandma doesn't

184

like Lorna. She's afraid she'll marry Daddy too.'

'You shouldn't tell me all this,' said Carol gently, 'your father and Miss Sheffield wouldn't like it.'

'I suppose not.' Lydia sighed again. 'It's hard to know what people will like, or won't, isn't it? I don't talk to everybody. Mrs—' she put her hand to her mouth—'the lady who stayed in bed till noon,' she explained, 'she was always asking me things ... about Daddy, about Lorna. I wouldn't tell her anything. I didn't like her. I like you. Will you come see my pony? I'd let you ride him, but you're too big. I'll ride him for you.'

Dawson caught up with them. He looked at his watch and said that he had to make a telephone call.

'Lydia, will you take care of Miss Reid?'

'We're going to see Starborn,' said Lydia, bouncing again. 'We'll come back from the picnic.'

Lorna came down the steps, as the chauffeur brought up a small open car. She said as the others reached her:

'I hate to go.'

Lydia threw her arms around her, and hugged her.

'Come home soon. It's empty without you. Give my love to Betty. When can I see the baby?' she asked.

Lorna bent and kissed the top of Lydia's

head. She said:

'There isn't a baby, Lydia.'

'Last time . . .' began Lydia.

'I know. Not this time.'

She smiled at Carol, spoke briefly to Dawson and presently drove off. Lydia said solemnly:

'I thought you just went to the hospital for babies.'

She shook her head, caught Carol's hand and tugged it. She cried, 'Let's go see Starborn, now. I promised him I'd come.'

CHAPTER SIXTEEN

They walked together to the stables and Lydia went in, beckoning Carol. She coaxed the little pony from his stall and led him out into the sunlight. Carol looked for the white marking on his forehead which she had expected. He had none. He was a sturdy brown pony, shaggy and sagacious.

'Did you name him?' she asked the little girl.

'Of course.'

'But he hasn't any star.'

'I didn't say he had. He's starborn,' said Lydia. 'He dances. You'll see.'

The pony followed her, like a dog. A stableman stood grinning in the doorway, watching. Carol asked, as they walked toward a small paddock, and went through the gate:

'But you haven't a saddle.'

'Stand still,' Lydia ordered her pony. She closed the gate. 'I don't need one. If you'd boost me,' she suggested.

Starborn was docile. Carol boosted. Lydia put her hands in his long mane and hung on. Her short fat legs dangled. She gripped hard with her knees. 'See?' she said.

Round and round the paddock, hanging on to Starborn's mane ... Starborn trotted, sedately, seemingly a little bored. Carol leaned on the gate and watched. The thick-cut close grass, the sun beating down, the sea wind, the child and the pony.

Presently Lydia rose up, spoke to Starborn, and slid unconcernedly off, over his patient rump. She gave him a friendly slap. She said, 'Stay out here for a while. Jim will fetch you in, later.'

She came up to Carol, smelling strongly of horse, and took her hand. 'Well?' she demanded.

Carol said, 'He didn't dance.'

'No,' agreed Lydia, with some impatience, 'not with us around. But he can, alone. He kicks up his heels and dances. I've seen him. He can't, with me. He knows he mustn't. He's a very intelligent pony.'

She looked at her hands. She said:

'Lorna would say, "Wash."' She slanted a twinkle at Carol. She added, 'I'm lazy, did you
187

know that?'

'I suspected it,' said Carol, laughing.

'I hate to wash,' said Lydia; 'It's a bore. Lorna has to keep after me. I don't mind. She likes to do it. Wash, clean teeth, take baths, change clothes ... pick up my room mornings right after breakfast. Sometimes at night I forget my prayers.'

'What about mornings?'

'I don't say them in the morning,' said Lydia happily, 'I say good ones at night. They last twenty-four hours.'

She trotted along at Lydia's side. She demanded:

'Do you like the radio ... do you listen to "Gang Busters" and "Sherlock Holmes" and "The Lone Ranger"?'

'Not often, I'm afraid.'

'Fun,' said Lydia. 'Lorna listens. She didn't like them at first. She does now. You would too.'

'I'll listen,' said Carol humbly. 'Do you read a great deal, Lydia?'

'I'm in too much of a hurry, I skip,' said Lydia, 'even when I'm being lazy.'

'What do you mean by that?' Carol asked.

'I want to find out what happened. Lorna reads to me. But it's more fun making things up yourself.'

Carol held her breath. She asked carefully:

'Why? Because you don't know what's going to happen if you make it up yourself?'

188

'No,' said Lydia earnestly, 'don't you see? You can make it go on as long as you want. Or you can stop it. You can make it happen right away or you can keep from making it happen ... ever.'

'I see,' said Carol.

They reached the house and went upstairs together. At Carol's door they paused.

'May I come in a minute?' asked Lydia.

'Do.'

Lydia came in and looked around the room. She said, with satisfaction, 'It's nice, when you're in it.'

'It's a lovely room,' Carol told her.

'I don't like it much,' said Lydia, 'it doesn't belong to anyone. People come and go in it. Next door too. They're just rooms. But Lorna's room is hers even when she isn't in it, and Daddy's and mine. Of course,' she added carefully, 'I've never seen mine without me.'

She looked at the beach robe lying on the bed. She said, 'That's Lorna's.'

'I know, she lent it to me.'

Lydia touched it, a blue toweling robe with a hood. She said:

'Lorna's like—like looking into the sky very early in the morning and again before the sun goes down. Just before. In summer, I mean.'

Carol knew what she meant. A stillness in Lorna, a serenity. A sense of endurance, of something eternal.

Lydia laughed. She said, 'I'll get my suit.'

The door closed behind her and Carol stared at it. A perfectly normal friendly little girl, with thick short hair and a gap where teeth had been. Freckles on her nose, a tanned, clear skin. A fat little girl who hated to wash.

She realized with astonishment that until Lydia spoke of 'making up' things she had not thought about the book, or indeed of Maynard and Hall, since before breakfast.

She undressed, stood under the bracing spray of the shower for a moment, put on her bathing suit and the beach sandals. Lorna had left a rubber-lined beach bag for her, with a bottle of sun-tan oil and dark glasses inside. She put her cap inside too and picked up the robe. It was evidently just back from the laundry but she fancied it had a distinctive fragrance, sun, salt, and something faintly like lilac.

Presently she went downstairs, alone. She was thinking of Lydia. She felt curiously guilty, as if she had been sent to spy, not to advise, as if she had been sent to eavesdrop on a child's luminous, unpredictable innocence.

She encountered no one except a parlormaid, who smiled at her. She went out through the French windows of the living room to the brick terrace where she had been on the previous evening. Mrs Wales was there, in a sheltered corner, in her chair. Jane Leaming sat beside her, sewing, with a green umbrella tilted over a table shielding her from the sun.

Carol stepped back but the old lady had seen her and beckoned imperiously, so Carol went on, the blue robe over her arm. Her bathing suit was a jade green printed with white sea horses. It had a brief flaring skirt. It became her very well. Jane, an angular girl, sighed. She could never hope to achieve such a figure, she thought sadly.

Mrs Wales demanded, 'Who are you, young woman?'

Carol shouted obediently. She was Carol Reid, Mr Dawson's house guest.

'You needn't scream,' said Mrs Wales, 'I can hear you. And I remember you. I hope you'll get that other woman out. You'd suit William very well, I should think.'

Miss Leaming shook her head slightly, glancing at Carol.

'Play the piano?' asked Mrs Wales suddenly.

'No,' Carol told her, 'I'm sorry. I'm not at all musical.'

'Lydia plays,' said Mrs Wales, 'she sings too. She'd make William a fine wife. But I don't want her to marry him. She's too young.' She grinned at Carol and her black eyes snapped. She added in a wholly normal voice, 'It's a lovely day, isn't it? I can't get enough sun. I like your bathing suit, it's decent as well as pretty. I used to be quite a swimmer.'

She closed her eyes, waved her hand as if dismissing an audience, and went to sleep, the

191

sudden sleep of illness and old age. Jane Leaming spoke hesitantly.

'You mustn't mind her, Miss Reid. She has this obsession about Mr Dawson. It hasn't,' she added, 'extended to me, as I've known Mrs Wales always and she still thinks of me as a little girl. Sometimes she smacks my hands, but not hard. I'm awfully fond of her really. She isn't hard to care for, I like to do things for her. She was awfully good to me and my family, she even put me through training.'

Carol looked down at the still face, composed in its temporary death, the yellowing skin, the many lines, the life gone now that the black eyes were hooded. She said gently:

'I understand, you mustn't worry—'

She heard Lydia's voice calling. 'Miss Reid!' called Lydia. 'Miss Reid!'

Her heart pounded suddenly. She smiled at Jane and went back into the living room. Lydia, in her red suit, looked more like a rubber ball than ever. She carried a brief robe, and her sneakers were laced with knotted unmatching strings.

'Daddy's in the garden,' she reported, 'he's got the hamper and the rug. He's waiting for us.'

They walked out of the garden and up the beach together, the three of them. The beach widened, the dunes diminished as they walked, there was driftwood on the sand and the gulls wheeled, crying their lonely, querulous messages. 'I don't like gulls,' said Lydia.

'Why not?' asked Carol. 'They're beautiful, the soft gray-white, the way they take off and land, they fly like airplanes, Lydia.'

'It's their eyes,' said Lydia. 'Like beads, sewed on. Mean eyes, I hate them.'

There was something in that, thought Carol, watching a gull walk along the wet brown beach, its delicate feet in the advancing, retreating water. Blank eyes, malicious because so empty of all awareness.

'What have you two been doing all morning?' inquired Dawson, walking beside Carol. Lydia was bouncing on ahead, running to wet her feet, drawing back again, stooping to pick up a shell.

Carol told him.

'She loves the pony,' he said. 'Later she'll have a good hack. She is perfectly fearless, she rides well.'

'She's a darling,' said Carol.

'Of course.' He smiled at her. He added hesitantly, 'You haven't considered ...?'

She answered frankly:

'I haven't thought about that at all. Does that surprise you?'

'No,' he answered, 'that was just what I meant. Now do you see? You came down here to meet her, to talk to me about having a book published. Then you forgot about it. She doesn't make you think of it. What did you

193

expect to find?'

She said, 'I don't know. Andy had described her, of course. You too. But I did expect something else.'

'Sophistication?' he asked.

'Not that ... you assured me she wasn't sophisticated—horrid word,' Carol interpolated vigorously, 'no, not that. But something—different. I can't explain.'

'You needn't,' he said quietly.

Lydia ran back to them. She had a very smelly starfish in her hands. It was dry and stiff. She said, trying to spread it out. 'It won't uncurl. Daddy, what's in the hamper?'

'Plenty.'

She cried:

'I'm hungry.'

She laughed up at Carol and added, 'I'm *always* hungry.'

Not far away was the special picnic spot, beside a small sheltering dune. You could sit there in a pool of yellow sunlight and peace, and listen to the gulls calling and the wet, white thunder of the waves.

'Here,' said Lydia. 'We always come here, Lorna likes it best.'

Grass grew on the dunes, yellow-green, stiff to the touch, stirring in the wind ... bright little flowers battled for their lives, sturdy blossoms, country cousins of the sweet pea, purple, magenta...

Dawson spread out the rug and set the

hamper down. He asked:

'Swim?'

Lydia took Carol's hand. She inquired maternally:

'You aren't afraid?'

'No,' said Carol, 'I like surf.'

'Daddy's going to take me to Honolulu someday,' said Lydia, 'Lorna and me. There are big waves there, you can ride a surfboard. You come with us!'

'I'd love to,' Carol said.

Dawson had taken Lydia's other hand. Linked, they ran together down the beach through the hot dry sand, shifting and soft, impeding, surrendering, to the harder, wet sand.

'Now!' cried Lydia.

They went forward to meet the advancing wave. The water was cold, it took your breath. They relinquished their hold of one another as Dawson said, 'Every man for himself.'

Coming out of a wet green tunnel, shot with light, Carol shook her head under the tight cap and looked for Lydia. There she was, swimming beside her father, her hair sleeked close to her head. Carol shouted:

'You look like a red seal!'

'There aren't any,' said Lydia.

'Does that matter?' Carol asked her.

Lydia giggled. She said, 'No, of course not. It's nicer. Red seals,' she added, swimming with her strong, funny little breast stroke,

195

kicking her legs like a dog, 'they're on letters.'

'What are?'

'Red seals,' said Lydia, delighted with her joke.

They came out, dried off, went back again. Once Dawson said with warning:

'Careful, Miss Reid—you mustn't burn ... Lorna will take off all our heads!'

Later, enveloped in the blue robe, the tight cap tossed aside, her hair free and curling under the hood, Carol watched her host and his daughter unpack the basket. Fried chicken, lettuce sandwiches, thin bread and butter, fruit, cupcakes, milk for Lydia, iced tea for her elders, hunks of good yellow cheese ... She said, 'I'm starved!'

'Fun,' said Lydia sleepily, her mouth half full. She added, 'Lorna will be sorry, she likes picnics.' She swallowed, and looked at Carol.

'What's your real name?' she demanded.

'Carol.'

'Carol. There's a girl in my class, her name's Carol too. She was born on Christmas Day.'

'So was I.'

Lydia asked, reaching for more chicken, 'May I have one more pickle, daddy?' She took it and went on. 'Being born on Christmas Day is special, I think, don't you?'

'I've always thought so,' said Carol.

'Except that you don't get as many presents,' Lydia said thoughtfully. She added, 'Could I call you Carol, Miss Reid?'

Her father said hastily:

'Lydia—look at the position you put Miss Reid in—she can't very well say no. And you're just a little girl.'

'She's not very old,' Lydia said swiftly, 'and if she'd rather I didn't, she'd tell me. I wouldn't mind.'

It was a tribute. Carol said:

'I wish you would call me Carol, Lydia, I would like it very much.'

'Daddy too?' asked Lydia.

Dawson reddened, expostulated, 'Lydia, please, that's not very—'

He had the most sensitive skin, Carol decided, amused. She smiled at him. She said:

'You were a friend of Andy's, you still are. We might have met long ago and known each other all these years.'

'People,' commented Lydia, going after the cupcakes, 'can be friends in two jiffs—or not at all, forever. Can't they?'

'She's quite right,' Dawson said gravely, 'Carol...'

After lunch, after Lydia and Carol had cleared away and repacked the hamper ... 'Lorna always makes us,' Lydia explained ... they lay back in the warm sand and listened to the drowsy beat of the sea. Lydia was singing to herself in a tuneless murmur, mixed up with the gulls crying and the sea coming in. Carol found that she wasn't listening, deliberately. She didn't want to hear. She didn't want to hear anything that might definitely set this child apart. Why?

Lydia stopped singing. She said sleepily:

'I made up a song about the sea—lots of songs, really ... Lorna wrote some down and I wrote some down.'

Carol asked, with an effort:

'Where are they?'

'Home,' said Lydia vaguely. 'I'll show them to you, if you like. I know a new one, no one's seen that, no one—'

She lay sprawled out on the sand, she was asleep.

Carol looked down on her. She thought frantically, hopelessly, Stay as you are, please stay as you are.

She felt Dawson watching her. She did not look at him but she felt him there, watching her and the sleeping child. There was sand on Lydia's cheek ... sand in her hair. She was smiling as she slept. Little beads of sweat were on her short upper lip.

Carol moved closer to her, to shade her a little, if possible. She looked up at Dawson almost apologetically. His eyes were not now on the child, but on her. She saw the liking in them, the warmth, the admiration. She looked away wondering if he could be aware how irrevocably she had fallen in love.

CHAPTER SEVENTEEN

The tide altered, the gulls screamed, the sun shifted. Carol leaned over to pick up Lydia's robe and put it over her bare legs. Brown legs, with the engaging shapelessness of childhood, fat, fuzzed with a golden down, scratched and scarred. Carol thought, No matter what angel—or is it demon?—has taken possession, she's a *child*. The round knees proved that, one of them bruised, and the nape of her neck. Lydia's head was turned on an outflung arm, she had not lost that touching and innocent signature of the sculptor's thumb, just where her short hair made a damp dove's tail.

Carol was appalled to find her eyes wet. She blinked them, smiled determinedly at Dawson. She said, softly because of Lydia, sleeping deeply, relaxed as a kitten:

'I wish I could sleep like that. It's a pity to grow out of the power to plunge yourself into instant unconsciousness.'

He commented, lying flat on his back, his crossed arms shading his eyes:

'Children and animals are wonderful in their response to hunger and the need for sleep.' He drew a long breath, added, 'We wanted a big family, half a dozen boys and girls. We talked of it, planned it. We were healthy youngsters, and we could promise children a certain

199

amount of security. We felt we owed it to ourselves, to the world perhaps.' He laughed shortly.

Carol said, 'Lydia's worth a dozen.'

'I know.' He turned on his side, looked up at her. 'A man,' he said, 'left alone with a child, a baby. It's a difficult problem. Oh, in my situation I was fortunate, other things being equal. I could pay for the best care, supervision. I used to think of other men in my position, those without means, who were away at work all day, leaving their children in the casual care of relatives, or with some slattern, or who had to part with them and who, once a week, scrubbed and dressed in Sunday clothes, would go see them in some institutional place. I was more fortunate, having found Lorna . . . no amount of money can repay her for what she has done and is doing. Understand, in common with most men, I knew nothing about children. The average man—I've talked to dozens—is afraid of children. Not until a child begins to walk, talk, exhibit a will and a personality is the father won. And I suppose a child's mother acts as interpreter for it, to the father, for some years. After that, if you're lucky, you grow into confidence, friendship even. For months after Lydia's birth I suffered intensely . . . horror, remorse, anxiety. As she began to grow up I—' he spoke self-consciously—'I read many books on child psychology. Some of them terrified me. I talked to pediatricians, psychologists. As if Lydia was a subject I must master.'

Carol said, gaining a clear picture of him:

'I see.'

He said, sifting the sand through his fingers:

'I thought of remarriage, before Lydia was two years old. To give her a mother, a home ... I was afraid I couldn't create one for her, or make up her loss to her. You understand?' he asked anxiously and when she nodded, went on, 'But it was no go. What woman would marry me for a child's sake? It would not have been fair to any woman.'

Lorna? thought Carol.

Lydia stirred, flung her arms about, sat up and rubbed the sleep and sand from her lids. She yawned widely, showing the gap in her teeth, her red tongue. She said crossly:

'I've been asleep.'

'Not long,' Carol assured her.

Lydia's cheeks were flushed, one more than the other. On the redder, there was an intricate delicate design stamped by the sand.

'Did I miss anything?' she demanded.

'Not a thing.'

'Was there a peach left?' Lydia inquired and hitched herself over to the lunch hamper on her round firm bottom.

Carol and Dawson looked at each other and laughed.

Lydia had her teeth in the peach. The juice ran down her chin. She demanded, 'When can

201

we go in again?'

'Later,' decided her father. 'We might have some games first.' He looked stricken, 'We forgot to bring the big ball,' he said.

'We can hunt shells,' Lydia told him. 'I want more for my collection. Lorna says they're dust collectors but she always brings me new ones when she goes to the beach, just the same.'

She got up and shook herself. Dawson held out his hands and pulled Carol to her feet. She was conscious of his warm, hard grasp, his strength.

They went down the beach, Lydia skipping ahead of them, running back to show them something, to cache a find of sandy or wet shells in the pocket of Carol's borrowed robe. She was singing to herself again. Once she remarked casually that gulls were probably drowned mermaids.

'How can mermaids drown?' demanded Carol.

Lydia slanted a gray eye at her. She explained, 'In the air ... out of water. Like fish. Then they're gulls. Have you read *The Little Mermaid*?'

'Often.'

'I hate it,' said Lydia, 'it's cruel. Lorna read it to me, years ago,' she added importantly. 'I cried. I used to cry a lot but I don't now. I'd dream ... walking on swords, her poor new feet bleeding. I despised it. But I read it to myself now. I don't know why. I know what's coming

202

and I don't want it to come.'

'But why gulls?' persisted Lydia. Dawson said nothing. He had fished a cigarette from his beach-robe pocket and was smoking it thoughtfully.

'They haven't any soul,' said Lydia; 'I told you about their eyes.' She put her sandy damp hand in Carol's. 'What *is* a soul?' she demanded.

Before Carol could answer, Lydia had seen something far up the beach and had run away toward it, the wind ruffling her hair. Carol looked at Dawson and laughed. She said:

'In the nick of time. I couldn't answer.'

He said:

'She rarely waits for such answers. Perhaps she knows them and is merely being polite, lip service to the alleged wisdom of her elders.'

When Lydia tired they went back to the picnic place, and then into the sea for a brief, tingling half hour. They dried off, walking back to the house.

Dawson said, as they crossed the sand and wild strong grass between the beach and the garden:

'It was an especially nice picnic.' He smiled at Carol, and added, 'You belong here with us, on picnics, I think.'

Her eyes were on Lydia's retreating back, ahead of them. She did not answer, perhaps she did not hear.

They went into the house, Lydia clattered off

203

to her shower, shells dropping on the polished floor, leaving a bright trail. Dawson in his own rooms, standing under the stinging water, thought that this day had been unusually happy. It was a long time since he had been so attracted by a woman. Andy's wife. What was the matter with old Andy, letting a girl like this leave him, slip through his fingers? He stepped from the shower, shook the water from his eyes, toweled himself vigorously. He thought, If I consent to have the book published, I'll see her often ... I won't need an excuse.

He stopped, startled. The book was Lydia's, the whole debate revolved around Lydia, her good, the right thing or the wrong thing. He could not remember that in any decision concerning his child he had been influenced by a need in himself.

Carol sat in a big tub, steaming hot, smelling of lilac bath salts. She had pinned her hair on top of her head. She found herself singing tunelessly, as Lydia had, but she had not Lydia's words. She thought, A lovely day—

When she went into the bedroom and glanced at the clock beside the bed she saw that it was half past three. They had been on the beach since before noon. She was drowsy and lay down across the cool wide bed for a moment, in a thin silk robe. The sun was in her blood, the sea and wind. She slept deeply and woke to a hammering at her door.

'Come in,' she said, bewildered, not

knowing where she was for a moment, hardly knowing who she was.

Lydia put her head around the edge of the opening door.

'Did I wake you up, Carol?'

'Yes. But it's high time ... or isn't it?'

She glanced at the clock. Four-twenty.

Lydia said:

'It's almost teatime. Lorna should be back.'

She wore a brief gingham dress. Her eyes shone. Her hands were full of papers. 'I brought you the songs about the sea,' she said.

Carol sat up and pulled the robe closer around her. Lydia came to sit beside her. Carol picked up a sheet of paper and looked at the words on it. Lydia had written them, in a careful round hand ...

Carol laid the paper on the bed and put her arm around Lydia's shoulder, with timidity. So many children hate to be touched. You mustn't affront their dignity. But Lydia came closer, confiding, warm, friendly. Carol asked:

'Would you leave them with me? I'd better dress now. I'd like some tea.'

She looked anxiously at the round face. Was that the right thing to say—casual, practical—or should she have remained there reading, with Lydia watching her? It wasn't merely a question of how to meet a situation in order to obtain the exact response.

'Hurry,' said Lydia, 'I'm hungry.'

She grinned, rubbed her cheek against

Carol's shoulder, remarked, 'You feel smooth, you smell wonderful,' hopped off the bed and out of the room. Carol released her breath. The right word, the right note. Lydia did not want to be regarded as anything save the child she was. Black words carefully set down on the white paper were part of her, nothing strange, nothing to be gaped at, exclaimed over, made important. That was the way it must be.

Carol picked up the sheets of paper, stacked them on the desk, weighted them with an onyx block, and began to dress.

Lydia's glass of tea was very weak and very sugary, Dawson's and Carol's strong, fragrant with mint. There were cinnamon buns, cookies, more cupcakes, cucumber and tomato sandwiches. Jane Leaming joined them, on the terrace. Mrs Wales was sleeping, she reported.

Lydia heard the car first. She set down her glass hard, it splashed and she ran through the living room and out to the drive. Presently she came back with Lorna. Lorna looked cool, she was smiling. She drew off her thin driving gloves and said:

'You all look very well satisfied with yourselves. I'm thirsty—I could drink a pitcherful.' She looked closely at Carol. 'You're sunburned,' she said, 'but not too much.'

'How's Betty?' Dawson asked her, as Carol laughed.

'Fine, she wants to go home, but can't for a

week. They'll bring the baby to see her tomorrow—' she turned to Carol, including her, explaining—'my niece, she's three ... I stopped to see her before I went to the hospital ... she's a darling.'

She put her hand out and touched Lydia's arm.

'Have a good day?' she asked.

Lydia told her about it, the gulls, the starfish, the shells, the water. And all she had eaten. She said, with her slanting upward look, 'Not too much, Lorna, honest.'

Jane excused herself, slipping away to see if Mrs Wales still slept. Carol leaned back in the long green chair and looked seaward. She felt as if she did not belong ... as if she intruded. Yet they made her one of them, drew her into their close circle.

CHAPTER EIGHTEEN

Lydia had her dinner at seven. Carol sat with her, and Lorna, at Lydia's request. She had her own small table in the windows of the big dining room. Lorna explained:

'Her father likes a late dinner, too late for Lydia, except on state occasions. She's in bed by eight.'

'Come see my room,' Lydia demanded, after she had eaten.

A corner room, big, with Venetian blinds to keep out the noonday sun. Next door a day nursery, filled with toys. Lydia walked Carol around the shelves, showed her the doll collection, the soft animals. A desk in one corner ... an array of balls, an electric train. She laughed tolerantly over the train. 'Daddy gave me that when I was six!'

Carol left her with Lorna and went off to dress for dinner. Shortly after eight Lorna knocked and came in, wearing the tailored frock of the evening before. She said, 'Lydia wants to say good night.'

They stood together by the child's bed. Lydia looked up at them. She said indignantly, 'I'm *not* sleepy! Lorna, you might have let me stay up a little longer.' A yawn betrayed her and she chuckled. She apologized, 'That wasn't me, really.'

Lorna and Carol went downstairs to join Dawson. Cocktails and then dinner. Afterward they went out on the terrace, still talking of books and plays they had discussed at the table. On the terrace Dawson lit Carol's cigarette for her. He asked:

'Have you come to any conclusion?'

Carol shook her head. She said, 'Lydia brought me some of her poetry.'

Lorna exclaimed. She said:

'That's a real compliment. She never voluntarily shows it to anyone outside the family. It isn't that she's shy, but because we've

208

tried not to make it seem—important, different. Of course, she knows that most children don't "make songs" as she describes it. But in her class at school there's a child with a remarkable drawing talent, and one who dances, another who sings, and still another who writes little stories. So Lydia doesn't feel strange about the poetry. She can do that, the other children can do other things. She particularly admires a little girl who can spit very accurately through the place where her teeth were recently. Lydia's tried it, but failed.'

Carol said slowly:

'You've done a wonderful job.'

Lorna said, after a moment:

'I've tried.'

The man said nothing, smoking in silence. And after a little Carol roused herself to turn to him. She asked:

'Shall we talk about it tomorrow?'

'If you like,' he said. He added hesitantly, 'Seeing you with her today—I realize that you understand what we—Lorna and I—are driving at, and that you wouldn't deliberately jeopardize ... Lorna, we've been over this again and again, and still you won't—?' Lorna said firmly:

'It's up to you to decide, Bill. I'll have no hand in it. It's too easy to decide the wrong way. I can't have the responsibility.'

Carol asked:

'Has either of you consulted Lydia?'

'I have,' Dawson said promptly, 'before you came down. I said, "How'd you like to have your songs published?" And she said, "You mean, in a book?" and when I said, "Yes," she said, "It would be fun," and went off about her own business. She hasn't mentioned it since.'

A servant came to call him to the telephone. When he'd left Carol said hesitantly:

'I wish you'd tell me honestly, Miss Sheffield—'

'Could you manage Lorna?' asked Lorna, smiling. 'I see that Lydia calls you Carol ... I hope you don't mind. She doesn't usually—'

'I like her to, Lorna. Tell me, truthfully, what do you think about this?'

'The book? I haven't any right to tell you,' said Lorna, 'I don't want to influence Lydia's father, one way or another. He's grown dependent on me so I have to lean backwards! He leaves almost all ordinary decisions to me. That's all right, they are within my province. This isn't.'

'And whatever he decides?'

'I'll abide by it,' said Lorna.

She's in love with him, thought Carol, and no wonder. But she has too much integrity to let it conflict with what she feels right for Lydia.

Lorna added, 'I think he's decided, because of you.'

'I haven't said—'

210

'I know, but he's been with you, he knows that you wouldn't want Lydia hurt and would try to guard her from it. That would decide him, wouldn't it?' asked Lorna. 'And that's what you're here for, I expect.'

'Yes, of course,' said Carol after a long pause, hearing Dawson whistle as he came through the living room on his way out to join them.

In the morning she breakfasted alone with Dawson. Lydia had gone to Sunday school and Lorna with her. 'She'll pay some calls,' Dawson explained, 'and then pick up Lydia. I believe there's a youngster coming to spend the day. Starborn's a great attraction.'

The house was empty without Lydia. After breakfast Carol walked with Dawson in the garden. Mrs Wales's wheel chair was not in evidence, she had had a bad night and was staying in bed, Dawson said.

'Let's sit down here a moment,' Carol suggested.

They sat down on a faded green bench in the rose garden. Cedars screened them from the sea wind. Carol said abruptly:

'I read the songs Lydia brought me. Last night.'

'Yes?'

She said:

'All the arguments still stand. This is a gift the world should share; it will endure if she never writes another line. It may grow, as she

211

does. Now it's perfect, as it is, self-contained, like a little world, like a star. Everything I said in the office is true. But I am going to advise you not to publish this book.'

'Why?' he asked quietly.

'We can't keep her as she is,' said Carol desperately, 'no matter how we try. She'll grow up, she'll no longer be a child. But must we hasten it? The moment you sign that contract you are under certain obligations ... to Maynard and Hall, to the people who will read the book. I would keep my promise, show you every line of publicity before release. Peter Tarrant would consult you on advertising. I would be present, if you wish, with the interviewers. We could keep the interviewing down to the minimum. But there'd be some ... we can't escape it. Lydia would take it in her stride, she would be interested and friendly. After a while she'd get used to it, she might even like it. Try as we would, there's that, there's always the possibility of the wrong person...' She stopped. 'You'll think I'm crazy. The child is more important than the gift ... I don't know whether it's because of the gift or not. That doesn't make sense. I can't possibly explain. But—once the publicity is launched, once the interviewers have come and gone—and even supposing that they do no harm—there are the readers. You'll be under obligations to them too.'

He said, 'I know, but—'

Carol said hastily:

'There'll be a certain encroachment ... you can't ward it off—you'll try to take the brunt, so will Lorna. But Lydia will bear the real burden. Oh, it isn't comparable to the pitilessly exposed life of a child motion-picture star. But it will all be there in a lesser degree. I'm trying to influence you—against my employers. I'm telling you—*don't*. Not till she's older. Not till it won't matter so much. Let her grow up like this, guarded at school, happy there, happy here ... with the pony and the beach and the picnics. When she's eighteen, twenty—there will be other songs to publish. These too. They'll be as they now are, perfect. They can be published under their date line if you like, if Lydia likes. The decision will be hers then, not yours. Or they can just be part of a book ... if she goes on writing. I think she will. If she doesn't, she'll still have these. I'm saying this very badly.'

He said, throwing his cigarette on the path, watching it smolder:

'A few weeks ago I would have welcomed this ... advice, for it's the way I feel. Lorna too, although she's never said. But Andy can be very persuasive. You were too, in the office the other day. And now you—you league yourself with us.'

'What do you mean,' she asked, 'by—a few weeks ago?'

He said:

213

'I never thought that I could be deflected, for a moment by a hairbreadth, from thinking solely of Lydia. Now I'm thinking of myself. If I sign that contract I won't lose you ... I'll see you,' he added, 'often.'

She was startled, her heart quickened. She said evenly:

'But what difference could the contract make?' She smiled, her dark eyes luminous. 'You can still see me, often, can't you?' She added, 'You and Lydia.'

'I never thought of that, Carol. I've just thought all along, She's here, she likes us—but...'

'With a business motive? You can forget that,' Carol told him.

Then he said, his face illuminated, 'I can't tell you what you've done. I was afraid to decide—afraid I'd be robbing Lydia. You make me believe my first thought was right, that if I signed it would be a betrayal. I'm very much more than grateful.'

He held out his hand and she laid hers in it, and he said, still holding her hand:

'You'll have the job of telling Andy I decided—the wrong way for Maynard and Hall.'

She said, 'They'll be furious,' and laughed, not caring.

'Andy especially.' He released her hand, with reluctance. He added, 'Andy will think you failed.'

214

Carol said quickly:

'But I'll tell him.'

'You needn't,' said Dawson. 'It—you can put it up to me, can't you?'

Carol shook her head.

'He'll ask,' she said, 'if I tried to persuade you. And I'll tell him the truth.'

Lydia came flying down the path, with a coltish, long-legged little girl in tow. She flung herself at Carol and at Dawson indiscriminately. She cried, 'This is Evelyn, we're going to ride Starborn. Please come, Carol—Daddy...'

Dawson drove Carol back to town after supper. They did not talk much on the way. But when he left her at her apartment he advised:

'I still think that you'd better let me take the blame.'

'No. Good night, Bill, and thanks.'

He said, 'I'll call you soon. I've a present for you, by the way—I wasn't to give it to you until now. Here it is.'

Carol took the long envelope, turned it over in her hands.

He said.

'The sea songs. Lydia copied them, before her supper, after Evelyn had gone. They're for you, she said. There's a new one ... the picnic one, the one about the gulls.'

She could not speak, over the tightness in her throat.

The telephone was ringing when she let herself into the apartment, and she hurried to answer it. Andy spoke to her, impatiently.

'Carol—? I've been calling you since eight.'

'I just this minute walked in, Andy.'

'Well,' he asked, 'what happened, will he sign?'

'No,' she said, 'no, he's decided against it.'

Andy swore. 'Well, that's that. I was afraid of it. So even you couldn't persuade him ... I thought the other day at the office that if anyone could—'

She could let it go at that. She could say, 'It's too bad, but there it is.' And Andy would never know.

She said steadily:

'I didn't try to persuade him, Andy. I advised him not to sign.'

There was a blank silence. Then Andy shouted:

'*Not* to sign? Carol, are you out of your mind?'

She said wearily:

'I don't think so. I did what I thought was best.'

'For whom?' he demanded.

'For the child.'

She had the envelope in her left hand. She held it tightly, as if it gave her courage.

'Are you working for her,' asked Andy, 'or for us?'

'Andy—please, I'm tired, I—'

216

He said, 'Hang up. I'm coming to your place as fast as a taxi will take me. You can call Dawson in the morning and tell him you've thought things over.'

'Andy—'

But the line was dead. It buzzed now, and the operator spoke. 'No,' said Carol, 'I'm not calling anyone.'

She replaced the instrument and went to the bedroom to take off her hat, to run a comb through her hair. Returning to the living room, waiting for Andy, she opened the envelope...

In what seemed to her a very short time, the bell rang.

CHAPTER NINETEEN

The bell rang twice. Between the first and second ringing Carol put the long envelope in the desk drawer. When the door was opened Andy stormed in. He was hatless, his thick hair in disorder. He demanded, without preliminary:

'What in hades has come over you?'

'Sit down,' Carol advised him, 'and compose yourself.'

She was conscious of inner laughter. Here was another Andy, one whom she knew very well, impatient, testy, exasperated. She had not seen him in many years. I, however, she reminded herself, am not the girl who used to watch Andy work himself up into a rousing good temper, the girl who'd been able to work up a temper to match.

He sat down and glared at her, then he smiled suddenly.

'Are you going to prowl?' he inquired, with interest.

Another of their intimate catchwords. Prowling. She had been quite a prowler in her day, she admitted to herself. She laughed, sobered, sat down on the love seat with him.

'Andy, do be sensible.'

He said, 'I've worked on this thing ... I set my heart on it—hammered at good old Bill, even dragged in the dear bygone Alma Mater ... and I was convinced you'd clinch it, after my spadework.'

'Is it so important to you—to the firm?' she asked quietly.

'Good Lord! The discovery of the year, of the era, of more than that, perhaps,' he said, staring at her, 'and you ask me if it's important!'

'The child's more important. I've been with, talked with, her, grown to know her. It wouldn't be good for her, Andy. I know it as well as I've ever known anything. Better. The poems will keep and the book will keep. In seven or eight years you'll have your book ... and no one will be harmed.'

He said, 'This isn't like you,' and she

218

was silent.

After a moment, he added:

'Richard and Steve will—'

She said quickly:

'I'll tell them the truth, if it costs me a job I like very much.'

The sound he made could be classified definitely as a snort.

'Don't be ridiculous,' he said shortly. 'You don't have to tell 'em anything. Bill Dawson refused to sign the contract, that's all there is to it.'

'Nice of you, Andy,' she said, 'but I'd rather not.'

He shrugged, his temper evaporated, and he wondered how much of his anger derived from the loss of his 'discovery' and how much stemmed from the fact that Carol, setting her will against his, had defeated him. He dismissed the thought with irritation.

'Let me at least try to convince you,' he suggested.

She heard all his arguments in silence; was not convinced. And when he left, almost an hour later, she felt herself drooping with fatigue.

In the hall he grinned at her.

'I could shake you,' he warned. He did so, his hands hard on her shoulders. She was very conscious of a desire to relax against him, put her head down, weep, from what cause she couldn't imagine. The awareness stiffened her

219

spine, and she drew away.

'Sorry, but that's the way it is,' she said.

'I saw Millicent yesterday. She tells me you're going up to Longfields next week.' He added, aggrieved, 'She didn't ask me.'

'She will,' prophesied Carol consolingly, 'another, more suitable time.'

The door closed, she locked it, returning to the living room to take the long envelope from the desk and carry it into her bedroom. Before she turned out the light she read once more the poem about the gulls. 'For Carol' Lydia had written, in her round hand.

Lovely gift, lovely—clear, burning, a cool flame. Lovely child. Andy had asked her about Lydia. He had asked, 'How could you come to know her in so short a time?' and she had answered carefully:

'I can't explain. I've never cared greatly for children or had much to do with them. The few I've known I've liked or disliked as I do adults. The age factor had nothing to do with that. This child appealed to me, instantly. You've met her. You know what she's like. I loved her,' she explained, with difficulty, 'almost on sight. I can't bear to have anything happen to her, to be instrumental in harming her, in any way. I feel she should develop naturally, grow—like a plant ... not be forced. If you can't see it, Andy, it's no use. Her father sees it ... he hasn't wanted this for her. I'll be honest, I could persuade him; you almost did, you know. But I

220

wouldn't, I won't.'

He'd looked at her, she recalled, with sudden gravity. After a little while he said, 'All right, Carol, I won't argue any more.' It was then that he'd risen to go.

The next morning Carol went directly to Maynard's office as soon as he came in and asked to speak to him and to Hall. When Hall joined them she told them bluntly what she had done, or left undone, and, as explicitly as possible, why.

Steve was like Andy at first, inclined to storm. But Maynard understood. He said, 'I won't say it isn't a disappointment. But, as you say, in time, she'll come to us. Or will she?'

'Of course,' Carol assured him eagerly, 'her father would see to that.'

'I can see his point,' Maynard admitted thoughtfully; 'in fact, I've seen it all along. I have kids. You too, Steve. And do you remember our one and only child prodigy, the year you came with us?'

Steve groaned.

'Exactly.' Maynard smiled, recalling the delicate high-strung boy, with the really outstanding gift. There were editions still sold of his one book, written and illustrated by himself. Maynard also remembered the child's mother, with compassion and horror. He knew what had happened to the boy, or rather what had not happened after a season's furor, interviews, pictures, and even lecture platforms. He shook his head.

He said, 'Forget it, Carol.'

She said, half smiling:

'I thought I might be fired. After all, my loyalty should be here. It is, really. Yet, in this case...'

Steve touched her shoulder on his way to his own office. He said, 'That's okay. You'll find Andy tougher to deal with, I'm afraid.'

'I've dealt with him already,' she admitted.

The rest of the week went by with its usual routine, conferences, a visiting author, a bookshop party, unusual during summer. Bill Dawson called her, on Wednesday, they dined together and went to a play. He called her again Friday before he left for Long Island. 'I talked with Lydia this morning,' he said, 'she wants to know when you're coming back. Make it soon, won't you?'

Millicent telephoned during the week. She was in town, she said, and would drive Carol up early Saturday morning.

On the way, she talked about her book. It wasn't until luncheon that she mentioned Andy. Then she said that she understood Maynard and Hall hadn't been able to sign the Dawson child.

'No,' said Carol briefly, looking out over the terrace to the fields which gave the place its name.

'I suppose you wonder how I know?'

'Andy told you,' said Carol with conviction.

222

She was conscious of resentment.

'I asked him,' admitted Millicent. 'He was disturbed about it. He said you'd done your best.' She looked, smilingly, at her guest. 'I should think,' she suggested, 'that the setup was perfect—a weekend in the country, a lonely widower—or isn't he? You should have done better.'

Carol nodded. 'I should have.'

Her heart was light, her resentment vanished. Andy had protected her. She was glad of that. She hadn't realized how much she disliked the thought of Andy's discussing her with Millicent. Which was pretty inconsistent, she admitted.

Nothing further was said, and the weekend passed pleasantly. Swimming, walking, an invasion of droppers-in, casual, uninvited guests—discussion for the most part of the forthcoming book, of the next book which Millicent was planning, of some short stories she had roughed out but had not completed. It wasn't until just before Carol left for the train Sunday evening that she returned to personalities.

'You don't like me much, do you?' she asked.

'Of course,' began Carol conventionally, bracing herself.

'No, I don't mind. I like you, rather. Do you know why I asked you here, this time?'

'I've tried to guess, and also I've wondered.'

'I wanted to see what attracted Andy,' Millicent told her.

Carol laughed. She said, 'My dear, what attracted Andy ten years ago and what would attract him now are as different as night and day.'

'I'm not so sure.'

Carol said lightly:

'The Andy I knew would writhe if he thought we were discussing him. I don't know about the present Andy.'

'He'd writhe too,' said Millicent carelessly. 'Men learn early, reading, writhing, arithmetic. It doesn't matter.'

'Try to make one adjustment,' Carol advised her; 'think of me in relationship to Andy now. It doesn't make sense. You never *knew* the man I married, Millicent, and you never will. He's gone, except, I suppose, in certain fundamentals. At all events he's grown up.'

Millicent said:

'Looking at you, being with you, listening to you, I cannot possibly imagine why you two—'

'There it is again,' Carol interrupted. 'You didn't know the girl Andy married, either.'

Millicent stirred restlessly. They were sitting in the long living room, heavy with the scent of flowers. The breeze was cool at the open windows.

She said, 'I amuse him, I interest him, perhaps I even excite him. But he's not in love with me.'

224

Carol said gently, 'Perhaps you don't want him to be, perhaps you'd rather it was this way.'

'I thought so,' admitted Millicent, 'until you came into the picture.' She stared at Carol. The room was dimly lighted but Carol could feel her regard. She added, 'Now, I'm afraid. I warned you before. I'm repeating it. I don't like forcing issues, but if you get in my way—'

'I won't,' promised Carol. 'But if I did, what could you do?'

It was a challenge. Millicent laughed, she did not answer.

The car drove up and Carol rose. She said, 'Train-time ... thanks very much, Millicent, for the weekend.'

'You'll come again?' asked Millicent, going to the door with her.

'I think not,' said Carol. 'Why should I?'

Millicent laughed again.

'I can respect that. Why should you? But I'm going to give an office party in the autumn. The Halls, the Maynards, Andy, some of the others—and you. You can't stay away, it would look very odd. Or do you feel at a disadvantage? Is that it?'

'I'll come,' said Carol, 'under those terms.'

Andy, taking her out to dinner, wanted to know what she and Millicent had found to talk about. She told him, 'You,' smiling over the edge of her wineglass, and was rewarded by his scowl. He said furiously:

225

'Women are the most indecent—!'
She said mildly:
'Millicent thinks we have you in common. Very common, you'd call it. I don't blame you. I tried to assure her that we hadn't.'

He didn't know whether to laugh, with relief—you could count on Carol but Millicent was unpredictable, her mind worked oddly, went around corners—or whether to swear because of the sharp stab at his natural male vanity.

They dined occasionally, lunched often, and when it was too hot to think of dragging themselves out on the blazing streets they shared bottles of milk and sandwiches on the polished surface of the conference table. Sometimes half a dozen of them had luncheon sent in, sometimes Carol and Andy were alone. She was seeing less of Bess and Jerry than she had expected. Now when Jerry went off on his trips, Bess went with him. But she saw a great deal of Bill Dawson.

He telephoned her every day, and they had dinner when she was free. It seemed natural that every weekend, or almost every other weekend, she would drive down to the Island with him. Late in August Andy commented. He said:

'You're certainly giving the office plenty to talk about.'

'Why—exactly?' she asked cautiously.

'First us,' he said, 'when it leaked out, in the

diplomatic way it did. That was pretty funny. People eying us as if we had suddenly become freaks. Now Bill—'

'I like him,' she said definitely.

'No doubt. If you didn't you would not waste your time. Going to marry him?'

'I've known him less than three months.'

'How long did you know me?' he inquired.

Her heart gave a startled, convulsive leap.

'It's hardly the same thing. I'm no longer eighteen,' she answered.

'Bill's all right,' he said casually, 'you could do worse. Plenty of money, a nice guy, if on the dull side. Or perhaps you don't find him dull?'

'I don't,' she said shortly.

'And,' he added, slowly, 'you're crazy about that kid.'

How crazy she dared not admit ... and how much of that love colored her growing interest in Lydia's father she did not know.

In September, Lydia spoke suddenly at the breakfast table one Sunday, 'I don't know why you ever go away, Carol; do you, daddy?' she said, and Dawson, coloring in his quick, helpless way said, 'I wish she didn't have to.'

'There!' said Lydia. 'You heard him. Grandma's always saying you'll come here to live.' She looked hopefully at Carol. 'You could sleep in my room,' she conceded.

Lorna, overturning a glass, apologized, and rang for a cloth. Glancing at her, Carol saw how white she was, how drawn. She thought, with hot remorse, I've had no business interfering in their lives like this. She must hate me for it. Yet Lorna had never intimated that she 'hated' anyone. She was unaltering, friendly, serene, maternal.

On their way back to town Dawson said abruptly:

'Lydia was my advocate this morning ... I haven't dared. Carol, would you come and stay—always? I think I've wanted to ask you ever since that first weekend. But ... I was afraid. Lydia and I are in love with you, dear.'

'Bill—' She was stammering, uncertain, now that he had spoken.

'Don't answer. Not yet. Think it over, I am not trying to hurry you.' He added gravely, 'I can't offer you what I gave Lydia's mother. You understand that? Once, it was you and Andy.'

'I know.'

'That was youth,' he said gently, 'and dreaming and a sort of miracle. This is maturity—it is different. I am not saying one is better than the other. You—like me, I think.'

She said soberly:

'I'm very fond of you, Bill.'

'There's Lydia,' he reminded her. 'You love her ... I know that.'

'Oh, yes,' she said, 'so very much.'

Falling in love, growing into loving, all this bright summer, the blue salty days and Lydia running across a beach or paddock, Lydia

228

coming into her room, mornings, now that they were intimates, sitting on her bed, talking, laughing ... Lydia, half asleep, asking Lorna, 'Can't Carol come tell me good night?'

Lorna.

If he had been going to love Lorna, she thought, he would have done so long ago. She was taking nothing from her, she would never do that. If she married Bill, Lorna could not leave them, ever, unless she herself married. Carol would explain that to her. She would tell her, Lydia's yours, almost as much as Bill's, more than she'll ever be mine. There was sorrow in that thought, but no jealousy. You couldn't stoop to jealousy of Lorna, you couldn't belittle yourself—or her.

She *was* fond of Bill. She liked him, he was her friend. She depended on him. She liked his strength, his shyness, the occasional awkwardness which made him seem young and vulnerable. She admired the man she did not know, the man who could control efficiently a large organization. They had grown during these weeks into companionship. She liked being with him.

Physically, he was not exciting to her. She liked the touch of his hand on hers, and being near him. If there was no desire, no delicate, disturbing consciousness of him in her blood, did that matter? Wasn't that something which could not endure? She thought, reluctantly, of her marriage with Andy and grew hot and cold by turns. But that couldn't come again. It shouldn't, for it had not lasted. This was better. And on such a firm basis of friendship and affection, surely she could grow into loving, into a different desire, with deeper roots, quieter, more satisfactory.

She said, after a long time:

'I can't answer now, Bill.'

He said, 'I don't want you to—when you can, you'll tell me.'

'Yes.'

'Is there anyone else?'

'No,' she told him. 'No one.'

'Then,' he said, 'I'll wait.'

CHAPTER TWENTY

When they reached town it was still not very late. Carol, alone in the apartment, and restless, found herself turning to the telephone. She thought, I want to talk to someone. Bess wouldn't be available. Andy, then?

But how absurd to think of Andy. Why should she turn to him? How could she discuss her present problem with Andy, of all people? You don't go to your ex-husband and say, 'Look here, Bill Dawson wants to marry me but I'm not sure whether I should marry him or not.'

She hadn't dreamed of consulting Andy

about Kim Anderson.

That had been different. She had known definitely that she could never marry Kim. She thought of him, and smiled. She had run into him perhaps four times since the last time she had dined with him. Of course, he hadn't left it there, that night, after the bus ride. He had written her a number of times, telephoned almost daily, sent flowers. After a time, however, he had apparently reached the conclusion that, rare among women, she meant what she said. So the letters, flowers, and telephone calls had ceased. But on the first three occasions of their accidental encounters, his face had become illuminated at the sight of her, he had tried to maneuver her into a corner, he had offered to take her home, had begged her to leave the party, to go somewhere with him, for a quiet dinner. But the fourth time he had not been alone; he had a girl with him, very dark and young, all sparkle and verve, and Carol had fancied, with considerable amusement, that he had been embarrassed at seeing her.

So it wasn't at all like Kim, this question of Bill Dawson.

Impelled by an urgency which she could not define, she picked up the telephone and called Andy at his flat. Howie answered, sleepy but courteous. 'No, ma'am,' he reported. Mr Morgan wasn't in town. He had gone to Connecticut for the weekend and he wouldn't be back till morning. He'd go straight to the office. If it was important Miss Reid could reach him at Miss Allen's. Howie had the number, written down.

'Never mind,' said Carol, feeling deflated, 'thanks. No, don't bother, I'll see Mr Morgan tomorrow.'

She went to bed, exasperatingly wide awake and wondered if Millicent was having a weekend houseful or if Andy was there alone?

Andy was there alone. You couldn't count the little gray creep mouse of a cousin. And at just about the time Carol was dialing his number he was sitting on the terrace with Millicent, looking across the garden, a tall glass beside him on a little table and a cigarette in his hand.

'How's Carol?' asked Millicent.

She had dressed for their tête-à-tête dinner ... as Miss Parker conveniently developed headaches whenever it was expected of her, she had, it seemed, a movable migraine ... in something long, simple, and flowing, innocent white in color, but not innocent in line. It had a jacket edged with sable against the possible chill of the September night. She wore rubies in her ears, on her hands and wrists, and her lips and fingernails were painted the exact shade, deep and glowing.

'All right, I guess,' Andy answered. He was comfortable and a little sleepy, too lazy to make the first move and say, If you don't mind

232

I think I'll go to bed. He should, he reflected, he had to be up at an ungodly hour in the morning.

'Is she going to marry her restaurant keeper?' inquired Millicent.

'Who? Oh, Dawson. I haven't the least idea.'

'It's a sensible thought,' said Millicent, 'she's getting no younger.'

'Oh, come, she's not fifty,' said Andy, vaguely irritated, 'she's thirty.'

'Must you leap to her defense?' asked Millicent, laughing. 'Look, you scared Reddy, poor beast.'

Redlock of Wakeridge stirred under her chair, barked in his sleep, and subsided again.

'Sorry,' said Andy, somewhat abashed by the loud, startled sound of his own voice, 'didn't mean to yell. But if you put Carol in that—last-hope, last-chance class—what does it make me?'

'Men are different.' She added dreamily, 'She'll go on slaving in that office—'

'Slaving? Good Lord!'

'Day in and day out,' she continued imperturbably, 'growing a little fatter—or angular, as the case may be—and getting a streak of gray hair, and a little more tired—'

'A pretty picture!'

'It must happen,' she prophesied serenely, 'not this year or next, perhaps not in five years. But in ten surely.'

'None of us knows what will happen in ten

years,' he said gravely.

'Don't get world-minded,' she said, 'we were discussing Carol.'

'You were, you mean.'

'And you won't?'

He found himself saying shortly:

'I'd rather not.'

'That's odd,' said Millicent.

'Why?'

'Men,' she mused, 'are nicer than women, aren't they? Carol doesn't mind discussing you.'

She didn't, did she? He found himself growing red in the darkness. And annoyed. He said:

'That's all right by me, if it amuses her.'

'I don't think it does,' said Millicent thoughtfully, 'but it's amusing to me—to draw her out, I mean.'

'Women have no—'

'Decency?'

He said, 'Well, that's it, I suppose.'

Millicent laughed. 'You don't know much about women.'

That irritated him too, as she knew it would. She said, laughing again:

'Have I annoyed you? Funny how the nicest men hate to think they don't know all about women . . . they don't, of course. Only the ones who aren't nice do—or those who aren't quite men.'

He said, 'This isn't getting us anywhere.'

234

She asked gravely:

'Would you mind if Carol married William Dawson?'

'Of course not,' he answered heartily; 'that is, not if she were in love with him and he with her ... he's a swell person.'

'I had an idea he was a little on the heavy side from things I've heard here and there. But perhaps Carol would like that.'

'How do you know what she'd like?'

'I don't. I know only what she *used* to like.'

He asked incautiously:

'What?'

'You, my dear.'

He said, after a moment:

'Well, that's obvious enough, as she married me.'

'I've been wondering about that,' said Millicent calmly. 'You aren't still in love with her, are you, Andy?'

'Good God, no!'

'You needn't be so emphatic. Isn't there something about ... protesting too much?'

He said, 'You needn't be concerned about Carol and me ... if you are concerned.'

'I am,' she admitted. 'It's troubled me ... I—you see, Andy, you've outgrown Carol. I would hate you to make the same mistake twice.'

He said, genuinely bewildered:

'Aren't you assuming a good deal, Millicent?'

235

'Perhaps. But you don't seem too enthusiastic about the possible Dawson alliance.'

He said, 'I wouldn't want her to have two bad breaks. She deserves better. She's a grand person. We have grown to be very good friends. Even if I get madder than—' he stopped and laughed—'in a business way, of course.'

'The losing of the book contract?'

'Well, yes.'

'She's besotted about that child,' said Millicent. 'I believe she will marry Dawson because of the youngster.'

'That's a crazy reason.'

'I know, but perhaps it's as good as any,' said Millicent. She rose and went over to a long couch heaped with cushions. 'Andy, do come over here. I hate shouting across space. I want to talk to you.'

He went obediently, and sat down next to her. 'What were we doing just now?'

'Not talking ... not really. Andy—do you dislike me?'

He said, 'I think you're a little goofy tonight.'

'Do you? I must know.'

'No,' he said; 'you're a damned attractive woman and you know it. I like you very much.'

'And is that all?'

He said against his will, 'No.'

She asked:

236

'Is it possible that you are a little in love with me?'

'It's quite possible,' he said. He tried to control his tone, to keep it even and light. 'It's even probable.' He found that his tone was neither even nor light and that he was definitely, disturbingly aware of her nearness, and of the perfume she wore.

She moved closer to him. She said quietly, 'I'm terribly in love with you, Andy.'

If he had any thoughts at all they stemmed from common sense and were therefore to be ignored. He took her in his arms and kissed her and was both appalled and enchanted by her instant response, and the type of that response.

He'd known she was a man hunter. But he had always imagined that once she had bagged her game—

He had thought her essentially cold. He had thought that any woman who could dissect the male and female emotions as she, with her scalpel of a typewriter, could do must be basically frigid ... or she could not be as inhumanly, maliciously detached.

Apparently he had been in error.

After a long while she drew away from him. She said, 'Andy?' questioningly, and he said, 'Well?'

'Is that all you have to say?'

It sounded utterly Victorian, it sounded like, What are your intentions? It couldn't mean that. Millicent Allen was an entirely worldly woman. A kiss didn't . . . wasn't the prelude to marriage . . . it needn't be prelude to *anything*. He thought, Good Lord, I don't want to marry her.

She was saying, 'A little bird told me that you are very conventional.'

'A little bird?' he repeated, wondering if she had lost her mind, descending to clichés.

'Carol.'

So they were back there again. He said, 'I am, extremely so. I read a chapter of Mrs Post every night before I retire.'

She pulled his face down to hers again. She said, after a breathless interval:

'Does Mrs Post say anything about this?'

'I'll have to check up,' he said, enraged to hear his voice shaking.

She said:

'Andy, we could be very happy—'

He thought, My God, it's arrived, it . . .

She was saying '. . . and very discreet. I'm in a position—I'm very fortunate, you know. My servants have been with me for a long time. And I am superbly chaperoned.' She laughed. 'Cousin Connie knows what I expect of her.'

He said, 'I suppose you know what you're saying?'

'Quite.' She added thoughtfully, 'You won't believe this. I've never had a lover. Silly, isn't it? I've never been able to believe that it would be worth it. I've always thought that no matter what temporary pleasure it might afford me I would eventually loathe the fact that I had surrendered myself. Can you understand that? I didn't want to be deeply involved ... ever.' She closed her eyes in the darkness, smiling, remembering Ollin Jones and his importunities. He had even offered to procure a divorce from the fat, intelligent, committee-loving Mrs Jones to marry Millicent Allen. That was a true flattery, for while there had been many women since he had stood at an altar with Mrs Jones he had never wanted to marry them.

Andy said gently:

'I don't think you mean it, Millicent.'

'Mean what?'

He said, floundering, feeling idiotic and gauche, as all men have felt since time immemorial, in a similar situation:

'It's just tonight ... and because we're attracted by each other. You'd be very ill-advised—'

She said wildly, 'I'm not looking for a job. Stop talking like that!'

'Millicent.' He took her restless thin hands and held them tightly. A stone cut her but she liked it. She enjoyed it. She sat there, passive, and let the ruby bruise her delicate flesh. 'Millicent. Please believe that I'm honored beyond words, that I—'

She pulled her hands away and said in a hard, tight voice:

'If you say you respect me as much as ever,

I'll scream, I'll—'

He tried to laugh. 'I've never,' he said, 'respected you particularly.'

'Well!' She was for once very nearly bereft of speech.

He said, 'Wait a minute. I mean, I don't think of you in stodgy terms. Sounds like mission furniture. Or is it *East Lynne*? I respect your mind and your ability. I respect your courage.'

'It took very little courage,' she said, and now her voice was normal again. 'I've wanted you for a long time. Are you trying to tell me that you don't want me, Andy?'

'If I told you that, it wouldn't be true,' he said sincerely.

'Then why—?' She broke off in exasperation. 'Carol was right,' she said; 'she knows you best, after all. You wouldn't be comfortable in an affair.'

He said, 'No, Millicent, I wouldn't be.'

'Do you mean to tell me,' she demanded, 'that since your divorce you haven't been interested in—'

'Several women,' he finished for her. 'Yes, I suppose you'd call those episodes affairs. It's a silly word, isn't it?'

'Then why?'

He said, 'I wasn't at all in love with them, my dear, nor they with me. There was nothing of any duration. A very fleeting attraction—and no regrets, on either side. Escape, release, call it

240

what you will—'

'And I differ?'

He said, 'Very much. I like you. We're friends.'

She said hysterically, 'And you publish my books. Does that—you can't mean to tell me that *that* makes a difference?'

He asked, 'Just how stupid would you think me if I said that, yes, somehow it does?'

'Incredibly,' she answered. 'Suppose we stop making conversation. You—won't?'

He drew a deep breath. He thought dazedly, I must be crazy. He answered, without perceptible hesitation, 'That's it.'

She began to laugh, quite naturally. 'There's another quotation, something about hell hath no fury—'

'I can't imagine you as a fury,' he said, 'and, moreover, you are not scorned.'

'Yet,' she pondered aloud, 'you're—a little in love with me, or so you said.'

'The fact remains,' he told her, 'I have never known a woman more attractive.'

'This,' she said, with petulance, 'is an extremely silly situation, a reversal of a very common one. I've been in your shoes, so to speak, a number of times.'

'I don't doubt it.'

'A courteous rejoinder,' she informed him. 'If I were a marrying woman...'

His heart did a sort of swan dive. He waited, literally holding his breath.

241

She went on, 'But I'm not. The very thought of marriage appalls and affronts me. Well, that's that. What happens next?'

He asked:

'Isn't that entirely up to you, Millicent?'

'Nice of you,' she told him. 'What do you want to happen?'

He said carefully, 'I like being with you, and working with you. I would be very much disturbed if I thought that—' he broke off and added, still keenly aware that she was very close to him—'how does it go—that you would forbid me to darken your door again.'

'The trouble is,' she reflected, 'that you won't darken it. Oh, I've no idea of giving you your congé—or is that phrase wrong here?— you're far too useful to me,' she went on frankly. She rose and he came to his feet with a definite sense of relief. She put her arms around his neck and kissed him. When she took her arms away she was smiling although he could not see her face clearly, 'I haven't given up,' she said. 'I don't know how one goes about breaking down a man's scruples and trampling upon his principles. But there must be ways and I'll try them all. So you are warned ... if you want to run away, I'll understand.'

'My dear Millicent...' he began.

But she had gone, quickly and lightly across the terrace to the living room, lights shone on the flagstones. The French windows closed behind her.

242

Andy put his hand in his pocket, discovered his cigarettes, struck a match. He felt like a fool. He was a fool. Practically every man of his acquaintance would think so. Even Richard and Stephen. They might not admit it, they would hardly encourage an affair between their managing editor and one of their authors—but they would think ... Oh, hell!

He went up to bed without seeing Millicent again. He did not encounter her at early breakfast nor until he was ready to drive away when she appeared briefly in the doorway, in extraordinary pajamas, but with every ash-blond hair in place and her face carefully made up for sunlight. She waved, and called, 'See you in town.'

Driving back, he thought, I wish I could ask Carol about this. That was a lunatic notion, as notions went. The idea made him laugh heartily, to the astonishment of a couple of early birds regarding him from a fence rail and an annoyed woodchuck scurrying across the road. Fine idea, that was. Go to your ex-wife and ask her soberly, What's the matter with me, if anything? Why can't I subscribe to a little interdicted excitement? Clever, damned attractive woman, her own mistress—no matter who else's—there's a sentence for you—whom else? he inquired, growing grammatically confused ... no furtive hole-in-the-corner business, merely a spot of pleasant, discreet indiscretion, no commercial angle...

243

He stopped thinking, in self-disgust. Carol would look at him in utter amazement. Or wouldn't she? What right had she to tell Millicent that he was conventional? What right had she to know that he was? He hadn't known it himself!

He had told Millicent that he was a little in love with her. Euphonious term. Had he been, even a little, he would have slapped her down and inquired when she would marry him. That's how conventional he was. If you were in love with a woman, you married her!

So what? So he wasn't in love with her. There was another word for it in any language. And he certainly didn't want to marry her. Well, he wasn't going to, he reflected, and let the car out a little on the parkway.

It would be awkward, seeing Millicent again. How did you greet a woman who had told you she was in love with you and who had offered you bed and board without benefit of justice of the peace?

He was annoyed to reflect further that any embarrassment would be on his side and not on hers. But he took refuge in the comforting thought that, well, she'd get over it—she'd think better of it someday and be grateful to him. Not that he could imagine a grateful Millicent.

CHAPTER TWENTY-ONE

In September the Dawson ménage returned to the big, old-fashioned apartment in town. Lydia's school would soon open, Lorna must get her ready. Carol went there for dinner, now and then, with Bill and Lorna, going early in order to see Lydia at her supper. Several times Lorna had occasion to telephone her. Once she had to go to Chicago to see her brother, once she was called to Southampton, another time out-of-town friends had come unexpectedly and wanted her to be with them ... was Carol busy, could she take Lydia to some promised treat, the Zoo, a movie, a walk in the Park, during the weekend?

After this fashion, almost imperceptibly, Carol was established in the family.

She often saw Bill Dawson alone. He came to her apartment for a cocktail, prior to dining out, or they dined there, at home. He did not speak directly of his proposal again, but all his future plans included her. 'When we take Lydia to Honolulu ... When we go abroad with Lydia...'

She saw him the night before she went to Longfields for Millicent's office party. Taking her home, he asked if he might come upstairs with her. They sat talking for a time, as it was early. Leaving, he took her in his arms and kissed her.

When he had gone, without a word, she thought how safe she had felt, how content, how sheltered. She had responded generously, with tenderness and affection. No more, she admitted; but surely that would come? If he had sensed a lack, he did not say so.

* * *

The office party was an occasion. The October woods burned under a deep-blue sky. Picnic grills had been set out and most of the Maynard and Hall staff had come, either by car or by train. The Halls were spending the night, the Maynards, Andy, Carol, Peter Tarrant and his current fiancée. The others would leave after a buffet supper that Saturday night.

Sumac running on scarlet feet through the woods, the last zinnias blazing in the garden, the ruffled heads of chrysanthemums. The sun was marvelously warm, and the trees a glowing sacrifice, burning themselves to glory for summer's sake, suttee trees, claret and burgundy, gold and pale yellow, brown and beige, rose, purple and russet.

Millicent was, as always, the accomplished, unhurried hostess. Food and drink were excellent and lavish. There were speeches. Her book had appeared, the critics had taken it to their hearts, the public would follow.

246

Everything was wonderful.

They'd had their outdoor picnic and their long afternoon, and were at supper when the telephone call came, for Carol.

She answered, wondering a little. She had told no one where she would be this weekend except Bess and Bill Dawson. She went into the living room where a fire sang on the big hearthstone and picked up the instrument.

'Carol—this is Lorna.'

'Yes ...?' Her heart twisted suddenly. She asked, 'Is anything wrong?'

'Lydia ... she's very ill.'

Carol said, stunned, 'But I talked to Bill yesterday.'

'We weren't sure then. We—' Lorna's voice broke, but she steadied it—'he didn't wish to alarm you, or spoil your party.'

Carol said frantically, 'Can't I do something?'

'She wants you,' Lorna said. 'Will you come?'

'Of course. As soon as possible. Give her—my love.'

When she hung up, and turned, Andy was there. She said, white:

'I must go, at once. Lydia's ill—they've sent for me.'

'Lydia?' he repeated, startled—'the Dawson child?'

She did not hear. She was thinking, I'll go as I am, throw things in a bag, look up a train ... it would be quicker than by car.

He asked:

'They sent for you? That means that you—'

'I don't care what it means,' she cried at him, hardly knowing what she said. 'I must go immediately, Andy, can't you see that?'

Millicent had left the dining room and come in. She said, 'I saw you—and then Andy. What's the matter?'

'I have to return to town,' said Carol. 'Is there a train?'

'Something wrong?' Millicent could see that something was, she didn't bother to finish her sentence. 'There isn't a train, Carol, but Fritz will drive you. I'll send for him.'

'Thanks,' said Carol, and started for the stairs. But Andy held her back, by the wrists. He said, unmindful of Millicent:

'Tell me . . . are you going to marry Dawson? You must be or you wouldn't—'

She wrenched away from him.

'Oh, let me go!' she cried. 'What business is it of yours?' She was weeping furiously, the tears pouring down her face.

Millicent sent a maid to help her pack her few things and came herself just as the maid finished. She said:

'Andy tells me that the little Dawson girl is ill—I'm so sorry.'

Carol did not hear her.

Fritz drove her through the dark October night. The moon had not yet risen. Wood smoke lingered in the air, the trees, deprived of light, stood thick and black, the wind made a cool sighing sound. Hurry, thought Carol, hurry!

Now she was thanking Fritz, now someone had come to take her bag, now she was upstairs and the familiar manservant was opening the door, his face drawn and quiet. Bill was coming forward, she was frankly in his arms for a moment, and Lorna found her there.

Carol drew away. She said:

'How is she?'

Lorna took her away, into her own room. She said:

'No worse … it's—' she hesitated, used the commoner term—'it's infantile, Carol.'

'*No!*'

'Yes. Everything's being done. Two nurses, besides myself. The best doctors, the latest treatment—the—'

'She may not walk again,' said Carol.

She could see Lydia running, bouncing like a ball, over the wet brown sand, a starfish in her hand.

'We hope it won't be—that way. There are very wonderful cures, Carol.'

'May I see her?'

'For a minute. She's asked for you,' said Lorna, 'over and over.'

The nurse rose as Carol and Lorna came in. Masked, she stood by the bed. The room was no longer Lydia's. It was a hospital room.

249

Lydia looked up at her. She said, 'You look funny. I don't like this. My feet are queer. I can't feel them.'

A moment later, Lorna drew Carol away. She said, as they went out, 'You mustn't cry like that. It isn't good for you—or her.'

She took Carol into her room, brought her something fizzing in a glass. Carol drank it obediently. 'Have you had dinner?' asked Lorna.

'No, I'd just started. It doesn't matter. I couldn't eat.'

'You must. I've ordered coffee, and something hot. I'll sit here with you while you have your tray. I'm on the first day shift, eight hours. Bill wants it that way. And he wants her here, at home.'

Carol said angrily:

'I won't think of what might happen. I daren't. How is it possible to feel like this about a child not your own?'

Lorna said:

'I can.'

'Of course. All these years. But she *is* yours,' Carol said, 'in a way she'd never be if I—'

'If you married Bill?' asked Lorna quietly. 'But she loves you very much.'

'She doesn't need me as she needs you. You mustn't ever leave her,' said Carol distractedly.

Lorna was silent. Then she said slowly:

'Bill needs you, Carol.'

Bill. She had forgotten him. She said, 'Oh,

poor—if there were anything I could do, or say.'

'You can be with him,' said Lorna.

A maid knocked, and came in. Carol choked down the coffee, tried to eat a thin bread and butter sandwich, touched the omelette with her fork. She said, like a child, 'I can't really.'

Lorna rose. 'Bill's waiting in the library,' she said.

Carol found him there, and sat down beside him on the big leather couch. He looked beaten. He put his head down against her. He said, 'Just so she'll *live*—'

She hadn't thought of that, she'd been thinking of the other possibility, the wind leashed, the sea stilled, the quick feet shackled.

She felt his head heavy against her, but not so heavy as her heart, drumming in her breast. She found no words with which to comfort him. They sat silent, waiting. For what? A door opened and closed. They heard Lydia's voice, 'Lorna,' she was calling, 'Lorna.'

Bill said dully:

'Her temperature's very high. She's been irrational. Did she know you?'

'I thought so,' Carol said.

'She keeps calling Lorna. I can't let Lorna wear herself out. She must get some sleep. That's why I insisted upon her taking day duty. The doctor will be here presently.'

He began talking about serums, about light cases, often recovering without a sign … 'the paralysis spreads for a few days, they say, then remains stationary—a week, four weeks, five ... After that, in a light case, recovery begins.'

She said, 'It *must!*'

'We were afraid yesterday. Today, we knew. Lorna knew how much I wanted you. So she telephoned.'

He added, after a moment:

'Lydia—she doesn't always know me. That's why I asked if she knew you. She knows Lorna, calls for her, clings to her.'

Calls for Lorna. Not for me, Carol thought. She never called for me. Bill wanted me, not Lydia.

I would have come, she thought, for Bill, but Lorna made sure.

He said, 'I haven't any right, to this,' and moved his head restlessly against her.

It was a long night. The doctor came and went. He talked to Bill in the library, and Carol stood at the window, half hidden by the heavy draperies and looked out over the Park. There was nothing new to report. They were doing everything that could be done. She heard snatches of conversation, half incomprehensible. She didn't want anything to become clear, or to understand that if the paralysis spread to the respiratory organs the iron lung held out the only hope.

After the doctor had gone, they sat there again, on the leather couch. Sometimes they were silent. Sometimes he talked and she

252

listened ... about Lydia, and Lydia's mother. She had been slim and dark, with an enchanting smile, 'like yours, Carol,' and a direct regard, 'yours too ... when I saw you first I was startled, you are so much alike ... in many ways...'

Lorna came in, before dawn. She wore a dark flannel robe, her hair in thick, dark braids. She said:

'You must get some sleep, both of you.'

'Sleep,' repeated Bill. He was half drunk with fatigue. He stumbled to his feet and stood there, swaying. Lorna put her steadying arm around him. She said, 'Of course.'

'You haven't had any,' Carol said.

'Quite a lot. Miss Rogers called me twice, the last time when the doctor was here. In between, I slept.'

Bill said nothing. He went off, without a word, in the direction of his room. Lorna stood looking after him. She said:

'The doctor left a sedative, for him. I'll take it in, later. The guest room's ready for you, Carol.'

A pleasant room, rose and turquoise, her night things laid out on the bed.

Carol sat down on the bed. She said forlornly:

'Lydia didn't want me. I don't think she knew me. It was Bill who wanted me. I haven't been able to do anything for him, Lorna.'

'You are here,' Lorna said.

She knelt, and put her arms around Carol. She said, evenly, 'It's going to be all right. You *must* believe it.'

Carol looked down into her steady eyes. Lorna was white, drained, as if she bled inwardly.

She knows so much more than we do, all the implications, Carol thought, she says nothing except the hopeful thing. She keeps us all—going. It doesn't matter what she does to herself.

She put out her hand and pushed Lorna's hair back from her forehead. The fine skin was wet, under her hand.

'I'm just one more complication,' Carol said quietly. 'I crash through all your lives, doing no good. You could have kept me out, Lorna, if you had tried, you had only to raise your hand ... I wouldn't have existed, for *anyone*.'

Lorna said nothing. After a moment she rose.

'Try to sleep,' she advised, 'as long as possible. I've left a tablet on the night table. It's harmless ... take it, and sleep.'

The door closed, and Carol sat listening to the light footfall. She heard a door open. Bill's. Later she heard Lorna come out and go to Lydia's room. She was there a very short time. Then she went back to her own room.

Carol rose, undressed, crept into the cool wide bed, lay there thinking, trying to think.

Lydia's her life, she thought, and Bill.

Equally. She remembered thinking idly when she first heard of Lorna Sheffield, *Trying to marry him, of course.* But she hadn't. She hadn't tried to do anything. She had simply given—to the man, to his child—unremitting, constant devotion. For eleven years.

He's blind, Carol thought, he can't see the trees for the forest—I'm new, I'm different, I remind him of Lydia's mother.

She forced herself to think further:

It was Lydia I wanted, not Bill.

If she married Bill she might have a child of her own.

Hers and Bill's.

Her heart beat no faster, she was cool, a little repulsed. No, not repulsed, indifferent, finding the thought vaguely distasteful. She did not want them, Bill, a home, children ... just Lydia, and not because Lydia was Bill's child, but because she was herself. Nothing in her of Bill, little perhaps of her mother.

She was growing drowsy. She could not think clearly. Presently, she slept.

CHAPTER TWENTY-TWO

The next day was the longest she had ever experienced. Looking back on it, it was not a day, it admitted no limitations of time. She woke, a maid brought her a tray, she dressed, and left her room. Lorna was on duty, Bill was in the living room. He had breakfasted, he said. He asked her if she had slept. People had been telephoning, flowers had come, masses of them.

She had to find something to do; she arranged the flowers, sorted out the cards, looking at them blankly. Names she had never seen, through which she was made aware of the life of this household and of acquaintances and friends, a whole network of people, events, circumstances, which had never touched her.

Jane Leaming came into the room, and Carol realized that she had completely forgotten her and her patient. Mrs Wales had not been well since their return to the city. She stayed in bed, these days. When she slept Jane did what she could, she was free now, she said, to take messages, do anything. Perhaps during the afternoon Carol would sit with Mrs Wales for a little while, the old lady knew she had come, and had asked to see her.

Later in the morning Carol saw Lydia for a moment. She was sleeping. She stood with Bill, feeling strange, unlike herself behind the precautionary mask, and looked at the quiet, flushed face. Lorna came to the door with them. She said, to Carol:

'Try to get Bill out, for a walk.'

Before luncheon they walked, in the Park. A brisk blue day, a windless sky. Sunday, and the children playing, throwing balls, running, laughing. She saw Bill wince, knew that she herself was raw. He said, 'Let's get out of this.'

They walked down Fifth Avenue, looking blindly in the shop windows, not talking much.

In the late afternoon when Lorna was off duty, Carol said:

'It would be better if I went home, I think.'

Lorna looked at her gravely. She said:

'If you'd rather—'

Carol tried to smile. She said:

'So many in the house ... I'd forgotten all about Mrs Wales ... you have your hands more than full, Lorna. I know you'll keep in touch with me. Tonight, and tomorrow, at the office?'

She had forgotten about the office. Now she remembered. She didn't belong here and she had a job.

Bill said, 'Of course, we'll call you—'

He did not need her either, not now. Yesterday, in his first bewilderment, he had turned to her, as he would have turned to anyone whom he trusted. Lorna was— occupied, Lorna was needed elsewhere.

Carol said:

'I promised I'd go see Mrs Wales.'

The old lady was peevish, propped up in bed, looking like something carved from unlikely material. She asked, 'What's the matter with this house? No one comes to see me.'

'Lydia's ill,' Carol told her gently.

'Lydia's never ill,' denied her grandmother

stoutly. 'It's something that woman's made up, to annoy me. When are you going to get rid of her?'

Carol put her hand over the dry little claw.

'Never. You couldn't get along without her, any of you.'

Mrs Wales jerked her hand away.

'All alike,' she said, 'all in league ... where'd the flowers come from?'

Some of Lydia's flowers, banished from the sick room.

'I brought them,' Carol said and the old lady smiled at her. It was like watching the earth's surface crack.

'You're a nice girl,' she said. Her black eyes brightened, the integrated look returned. She whispered, 'Too nice—this is someone else's house. You ought to have your own.'

A moment later she was scolding Jane because she'd forgotten the hot-water bag. It was there at her feet. Jane took it away, and brought it back again, smiling at Carol.

A little later Bill went downstairs with her and put her in his car. He held her hand a long time. 'I won't try to thank you, Carol,' he said. He was, she saw, in complete command of himself. He looked older and his face was dark with fear. But he was not the man with whom she had sat all night long in the quiet library, listening for sounds from another room. He added, 'I'll call you, later in the evening. And tomorrow...'

She said, 'Ask Lorna to let me know when I may come again.'

She drove away, turning to watch him go back slowly into the house. The chauffeur, twisting to look at her obliquely, asked anxiously, 'How is she, Miss Reid?'

'No worse,' Carol said, 'it's just—the waiting...'

'My kid brother...' he began, but stopped, silenced, watchful of his driving.

At Carol's apartment they told her that Mr Morgan had called several times.

She telephoned him, later, but no one answered. He may still be at Millicent's, she thought, probably is. She wouldn't call him there. She took off her hat, conscious that her head ached badly. If Andy was in town, she'd ask him to have some supper with her. She hated being alone. She called Bess, but Bess was away. She thought of other people, old friends, new. There was no one she wanted to see. Lately she'd seen so few, she had offended more than one. Her job, Bill and Lydia, had occupied most of her time. She couldn't pick up threads again because she was lonely and afraid, and it seemed expedient.

She made some tea, some bread and jelly sandwiches, a salad. She ate very little.

At eleven her telephone rang.

'She's a little better,' Lorna said, 'her temperature's down. Bill wanted to call you,

Carol. But I made him go to bed, and get a good night's sleep. The doctor's been and gone.'

Carol thanked her, hung up and went back to bed. She tried to feel nothing but gratitude. A little gained ... it might mean everything.

When she went into the office on the following morning she was conscious of a change of atmosphere, a stir of excitement. It was Peter Tarrant who told her why, coming into her office grinning. He asked:

'Why'd you barge off?'

'I—Oh, from the party? It seems very long ago. I came back to town because of—of a friend's illness.'

'Of course. Sorry, hope it's not serious,' he said. 'I'd forgotten. The furor after supper put it clean out of my head.'

'What furor?' she asked idly.

His jaw dropped and he looked embarrassed, a most unusual circumstance. He stammered.

'Lord, I thought you knew ... didn't Millicent tell you before you left—or Andy?'

'Tell me what? Peter, do stop dithering.'

'About their engagement. Millicent announced it, after supper. It was quite an occasion. Champagne and everything.'

She thought, So she brought it off. She was aware of shock, as if she had been struck a blow. No pain, just a numbing sensation, very odd.

260

She said, 'No, they didn't tell me. I dare say I wasn't in any condition to listen. But—it's marvelous, of course.'

She didn't think it was marvelous. She thought it was idiotic. Millicent Allen was the last woman in the world with whom Andy would be happy. But how do I know that? she inquired of herself. He wasn't happy with me, was he?

She said, laughing:

'Peter, don't stare at me. I think it's fine.'

'Well, it's one way to hold an author, of course. Pretty drastic, if you ask me,' Peter said.

He went out, whistling. Elsie Norris came back from Olga James's office. Dot Owen appeared, late, and sat down to rattle her keys in a fury of concentration. The conversation, if any, always returned to the engagement. But when Carol was present it was a wary discussion. Carol thought impatiently, They handle me with kid gloves.

She didn't see Andy until later. When she did, half a dozen of them were in a huddle over the conference table. She had no word with him until the meeting was over. She touched his arm, as he was leaving the room.

'Congratulations,' she said.

To her astonishment he turned scarlet. He muttered something, and escaped. She stood looking after him, amazed, and turned when she heard Steve Hall's laughter.

'You missed doings,' he said. 'I wish you'd been there.'

'What was it like?'

'Millicent was cool—but a little coy. I never saw her coy before. Old Andy,' reported Steve, chuckling, 'was all of a heap. You'd think he hadn't known anything about it. Perhaps he didn't, for she said they hadn't intended to announce it for a while yet, but that it seemed an auspicious moment to her. Anyway, there was much chattering, exclaiming and goings-on ... Andy got plastered, completely. Tighter than an economic royalist. It was most interesting. Richard and I put him to bed, quite a job.' He asked abruptly, 'What do you think of it?'

She asked, smiling:

'What am I supposed to think? The entire staff treats me as if I might bite.'

'Well, it's a funny situation,' said Steve, 'as you must admit,' and held the door open for her.

During the morning Bill called. Nothing new, he said, would she come and have dinner with them?

'I'll come after ... I'd just be in the way. The servants have enough to do, Bill.'

He didn't urge her, and presently rang off. When the desk telephone rang again, it was Andy.

'Lunch?' he asked.

'All right,' Carol agreed.

They left together, followed by carefully careless eyes. In the elevator, 'That place is like a beehive,' Andy commented.

Over the lunch table, 'I'd like to explain,' he began.

She asked, 'Why? You and Millicent are getting married ... when, by the way?'

'No date, she—we haven't decided.'

'Is any further explanation necessary,' she demanded, 'and why—to me?'

He said, 'I called you last night to tell you.' He looked stricken. 'I forgot,' he added, genuinely ashamed, 'it's unpardonable of me. How's Bill's little girl?'

She told him, watched his face grow grave.

'I'd no idea,' he said, 'I'm so sorry. If there's anything I can do—?'

'Nice of you, Andy,' she said sincerely, 'but there's nothing.' She was silent a moment, then she added:

'I hope you'll be happy, Andy. I mean it.'

'I know.' He looked away, not meeting her eyes. He said, 'You're a swell girl.'

Anger rose in her, inexplicably.

'Because I'm taking it so well? Andy, you idiot! You—and for that matter the entire staff—behave as if I were still your wife—' She caught herself up, with irritation. 'I didn't mean quite that. But they treat me as if I had grounds for complaint, and you, as if you owned me ... as if we were married, yes, that is it, and you were telling me you wanted to marry someone else!'

He said, exasperated:

'Well, good heavens, aren't you even interested?'

'Naturally ... but hardly to that extent. The office misjudges me,' she said, 'and you flatter me.'

His temper was tinder to the spark of her anger. He said:

'Okay, I understand. Millicent said you wouldn't give a good little goddam!'

'She did, did she?' Carol retorted.

'Sure. And she was right. When are you marrying Dawson?'

'I'm not.'

He looked at her, incredulous. 'Not!' he repeated. 'After rushing off to be with him most of the summer, going places with him every other night, acting like a crazy woman because his child's ill and—'

'That's enough,' she said, white. 'We won't discuss Bill or—'

'You might have told me!' he said.

'Why? What business is it of yours? No more than you and Millicent are my business,' she said furiously. She pushed her untouched plate aside and leaned forward. Their voices had risen, people were looking at them, they did not know and they cared less.

He said:

'My God, women are hard! And they talk about men ... We've been friends, haven't we?'

'We've been friends,' she agreed, 'and we were married to each other a thousand years ago and that's that. But I don't care whom you marry or how often ... and whether I marry Bill Dawson or not I—'

He caught her up.

'So you are going to marry him!' he said, triumphant.

'I'm not!' She was practically shouting and the fat proprietor looked alarmed. A girl near by laughed, openly, and Carol, flushing, lowered her voice. 'I didn't know it,' she admitted, 'until last night. But that has nothing to do with you. I'll marry or I'll not marry, as I please.'

'Millicent went upstairs while you were packing your bag. You told her that you and Bill—'

'I never mentioned him to her!'

Andy picked up his beer glass and took a long drink. He set it down. 'One of you is a liar,' he said definitely.

'When we were living together, did I ever lie to you, Andy?'

'No, you didn't. Not even when it would have been—' He broke off. 'You've changed,' he accused her.

'So that's it. So I've changed, so I'm a liar!'

'I didn't say ...'

She regarded the pastry on her plate. A vanilla éclair. It looked smug and innocent and sickening.

'Get your check and let's get out of here,' she said.

They went, the proprietor breathed a sigh of relief, the girl at the next table demanded of her companion, 'What was *that* all about?'

'How do I know?' he answered and touched her knee under the table. He said, 'Look here, baby, Miami's a swell place, this time of year.'

She was twenty-two and had all her wits about her; he was fifty-one and had lost his. She liked diamond bracelets better than Miami ... you can't, in the wrong kind of pinch, hock someone else's palm trees.

Andy and Carol walked back to the office. They walked fast, not speaking. Carol spoke first.

'We're being childish,' she said firmly, 'and I do wish you happiness, Andy.'

'Thanks,' he said glumly.

They weren't really looking where they were going, they began to cross before the lights changed. Andy clutched her arm and dragged her out of a taxi's path. The driver made a few trenchant remarks which bore a faint resemblance to prayer.

'You hurt,' complained Carol, landing safely, in one piece, on the opposite curb.

She rubbed her arm ruefully, as Andy said:

'You deserve it ... flinging yourself in front of cabs like that!'

'I didn't fling...' She looked at him and began to laugh. 'Oh, my poor Andy,' she said with genuine gaiety, the first she had experienced for many hours, 'is it possible that you are flattering yourself again?'

CHAPTER TWENTY-THREE

Bill, or Lorna, telephoned her twice a day, and after work she would go to the apartment, or after dinner.

Lydia was better, and looked forward to her coming. The paralysis involved some of the muscles of one leg. It remained static, did not spread. The doctor was cheerful, hopeful in the extreme. During her convalescence she was normally impatient, fretting because of the sandbags. When the pain of the acute stage had subsided, her nurses began massage and passive exercising of the affected leg.

'Silly,' said Lydia.

She turned her head and looked at Carol. She said, 'Lorna says I can ride Starborn this summer. Do you think so, Carol?'

'Of course, if Lorna says so.'

'That's right,' said Lydia, understanding. She shook her head. She said, 'Sometimes I dream I can't walk or run ... ever.'

'It's just a dream,' Carol told her.

'I suppose so. I made some songs, this week. About not running. About things which can't run ... trees and mountains.'

267

'Where are they, Lydia?'

'Lorna took them,' Lydia said. After a moment spent in fitting together pieces of the puzzle Carol brought her, she said, 'Perhaps by Christmas—?' She looked hopefully at Carol.

She was well before Christmas, but not running. Walking, however, with a slight dragging of the right leg, which was a hurt in Carol's heart when she watched her walk. But the doctors had assured them that it would not be forever. There would be, they were confident, a complete recovery.

Lorna showed Carol the poems. They were not sad, nor patient nor resigned, nor any of the things they might have been. They were quick with awareness of life, motion, freedom. Carol thought, afterward, There's no use trying to divorce her from her gift; you can't, it's integral. Yet she did not believe the gift wholly responsible for her own infatuation ... the child came first. Yet without the gift would she not have been a different child?

The office was busy. The fall list having been accomplished, the spring list was now in order. But things didn't boil down to seasons, there were always books in preparation, on option, books being planned, discussed, hoped for, expected. And, of course, special books for the Christmas season. Now the visiting authors were coming in droves, the lecture season was well under way. Shortly after Thanksgiving, which she celebrated with Lydia, Carol flew to

Atlanta to hold the hand of a particularly timid writer-turned-lecturer, a brilliant, bewildered woman whose prose was smooth as cream, but who wasterrified of the press, of people, of the world in general. There were other jobs. A campaign to plan for Laura Thurston,ding

departure for foreign parts. Europe was barred now but South America had possibilities.

Millicent came frequently to see Andy, although why she need, reflected Carol, was not apparent as, having moved back to town, she could, and did, see him after work. They went to first nights, to cocktail parties, they spent a weekend on the Eastern Shore with the elder Allens. Andy returned from that trip looking worn. He came into Carol's office and sat on the edge of her desk. Elsie was not present, Dot Owen had gone to lunch.

'Have a good time?'

'Sure. They're swell people.'

'You haven't known them before?'

'Very casually. They stay in Maryland most of the time, until summer. Then it's Bar Harbor.' He sighed heavily.

'Tired?'

'It's an upsetting crowd,' he confided, 'and there seems to be an unusual number of relatives. All Millicent's aunts and uncles must have the patriarchal conviction. I never saw so many young things in my life. It appears to be the huntin', ridin', fishin' set, if there is such a thing. The energy consumed must be astounding. Quoted in ergs—or don't you care to quote me an erg—?'

'Ergs, forty-five cents a dozen,' said Carol gravely, 'new laid.'

'Quoted in ergs,' he went on, ignoring that, 'they could move mountains and give the utility companies competition.'

'Still uncertain about your wedding date?' Carol asked.

'Spring, I suppose.' He looked gloomy. He added suddenly, 'There's a catch in it.'

'Isn't there always?'

'I'm not being funny. Millicent wants me to give up my job.'

'Andy!' Carol looked at him, startled. 'Would you?'

'Of course not,' he said crossly, slid off the desk and was gone.

They had thereafter little intimate conversation. Now and then they lunched together or dined, very occasionally, when Millicent was otherwise occupied. Why so much was permitted Carol couldn't imagine. She asked once, on an unholy impulse:

'Doesn't Millicent mind your taking me out?'

'Don't be absurd.'

'I mean it. Or don't you tell her?'

'Naturally I tell her—' he added cautiously, 'if she asks.'

Carol laughed. She inquired:

'What does she say?'

'Nothing.' But she could tell that Millicent had not received his report in silence. She said demurely:

'Nice of her to give you permission.'

'Permission?' He glared at her. 'Man or mouse?' he demanded.

'Amiable mouse,' she decided serenely, 'and do be careful or you'll choke.'

Carol spent Christmas Day with Lydia, in the apartment filled with the spiced green scent of the biggest tree Bill could find. The ceiling of the room was high and the topmost bough brushed against it, branching out full and thick from the very bottom. Lorna and Bill had trimmed the tree. They'd asked Carol, but she had made an excuse. At home alone Christmas Eve she was conscious of a very real sacrifice. She thought, Just because I *want* to be there, helping trim Lydia's tree, I've no right. They've trimmed her trees for her all these years ... I don't belong in that picture.

Green globes and red, in the old tradition, snow-sprinkled, and silver and blue tinsel dropping, animals and cherubs and angels and Santa Clauses peering from the branches, little gingerbread-looking houses, long peppermint canes, popcorn balls ... and under the tree, the packages.

Mrs Wales was better, she came to the table in her wheel chair and said petulantly that the turkey was tough. It wasn't. But no one minded. It was a clear bright day with a frosting of snow. After dinner, Lydia went to take her nap. She didn't want her nap; she hadn't, she complained, napped in years! But she must sleep, after her massage. Lorna went with her, her arm about the child's shoulders.

Carol commented, looking after them:

'She's grown so much.'

'They do, in bed,' agreed Bill.

'She's thinner, the puppy curves going.'

'I know.'

Carol walked over and stood by the great tree. She said:

'Such a happy Christmas...'

'Carol?'

His tone was altered. She braced herself, waiting.

'Yes...?'

'Ever since Lydia was taken ill—' His voice roughened for a moment. 'You understand? I haven't said anything, but you know, don't you? Now, with things clear before us again ... I've not urged or hurried you, Carol, but you must know by now.'

She stood there, facing him, wearing the dark-red woolen frock which Lydia liked so much. She clasped her hands behind her back, steadying herself.

'I do. It's no use, Bill ... I'm sorry.'

His face changed, became younger, eager, unhappy.

'I had hoped—'

She moved forward, and put a hand on his.

'I had too ... I don't love you, my dear,' she said, 'and I won't cheat you, not even to—to see Lydia every day.'

He moved away from her, toward the windows. She followed, to stand beside him, waiting for him to speak. He said finally:

'Perhaps it's best. I don't know. Last summer ... I thought I'd recaptured something ... And you're such a darling, Carol,' he told her gently. 'Then when Lydia was ill it seemed to me that I hadn't room for anyone but her. Maybe that's so, and I would have been cheating you.'

She said, 'We'll leave it this way—' she put her hand on his arm and kept it there—'and we'll be friends? That doesn't often happen, I think, but in our case it must. We won't see each other so often for a while. I suppose Lydia will be returning to school soon, so she won't—think it strange. But I mustn't lose either of you entirely.'

'Aren't you thinking of Lydia,' he asked, 'rather than of me?'

She was silent for a moment.

'I have never believed it possible that I could care so much for a child not my own ... but she has that special quality,' she told him.

'I had hoped that *because* she was mine ...'

Carol shook her head.

'No.'

Lorna could care for a child not her own,

273

because of the child and because of the child's father. She could love them each as an individual, and dissociated, but she could love them, too, because they belonged, one to the other. He would know that someday.

'I see,' he said. 'Well—that's all, I suppose.'

'Bill, if it isn't imperative that Lydia return to school now—and surely it isn't—she can make up the lost time easily, she's so ahead of her grade—couldn't you take her and Lorna south?'

'Dr Renwick spoke of it,' he said, 'Warm Springs ... and then perhaps Florida. But before we made plans, I had hoped that you—'

'For Lorna as much as for Lydia,' Carol urged him. 'Can't you see what this has done to her?'

He turned and regarded her in astonishment.

'Lorna?'

'Yes. She keeps things in, she doesn't let go. She can't even cry. In a way, she's had all the burden ... as much as you have had, Bill. Her way.'

'I never thought of that,' he said slowly; 'she always seems the same.'

'She isn't,' Carol said; 'you'll see.'

She had done what she could, for Lorna. Someday he would see. Not now, not right away. Perhaps in the South, with the wind in the palms and the ocean at their feet ... perhaps this coming summer, watching Lydia run free again, seeing the shadow lift from Lorna's quiet eyes ... sometime, surely.

I am out of the picture, she thought, not without sorrow, and he'll turn back to her. No, not back. He'll turn *to* her. She's always been there, and he's not known it. I interrupted that not-knowing. He'll be more aware of her now, he's bound to be....

Lorna came silently in the room and found them standing there. She looked from one to the other, and Bill smiled at her with an effort. He said:

'She wouldn't have me, Lorna, not even as a Christmas gift.'

Carol thought, She urged him to this, he's talked to her about me, she's said, Why not today, why not on Christmas?

Lorna said, looking not at Carol but at the man:

'I'm sorry.'

He said abruptly:

'If you girls don't mind, I think I'll walk down to the club.'

When he had gone Carol spoke. She said,

'I'll go along too, presently. Lorna, you're angry with me.'

The quiet eyes were less quiet than she had ever seen them. Lorna said:

'It isn't your fault, I suppose.'

'You think I led him to believe ... Perhaps I did. I wasn't sure myself, and there was Lydia, all mixed up in it,' said Carol honestly. 'But it's

275

no good. I don't love him, Lorna, and I find, after all, that the substitutes aren't enough for me ... they wouldn't be for him either.'

She went to get her things and Lorna came with her. Standing in front of the mirror Carol tilted the black hat with the gay red feather over her eyebrow. She said, 'Funny how we fool ourselves, isn't it?'

'As long as it's just ourselves we fool,' Lorna said.

Carol looked in the glass at the other woman, standing behind her, leaning against the bedpost.

'Lorna, try to see it clearly. Bill's not hurt. I was new, I was on the side of the angels where Lydia and the contract was concerned ... that pleased him. Then, it became a matter of propinquity, I suppose...' She halted a moment, considering that propinquity in Lorna's case hadn't proved valid. She went on hurriedly, 'And besides, I reminded him of someone he had loved.'

'You are like her, rather,' Lorna said, 'I didn't notice it until Bill spoke of it recently. Taller than she was, older than she was when I knew her. She was very ill then, too. But I can see what he means, especially from her pictures.'

'That's all there is to it ... plus an attraction—a chemical reaction, one hears.'

'It takes two elements...' Lorna began slowly.

'Exactly. In a few months things will be as they were. You throw a stone into a pond, there's a ripple, it eddies away, toward shore, the pond's still, there's no trace.'

'On the surface,' Lorna qualified.

They went to the hall door, and shook hands there, a firm, close clasp.

'Don't be angry,' said Carol.

'It wasn't anger,' Lorna said, 'perhaps resentment ... What a mistake a woman makes becoming as involved as I have. But it's done now. Where anything affects Lydia—or Bill—I'm the proverbial hen, squawking after the chickens.'

Carol beckoned a taxi and drove home, through the darkening, cold air. Bess and Jerry were coming for late supper. She wouldn't be alone Christmas night. It had been tacitly understood that she stay at the Dawsons' the remainder of the afternoon, but Bill would understand, and Lorna would explain to Lydia, a reasonable child. Carol thought, I hope she isn't too reasonable about me, always. But I can see her often when Bill's not there, before they go away.

In her apartment upstairs, her small tree waited to be illuminated, the opened packages were on the table. Andy had sent flowers and an absurd hunk of junk jewelry, a crazy little horse—'Pegasus of publicity,' he'd written on his card. There were Bess's gift and others, including the perfume from Millicent, in a

277

bottle carved like a flower. A fantastically expensive thing . . . Carol had seen duplicates in gay Christmas windows. It was extravagant, and without warmth. Costly, delicate, sharp with sophistication, not too sweet. Very like Millicent.

Under her door, the yellow warning of a telegram.

She stooped and picked it up, tore it open, hanging her handbag on the doorknob with Lydia's present in it—an old, old ring, two small gold hands, clasped. Bill had sent a plant; Lorna, handkerchiefs. Lydia's gift was *the* gift . . . she wondered, had Bill selected it?

She read the wire, standing there:

Lunch with me tomorrow my apartment one o'clock please come if humanly possible imperative I see you.

Millicent

CHAPTER TWENTY-FOUR

Christmas fell on a Monday that year, and on Tuesday the staff returned to the office wearing the slightly overfed look which results from a long, festive weekend. Everyone was exhibiting something in the way of a Christmas gift. Dorothy Owen could hardly hit the right keys on her typewriter for admiring the diamond on her left hand, which symbolized a spring wedding and a new secretary for the publicity department. Elsie Norris wished that something would happen to the building's heating apparatus so that she might preside over her desk clad in the short fur jacket which had been the gift of an affluent sister. The gentlemen in the office were self-conscious in startling ties or new cuff links, or in displaying wallets and cigarette cases. 'Why is it,' asked Peter Tarrant—his case was thin and gold, 'that them as has gifts?' Peter's red head was brushed and burnished but he looked slightly fatigued. He put the new case back in his pocket. Three fiancées, three cases. He never returned them when the engagements ended. Too embarrassing for the poor girls, with the loving messages in their own dear little finishing-school script inside. However, he assured himself, this was positively his final appearance as a fiancé. This time it would take.

Carol had pinned the jaunty little horse on the lapel of her jacket. She liked his fabulous blue glass eyes and the look of his emerald glass hoofs. But Andy did not come in to be properly thanked.

Inquiring of Kate, she was informed that Andy wouldn't be in at all during the day. He had had to fly to Washington to confer with one of their political authors on a number of matters, embracing radio talks, magazine articles and, of course, a book.

Just as well, Carol thought, plunging into her routine. She wondered, if she had seen him, whether or not she would have mentioned the imperious telegram from Millicent. Probably not, for if he had not known that Millicent planned to see her, it might have been embarrassing. For him, at any rate.

Carol cleared her desk, commiserated with various associates over their white gift elephants, congratulated those whom Santa Claus had treated with intelligence, and shortly before one o'clock took a cab to Millicent's Sutton Place apartment. It was snowing, lazy white flakes, starry and soft, and the sky was a drowsy gray.

Her cab driver wore an optimistic spring of mistletoe in his buttonhole, and sang 'God Rest Ye' with more vigor than tune, as they slithered eastward.

Millicent's apartment was perfect with the clean perfection of a precision dancer. Very modern in décor, very becoming—living room, bedroom, dining room, study had space, air, light, and fireplaces. The coloring was mainly pastel, but with warmer sudden notes of color for contrast. The furniture was simple, in beautiful woods. Carol had been there several times, on business conferences, and now, waiting for Millicent, she looked around and decided that the white and silver tree was sufficiently formal and cool, but that the holly struck an incongruous note. It was a curious

280

apartment, it looked as if no one had ever lived in it.

Millicent came in. She wore a beautiful Chinese coat over heavy black satin trousers, her hair shone, her nails glittered with opalescent polish, her lipstick was dark, like wine-colored dahlias.

She said:

'I'm glad you could come.'

She was not, Carol decided, looking her best; there were faint blue smudges under her eyes, a worried line between her brows.

'I'll have to write properly,' Carol told her, 'to thank you for my perfume ... it's superb. The trouble is I shall have to go into debt to buy the right evening frock for it. It calls for lamé, sables, ropes of pearls...'

Millicent's smile was absent, although present. She said, 'I like that silly horse you're wearing,' and Carol said, 'So do I,' and there was a brief silence, interrupted by the appearance of cocktails.

'Or would you rather have tomato juice?'

'If I may?' Carol answered. 'I don't often indulge in the middle of a workday and last night friends came in for supper and brought champagne. I feel a little on the fuzzy-minded side as it is.'

Luncheon was announced, they were served in the white dining room with its view of the river. Pearl-white walls, a Monet over the mantel, pale-turquoise draperies. What a

281

mannered sort of place, thought Carol, feeling slightly irritated.

During luncheon, which was excellent, on the light side, and guaranteed not to alarm you when you stepped on the scales, Millicent talked of Christmas, of the skiing at Sun Valley, of a possible trip to Placid, and of the fact that her parents had been very much disturbed because she had not come to them over the holiday. This brought them to coffee, to the disappearance of the butler, and so, to Andy.

'But I wanted to spend it with Andrew and he wouldn't go to Maryland with me,' she said.

'Too bad,' said Carol. The coffee was too hot. She set her cup down.

'Stubborn of him,' said Millicent. She widened her eyes. 'I never dreamed he was so stubborn.'

'Didn't you?'

Carol was beginning to enjoy herself.

'No. Did you?' Millicent asked her.

She answered cautiously:

'It dawned on me, after a while. Of course, it's will power, really.' She wanted to laugh but succeeded in looking preternaturally grave.

'That's what he says,' said Millicent. 'I don't think you—Oh, you were being funny!' she deduced with some annoyance.

'Not very, I'm afraid.'

'I didn't mind staying in town ... we had dinner here, and went out to an eggnog party

282

and then had supper. We quarreled, rather badly,' she said abruptly.

Carol was silent.

Millicent took a cigarette from the hollow back of a crystal swan.

'Aren't you interested?' she asked.

'No,' Carol told her frankly, 'I'm not.'

'But you must help me,' Millicent said.

'I?'

'He'll listen to you. He said last night that you had more common sense than any woman he had ever known.'

'A dubious compliment,' murmured Carol. She felt herself shrinking, broadening. Her suit became a hairy tweed, her shoes flat-heeled brogues. She carried a stick, and was full of good works. She did not like the picture.

'He said you had integrity.'

That was better, and Carol brightened. She commented carefully:

'Kind of Andy. But I don't see why I—'

'I want him to give up his position,' said Millicent. 'I don't see why he won't. There's no sane argument against it.'

'Except that he hasn't any money,' Carol reminded her. 'That's why. Or so I assume. Also, he likes his work. He's crazy about it. And good at it.'

Millicent frowned.

'But I've plenty of money. One day I'll have more than I need,' she said.

'Impossible!'

'I mean that. My tastes are very simple.' She looked around the room and Carol could have shouted. Simple ... very simple, Longfields and Sutton Place. Nice upper-bracket simplicity. People could be pretentious on half what Millicent spent on simplicity.

Millicent put her elbows on the table and leaned forward. The cigarette smoldered in a crystal tray.

'We can travel,' she said, 'we can live where we please, as we please. I'll go on writing. He will help me.'

Lovely prospect. Courier. Escort. Private editor and critic. Carol shuddered.

'It sounds fascinating,' she said. 'And how does Andy feel about it?'

'He won't do it,' said Millicent sullenly. Sullenness sat oddly upon her delicate face, she wore it like a Halloween mask.

She rose, 'Let's go into the other room,' she suggested.

Carol followed, sank into the corner of a pearl-gray divan heaped with pale-coral cushions. What in the world was this apartment like ... Noel Coward with the spirit of Emily Dickinson hovering over the background? She couldn't decide. One thing she knew, she couldn't see Andy in it, with his big feet and his stupendously strong pipe...

'You *must* persuade him,' said Millicent.

'I? Good heavens!' Carol answered, genuinely amused. 'I haven't the remotest influence ... Remember, I told you that once?'

'You have,' said Millicent; 'he values your opinion. He's as much as told me. Look at what it will do for him, take him away from that daily grind, give him new interests.'

'Travel,' murmured Carol, 'is so broadening ... but it's narrowed down these days.'

Millicent was paying little attention. She was, Carol realized, completely unaffected at the moment. She'd laid aside her brittle air, her Venetian-glass figure manner. She was not being witty or cool or fragile. She was being earnest, and rather dull.

'I told him,' Millicent said, 'that we could make a bargain. If, after five years, he found himself bored, I'd set him up in his own publishing business.'

In another alley, thought Carol absurdly; no, the same alley, bigger and better. Aloud she asked,

'And he didn't want that?'

'No. I don't understand him, Carol.'

Carol said, after a minute:

'Perhaps I can help there. As a kid in college he wanted to have something to do with books, he wanted to write them. Then circumstances pitchforked him into the sort of business he hated. But he was good at it, everyone was in those days, he made a lot of easy money which he spent as easily. He led,' she went on, half to herself, 'the craziest sort of life ... no stability, no roots. Well, came the melancholy days and

285

the wailing wall ... and he was out on his ear. By degrees he struggled back to normality and, to his intense gratitude, found the sort of work that satisfied him. I can't see Andy racketing around the South Seas, Millicent, with nothing to do, nor can I see him letting any woman, not even his wife, buy him a business the way you'd give a baby a new toy to keep him quiet.'

Millicent crossed one leg over the other. She said:

'Well, that's how it is.'

'And neither of you giving an inch?'

'I'm afraid so. If he won't leave Maynard and Hall, I won't marry him.'

Carol said pleasantly:

'I'm amazed that you—want to marry him. You told me once that you didn't.'

Millicent shrugged. For the first time in her knowledge of her, Carol saw a faint betraying color creep under the fine skin.

'You were right,' she admitted after a moment; 'he is basically—conventional.'

Well! Carol drew a deep breath and put a silencer on exclamation. So that was it. Millicent couldn't have her cake and eat it too. She couldn't have Andy as her lover *cum* editor. So she was willing to sacrifice her lack of principles and make an honest man of him. Only that hadn't worked either. It was high comedy.

Carol said faintly:

'So you found that out?'

286

'I did. Before the office party at Longfields. I don't know why I bother with him, really,' said Millicent crossly. 'He's stupid, in the last analysis. And it's such an *unmasculine* point of view!'

'You must know very interesting men,' said Carol sweetly.

Millicent let that pass. She said:

'Then, at Longfields ... right after you left ... I said to him, "All right, have it your way," and announced the engagement.'

I'll bet, said Carol to herself, that it wasn't his way ... any more than it was hers. I'll stake my new winter hat that marriage hadn't been mentioned between them and that he was the most astonished man in New England when she said, in effect, All right, darling, if you won't let me keep you any other way, I'll marry you. Well, I'll never know, she thought, as Millicent wouldn't tell her and certainly Andy wouldn't. But she was never more sure of anything.

She said carelessly:

'By the way, you told Andy that I was going to marry Bill Dawson, didn't you?'

Millicent's face altered. It became still and wary. She asked:

'You are, aren't you?'

'No.'

'But I assumed...'

'Evidently. You did tell him ... you told him that when you came up to my room, to see if

287

the maid had come to help me pack, I'd confided as much to you.'

'Andrew told you?' said Millicent.

'Yes.'

'I came into the living room,' said Millicent. 'You and Andy were there, you'd just had the telephone call. You were standing there as if you *belonged*. If I told him that, I was merely anticipating events, or so I thought. It wasn't a lie because I was certain that you and Mr Dawson...'

'Bread into roses?' said Carol. 'Only this time it remained bread. Why did you find it necessary, Millicent?'

'I've told you.'

'Not altogether. If you're afraid of me, why do you ask me to help you now?'

'I'm not afraid!'

'That's good,' said Carol. She rose and stood looking down at her hostess. 'Because I won't help you. I like Andy well enough to believe it would be the worst possible thing for him. Far worse than if he had the privilege of staying here after your other guests leave, or of coming back and using his own latchkey.'

Millicent got to her feet. She said, with considerable heat:

'You want him yourself. I've always known it!'

'Have you?'

'Yes. I told him so last night. He looked as if I'd struck him. He's not in love with you, he won't ever be again, he's in love with me, he—'

It was embarrassing, and a little disgusting.

Carol went to the door. She said en route:

'You'll have to work out your own problem, Millicent. I can't and won't help you. If I've any influence over Andy, which I doubt, I'll use it against you. He's a friend of mine. I don't want to see him warped and wasted.'

'I was a fool to ask you to come here. I might have known that your conquest of William Dawson, your paraded devotion to his absurd child, was to attract Andrew's attention and to make him believe he'd lost something worth keeping.'

Carol could have shaken her until the jade buttons on the coat rattled. She didn't. She managed to say serenely:

'It's an interesting theory, at any rate.'

'After all,' said Millicent, staring at her, 'he couldn't hold you.' Her face had changed again, she had forgotten her miniature tempest.

'That's right,' said Carol cheerfully, wondering where this was leading.

'You're pretty,' said Millicent, 'and intelligent enough. But, if Andy couldn't hold you...'

'Of course. He couldn't be expected to hold *you*,' agreed Carol calmly, 'even though he's had ten years in which to grow up ... or wasn't that your thought? Thanks for the lunch,' she added, 'and the entertainment.'

The door closed behind her.

Millicent walked back into the living room. She picked up a chaste white lamp and hurled it at the wall. In the kitchen the servants grinned at each other. She went to the telephone table, looked through her address book, and dialed the number of a travel agency.

CHAPTER TWENTY-FIVE

On Wednesday Andy returned to the office. He called Carol in conference and they went over some projected releases in connection with the political writer. Kate clacked cheerfully at her typewriter, and the increasing snow slurred against the panes.

'I saw Millicent yesterday,' Carol remarked, preparatory to leaving, 'and, oh, I haven't thanked you for the flowers and my horse ... I loved them both.'

'That's all right ... You saw Millicent?'

'Yes, she asked me for lunch. She wants me to use my influence with you. I was flattered. My turn.'

He said:

'Look here, Carol, I want to explain. May I come to see you tonight? Or are you busy?'

'I'm not busy. Come along then, about eight ... if you must.'

'What do you mean by that? It's hardly the

height of hospitality.'

'I mean, if you feel you must explain. I don't. However, come along.'

Eight o'clock. The little tree lighted. The holly still fresh. Carol had changed into the dark-red frock. She slipped her grandmother's heavy braided gold bracelet over her right wrist, and put Lydia's ring on her left hand. She made a face at Millicent's perfume bottle and took the stopper from a lighter, gayer scent.

When Andy had come she shooed him into the most comfortable chair and put cigarettes at his elbow. 'Your pipe if you'd rather,' she conceded. 'And when you're thirsty there's beer in the icebox, and some cheese and crackers.'

He announced abruptly:

'Millicent's flying to the Coast and taking the clipper to Honolulu.'

'It's nice work if you can get it,' she managed to say feebly. She had always longed to see the Islands. She remembered Bill's saying, 'We'll take Lydia to Hawaii.' That was as near as she would ever come to it, she thought. Lorna would like Honolulu—someday.

He said reluctantly:

'We had a showdown.'

'So she told me.'

'Why *does* she drag you into this?' he demanded angrily. 'Women have no regard for the decencies.'

'So you've remarked before. She doesn't consider me quite an innocent bystander. Having been your wife, I become an accessory before the fact, also after.'

She was saying anything, suddenly, not knowing, not caring. It was lunatic. She'd reminded herself—and Andy—before this that she had been his wife. But saying it, like that, just now, telescoped the ten years, she was back again, they were together, in a place of their own. Andy's pipe, beer and cheese and crackers...

You go along, you remember, you admit it, you look upon your memories with detachment, they do not touch you. It's like turning the familiar pages of a book you've read often. You know the beginning and the end. Then, suddenly, it's real, for no good reason, it comes to life, it isn't a book, after all, it's you.

He asked:

'Did she tell you she wants me to give up my job?'

'Yes.'

'I won't!' he said. 'She's out of her mind.'

Carol said carefully:

'To do her justice, she believes it would be the finest thing that could happen to you ... release from worry, grind...'

'I don't worry,' he shouted, 'and it isn't a grind!'

'Millicent thinks so. Travel, strange places,

292

new people. Then, when and if you grew tired, your own business.'

'She told you that too!'

'She believes herself generous ... perhaps she is. Andy, don't you see? It's not only that you attract her, and that she's as much in love with you as—' She stopped. That wasn't fair. She couldn't say, 'as it is possible for a woman of her type to be—'

'As what?'

'Skip it. She needs you. I believe her work has come to matter tremendously to her. It's good work, too. But I can see now how much you've helped.'

'It was my job,' he said angrily.

'Of course. So there you have it, a lifetime job, Andy, a one-author editor. It's been done before. I could name you half a dozen examples, people I've learned about since I came to the office.'

He said:

'Millicent accused me of lack of ambition. Possibly she's right. I like what I'm doing and what I have. I told her so. I told her, here are my terms, take 'em or leave 'em.'

'Terms?' asked Carol. 'Reactionary notion that she should live on your salary and buy cigarettes with her income? Don't tell me that was your world-shaking idea.'

'Certainly not ... I'm not a dope,' he said. 'You've been reading our spring list.'

They laughed, the tension snapped. He

added soberly:

'But I did want the whole situation put on a more equitable basis and I certainly wouldn't consider giving up my work. The whole thing was a mistake,' he concluded heavily.

'A reversal of the usual situation,' Carol told him. 'Millicent isn't the marrying type—she says so. Frankly. Therefore, she made a real concession.'

'My God,' said Andy, staring, 'she even told you that!'

'I find that writers are rarely reticent,' Carol said, smiling; 'perhaps it's their plot sense. I wouldn't know. Andy, don't look so—humiliated. I seem to have lost my reticence by example. I apologize.'

'Well, as long as she isn't broadcasting—' He halted, realizing that of all people in the world Carol was the last person he'd want to know about this. It couldn't be helped now. Women!

'So,' said Carol, 'the engagement's off. It was never publicly announced, you've that consolation. Just as an interoffice memo ... and, I assume, to Millicent's people.'

'She hasn't told them,' said Andy. 'She was going to wait until the newspaper announcement after the New Year.' He grinned sheepishly. 'They didn't take to me,' he confessed; 'I must lack glamour. But Millicent was sure she could persuade them into an attitude of, at least, technical approval.'

Carol went out to the little kitchen, snapped the top off the beer bottle, brought it in on a tray, with the crackers and cheese.

'It's over,' she said; 'the shouting and the tumult die. Here's your beer.'

Presently he looked at her as gravely as was compatible with a frothing white ring around his nice mouth.

'Suppose you think I've been a fool?'

'Not exactly. Must I render a verdict?'

'No, let it pass.' He scowled, adding, with the most unloverlike anxiety, 'Do you suppose she'll leave us? We have her sewed up, on a three-book contract, but no more.'

Carol laughed until she was helpless, until Andy became alarmed. He came over to thump her soundly on the back. He said, 'Here, here,' as if she were a fractious puppy.

'I'm all right, Andy. For heaven's sake stop whamming me.'

'What's funny?'

'You. You can lose a fiancée without, apparently, a qualm, but when it comes to losing an author you're all of a tizzy. No, I don't think she'll leave M. and H. You are still valuable to her as an editor. When she comes back from her trip, you'll see. You'll find yourself adjusting to an entirely new relationship. I don't say there won't be a touch of it-might-have-been and when-I-was-one-and-twenty. A lifted eyebrow over a cocktail glass and fond memories. But in the

295

sophisticated manner. No waltzes, no lavender and old lace. Apparently you know how her creative mind works, at least, and are able to help her. As long as you can be of that service, she'll stick with M. and H. ... Or am I being unkind?'

'You may be right. I wouldn't know,' he said glumly.

As he was going, Carol said, smiling:

'If you don't tear off to Honolulu, or bombard her with cables, and clipper letters, she'll blame it on me. I warned her I would do my damnedest to influence you—your way, not hers.'

'Why?' he asked. His hair stood at odd, disheveled angles, and his tie was under his ear.

'I didn't want you to marry her,' Carol said frankly. 'I like you too much to want a second disaster to come your way. But if you like I'll pick out exactly the right girl.'

He said grimly:

'Give me time to recover from this one.' He took her hand and shook it hard, released it. 'Carol,' he said hesitantly, 'you'd have thought better of me—wouldn't you?—if I'd come here done up in crape and singing the blues, uncertain of the wisdom of my decision, in short, thoroughly miserable and carrying a very large torch.'

She shook her head.

'Not in these circumstances.'

'But you haven't all the picture,' he added;

296

'you won't have, ever.'

'That's all right, Andy. It's a jigsaw, maybe I can fit in the missing pieces. And don't look so crestfallen. Few men enjoy the role of Joseph or enjoy being shanghaied.'

Her laughter followed him into the hallway.

When she went back into the living room, she realized that they had not once spoken of William Dawson.

Bill, Lydia, and Lorna were leaving for Warm Springs and then for Florida shortly after the New Year. Lorna called her, toward the end of the week.

'Are you busy New Year's Eve?' she asked.

'I hadn't made any plans,' Carol answered, 'I rarely do ... sometimes people drop in ... I haven't been out on New Year's Eve for years.'

She remembered fleetly, sharply, the first New Year's Eve after she and Andy were married. They'd been on a big party, noise, people, too much to drink, balloons exploding, music, laughter, voices. But when the lights went out, his arm around her and his voice in the darkness saying, 'A new year, every year's going to be new, darling, and every year will be ours.'

Lorna said:

'Bill would like you to come to us for dinner, he has theater tickets. And we promised we'd wake Lydia when we come in.'

'I don't know ...' began Carol hesitantly.

'Please,' begged Lorna.

297

'All right ... if you think so,' Carol told her obscurely.

They dined at home, with Lydia coming in in her pajamas to wish them good night. 'But promise to wake me at twelve,' she said, with her head against Carol's shoulder, her hard round head with its straight thick hair.

The play was amusing, and when they went back to the apartment supper was waiting for them. A few minutes before midnight Bill went into Lydia's room, picked her up, sleeping soundly, and carried her back to the living room. Lorna went for a blanket and wrapped her in it. She sat propped in a couch corner, blinking and smiling. The whistles blew, the bells rang, the radio announced that it was 1940. From an opened window the cold clean air came racing in. Lydia had a sip of her father's champagne and remarked, laughing, that it tasted as if her foot had gone to sleep ... But she was grave, instantly, remembering when her foot had really gone to sleep. Yet it was nearly awake now, and one day it would be wide awake. Lorna had promised and Lorna had never failed her.

Lorna took her back to bed, stumbling, the blanket trailing around her. Bill, putting down his glass, came to stand close to Carol. He turned her around, his hands on her shoulders, bent and kissed her unresisting mouth.

'There,' he said, 'for the New Year. It isn't any use, is it, Carol?'

'No, dear.' She smiled at him, her eyes wet.

'When we come back from the South,' he said, 'you'll keep your word, you won't give us up—'

'Not even for Lent,' she told him, trying to laugh.

Lorna came in. She said, 'Bill, Lydia wants you. She has something special to tell you … she won't tell me.'

Bill went off to Lydia's room and Lorna looked unsmilingly at Carol. For the second time Carol shook her head. She said:

'If you had an ulterior motive, it didn't work.'

Lorna flushed.

'I just thought—'

'Of everyone but yourself?'

Lorna said hastily:

'Carol, are you free next Saturday? Would you take Lydia out? I thought, for tea perhaps … a walk, if it's nice. She'll want to see you, alone, before we go away. She has such fun with you. I'll be busy getting things organized to go.'

'I'd love it. Lorna, we won't speak of this again,' Carol told her, 'but you love Bill very much, don't you? Don't answer, you don't have to. He's your life, and so is Lydia. Both of them. Self-preservation's the first law. You'd do anything, sacrifice anything, to preserve them, your other selves … and their happiness.'

299

Lorna said hardily:

'I can't help it, Carol. It's the way I'm made.'

'I didn't mean you went around indulging in noble gestures. Nothing you do is a gesture.' Carol moved closer to her, kissed her cheek. 'I'm not given to this sort of thing, you know. I hate women who kiss each other and then stab. I want you to know I think you're as swell a person as I've ever known.'

Lorna said huskily:

'If I thought for a moment that because of me you've refused to—'

'Oh, hush!' said Carol. 'I'm not noble. I don't love him, my dear. And you do. Men are idiots. Nice idiots, of course, but there you have it. Don't look so frightened. I promise not to interfere.'

When Bill returned, they were smiling at each other, Carol with frank, affectionate amusement, and Lorna a little warily, as if she weren't quite sure what was making her smile.

Going home, Carol thought, I won't see Lydia till spring.

Her throat ached, her arms felt empty. But in the spring she would see her and, please God, for many springs thereafter. She thought of Lorna, giving Lydia to her for an afternoon, for as many afternoons as could be managed. Bless her.

She hasn't much humor, Carol thought, she hasn't any, really. Well, neither has he. If they had they'd find each other quicker. But they'll

300

stumble on the lovely, comic truth someday. No humor, no devices, no artifices. Some of us have too much, too many for our own good. Not Lorna.

She remembered Andy saying gravely 'quoted in ergs...' and fell to laughing foolishly as Bill's car drove her homeward through the still noisy and excited crowds on the streets.

CHAPTER TWENTY-SIX

Saturday afternoon Carol went to the Dawson apartment to find Lorna completely surrounded by luggage. While Lydia was getting ready, Carol went in to see Mrs Wales. But the old lady did not know her.

Jane Leaming said, outside in the hallway:

'She's slipping more and more into childhood. She doesn't know Lydia at all, doesn't even confuse her with the other Lydia. She thinks Mr Dawson is the doctor.'

'Will it go on long?' asked Carol, distressed.

'Months, possibly. Her heart's very strong.' Jane sighed. 'I've become attached to her,' she admitted, 'as if she *were* a child, quite helpless, dependent on me. At home, I was afraid of her and hated being grateful, but it's different now.'

Lydia was waiting, in her Christmas

elegance, squirrel coat, squirrel cap and muff. They went out, and walked over to the Park. It was a windless day, very bright. Snow still lay in frozen heaps, and the lakes were brushed with a thin, sparkling veneer of ice.

'You won't be able to wear your new coat when you reach the South,' Carol told her.

Lydia stroked herself, lovingly.

'I love it,' she said, 'when I can make myself forget about the squirrels.'

They spent a happy afternoon walking, resting on the green benches, watching the children at play. When it grew cold they took a cab and went to Maillard's for tea. Lydia had a cup, very weak, sandwiches, a piece of cake, and a plate of varicolored ice cream. She prophesied:

'I'll spoil my supper, but Lorna won't mind. She knows it's a party.'

She put down her spoon and looked sadly at the melting mound.

'I can't manage another bite,' she said. 'Maybe if I wait a little?'

She looked hopefully at Carol, adding:

'I'll miss you, Carol. Can't you come with us?'

'I've got a job,' Carol reminded her, 'so I can't. I'll miss you too. But you'll be happy with your father and Lorna.'

'Of course; we always are.' Lydia looked away across the tables. She cried, 'There's Mr Morgan!' and waved heartily.

'Mr Morgan?'

Carol turned, astounded, and Lydia explained, still waving:

'He's a friend of Daddy's, he's nice, I like him ... don't you know him, Carol?'

'Yes,' said Carol.

It was really Andy, standing at the counter, buying something. Lydia's high clear voice rose. 'Mr Morgan,' it stated definitely.

Andy turned and saw them. He took his change and his package and came over. He said:

'This is an unexpected pleasure. Hello, Carol, hello, Miss Dawson.'

Lydia giggled. She asked politely:

'Won't you sit down?'

He did so, disposing of the package. Carol demanded, still amazed:

'What on earth are you doing here?'

'My dear child, it's a public place. I'm buying candy, if you must know. In a lavish satin box, hand-painted with cupids.'

'For your little girl,' deduced Lydia.

Andy smiled at the small face, not as round as it had been, under the squirrel cap. He said:

'I haven't any little girl, I'm sorry.'

'So am I,' said Lydia cheerfully. She looked at Carol. 'I think I can manage a little more of the ice cream.' She added, 'If you had a little girl, Mr Morgan, I'd teach her to ride Starborn. Carol's too big. Starborn,' she explained carefully, 'is quite a little pony.'

'May I order some more tea?' Andy asked. He beckoned a waiter, ordered, sat back. He said, smiling:

'I'm sure you young ladies are consumed with curiosity.' He indicated the package. 'Aren't you?'

'If it isn't for your little girl,' said Lydia, entering into the guessing game, 'it's for your mother. Or maybe Mrs Morgan?'

'I haven't a mother,' said Andy.

'I haven't either,' said Lydia. 'It's too bad. It must be fun. But there's Lorna.'

How right I was, thought Carol, how could I have been so insane? How could I have entertained for a moment ... selfishness, fear, a form of escape—and Lydia, of course?

Andy nodded. He said:

'There isn't any Mrs Morgan either.'

Lydia looked at him with her clear, luminous regard. She said:

'But there could be.'

Andy laughed. The waiter hurried forward with the tea. He said, 'I won't keep you in suspense. The candy's for a nice old lady. Her son was a friend of mine years ago. They've come to New York and I'm going to have dinner with them tonight.'

'Anyone I know?' Carol asked, pouring the tea.

'Frank Smithers—of course, you know him. Why don't you come to dinner too? They'd like seeing you,' he said eagerly.

'It would be a little odd,' Carol reminded him, 'under the circumstances.'

'Aren't you coming home with me?' asked Lydia. And when Carol shook her head, she added, to Andy, 'Carol's my very best friend, next to Lorna.'

'Lorna someone in your school?' asked Andy.

'You met her, I think,' Carol interposed. 'Miss Sheffield.'

'Of course. I didn't know her name.'

Lydia said:

'We're going away, you know, Mr Morgan.' She explained at some length. Carol watched them in silence: the big man, with his eyes intent on the child; Lydia, chattering, digressing, as was her way, confident of his interest. Her heart began to ache physically, she felt heavy and old and depressed. She thought, I hope I'm not coming down with something.

Presently the ice cream was gone, and Andy's strong, heavily sugared tea. They left Maillard's after a short, sharp struggle over the bill, witnessed by Lydia with some trepidation. Andy won. Lydia, putting her hand in Carol's as they rose, said in a confidential, but audible whisper, 'I thought you were really mad at each other.'

'Perhaps we were,' said Carol, laughing, 'but Andy has to have his own way.'

'Is that his name?' said Lydia. 'I like it.

You've never told me about him before.'

'We work in the same office, at Maynard and Hall's. It was through Andy that I met your father.'

On the street, 'Taxi?' asked Andy.

'Let's walk,' said Lydia, 'it's nice.' She looked up and added, 'If you look high enough you can see the stars, even in the city. I suppose people forget or buildings get in the way. Lorna and I saw a sunset the other day, coming home. We looked to the west and there it was all rose and gold, and the streets were so narrow and the buildings so dark against it . . .'

'I've always thought,' said Andy, 'that the sunset hour in Manhattan is the loveliest. Until the lights go on . . . and then I like that best. Did you ever drive over the Manhattan Bridge, Lydia, at night, when the scrubwomen are busy in the offices? Or at sunset?'

'No,' said Lydia. 'What's it like?'

'You'll have to see for yourself. Perhaps you'll let Carol and me take you someday. The boats go by on the river and the towers are tall against the sky, not quite substantial.' He forgot he was speaking to a child. 'They float in an atmosphere of their own, a dusty gold.'

Lydia said, delighted:

'You make up things too!'

Andy laughed, self-consciously.

'I didn't know it,' he said.

She walked between them with her slight limp, a mere lessening of grace, a retarding of perfect freedom. Over her head Andy's eyes met Carol's.

Carol said gently:

'It's getting late, perhaps we'd better take a taxi.'

'Can Mr Morgan come too?' asked Lydia anxiously.

Andy whistled for a cab and put them in it. Lydia was between them. She said:

'I believe you've been friends for ever so long.'

'Why?'

Lydia giggled again. She said, 'The way you fought. Strangers wouldn't ... it's rude, with strangers.'

'She's read a book,' Andy told Carol. He added, 'We are old friends, we've known each other a dozen years.'

'A dozen years?' said Lydia. 'Why, I wasn't even born then.'

'No.'

'Was Carol a little girl?' asked Lydia. 'What kind of little girl was she?'

Andy said gravely:

'Delightful. A bad-tempered, funny little girl with her hair cut almost as short as yours. When she wasn't crying she was laughing.'

Lydia looked at him, the lights at a crossing on her face.

'You weren't a boy,' she said decisively. 'Your hair's quite gray, grayer than my father's.'

'That's Carol's fault.'

Lydia enjoyed the extravagance. She demanded:

'What did you do to him, Carol?'

Carol stirred in her corner. She asked, 'Andy, is this quite necessary?' Yes, she must be going to be ill, she had never felt this way before, defeated, nostalgic, inert.

'Lydia,' said Andy—'may I call you Lydia, Miss Dawson?—is a good friend of ours. And I value her opinion. I'd like to have it. Lydia, what do you think of two people who once loved each other and they quarreled over nothing at all—at least, it seems like nothing now—and then who didn't see each other for years and years?'

'I'd think,' said Lydia promptly, 'that they'd wasted a lot of time.'

'Don't listen to him,' Carol advised, 'he's just trying to be funny.'

'He doesn't sound funny,' said Lydia. 'Do you mean you and Carol, Mr Morgan?'

'That's right.'

Lydia asked, interested:

'What did you quarrel about?'

'Lots of things,' Andy said: 'money for one and people for another, and how untidy I was and the way I swore when things went wrong, and the sort of hats she bought, and the trouble she had finding—and keeping—a decent cook, and sometimes I came home having had too many cocktails—'

'Home?' repeated Lydia, puzzled.

Andy said gently:

'Carol and I were married, Lydia, a long time ago.'

'Aren't you married now?' Lydia asked. She turned accusingly to Carol. 'You didn't tell me,' she said.

Carol said dully:

'I didn't think you'd be interested, Lydia. Yes, we were married. And then we were divorced. Perhaps you don't know about divorce.'

'Lorna told me,' Lydia said. 'It's when two people don't love each other any more. They get unmarried. Is that what happened?'

'Yes,' said Carol.

Lydia spoke through a silence.

'But if you're sorry—?'

The cab stopped, the driver opened the door. Andy got out, helped Lydia, then Carol. He felt her flinch away from his touch on her arm. He said, low:

'You'll forgive me?'

'It was stupid,' Carol told him, 'and it didn't make sense.'

Lydia shook hands with Andy, remembering her manners. 'Thank you for the tea, Mr Morgan,' she said, 'and the ice cream too.'

In the elevator she put her hand in Carol's.

'Don't look so sad, Carol.'

'It's because you're going away.'

'I'll be back. But it isn't because of me. It's Mr Morgan ... shouldn't he have said what he did?'

'No. It was silly of him, Lydia.'

'I couldn't help thinking he wasn't really talking to me,' Lydia said.

On the way from the elevator to the door Lydia stopped, her hand at the bell. She said:

'That's why you didn't come to live with us, after all.'

'Why, Lydia?' Carol asked, with an effort.

'Because of Mr Morgan. Being married to him. Oh, I forgot, you aren't. But maybe,' said Lydia frowning, 'you never really believed in the unmarrying part.'

She rang the bell.

CHAPTER TWENTY-SEVEN

Carol went down to the street again. The cold air struck her, she shivered. She was too tired to walk over to her bus. She called a taxi. These extravagances, she told herself, will ruin me. But it wasn't a very funny thought, after all. In the taxi the air seemed stale and hot. She let down a window and at once was cold again.

She had a dinner engagement with Bess and Jerry. She called Bess as soon as she reached home. 'I can't make it,' she said, 'I feel wretched. I think I've a cold. Tomorrow's

Sunday, thank heaven, I'll stay in bed all day.'

She had an uneasy night. Waking, shivering, sleeping heavily, waking, burning. She thought once, in a panic, turning on the light, I'm really going to be ill. But perhaps not.

Sunday.

The relief maid came in to tidy up and found Carol still in bed. She looked at her with concern. 'Have you got the flu, Miss Reid?' she said, 'You look very bad.'

'I feel it.' She hadn't been ill for years ... oh, a cold now and then, but always something that yielded to staying home a day, eating lightly, dosing herself with common remedies. She thought, I don't know a doctor in this district.

She reached out to dial Lorna's number. Lorna, she knew, would come right over. But she mustn't. They were leaving for the South the next day. She couldn't upset their plans. She knew that Lorna would organize things for her, nurses, doctors. She dialed Bess, but Bess had gone out.

The rest of the day was a blur. She lay quiet, aching furiously, from her head to her feet. She ached more if she moved. She was very thirsty.

She could telephone someone from the office, Elsie or Dot or Kate. She hadn't the energy. Besides, Dot lived in Jersey, Elsie in Brooklyn.

I'll be all right tomorrow, she assured herself.

During the evening the telephone rang and she dragged herself up on an elbow and answered it.

'It's Andy, Carol, is that you?'

'Yes—' She began to cry, suddenly, helplessly.

'I called to—Carol! What's wrong?'

'Andy,' she wept, 'I'm so ill—'

She heard him swear. He said, 'Hang up, I'll be right there.'

She fumbled, returning the telephone to its cradle. She lay back, lightheaded, weak. But she wouldn't be alone. Andy would know what to do.

When the bell rang she realized she had to answer it. She crawled out of bed, threw a robe over her shoulders, thrust her feet into mules and went to the door. She staggered a little.

'You took long enough...' he began. 'Look out!' He caught her in his arms, carried her back, laid her on her bed and put the covers over her.

'Andy, be careful, you'll catch it. Lydia,' she tried to sit up, 'if Lydia caught...? I kissed her goodbye. I must phone Lorna, I *must*...'

She was frantic. Her face was scarlet, her eyes too bright, her lips very dry.

'Lie down,' said Andy, 'I'll attend to it.'

He called his doctor first.

'Dr Bridges' office? ... John ... This is Andy.' He explained. 'I'll wait here,' he concluded. 'Come as soon as you can.'

312

'Lorna,' Carol said.

'Shut up,' he ordered savagely and she lay back, tears crawling under her lashes. He needn't be unkind, she thought, I didn't ask him to come.

'May I speak to Miss Sheffield? ... Miss Sheffield ... This is Andrew Morgan.'

Through the curious swimming haze Carol could hear him explaining. 'She's terribly distressed, she feels she's exposed Lydia. Yes, it looks like flu. No...' He turned to Carol. He said, 'Miss Sheffield wants to come.'

'Don't let her,' said Carol, 'please, tell her I insist.'

He told her. He added, 'She appreciates your wanting to come. No, she thinks you shouldn't. Because of Lydia ... I understand you're going South tomorrow. Yes. Of course, we'll keep in touch. My doctor's on the way, we'll have a nurse.'

Presently he hung up and rose.

'You're going!' wailed Carol.

'Not far.' He went into the bathroom, came back with cold water. Her teeth chattered against the glass. Afterward he brought a wet washcloth and a towel, bathed her face and hands. 'Haven't you a basin?' he asked, getting ice cubes from the kitchenette. 'You wouldn't! I'll find something in the kitchen.'

He broke a dish, swore, almost shut the icebox door on his fingers, swore again. Her head ached so, he made a good deal of noise.

But she wasn't alone.

The doctor came, brisk, competent, thorough. He telephoned a drugstore. He telephoned a nurse who did twenty-four hour duty. He said finally:

'Miss Sims will be here within an hour—meantime—'

'I'll stay,' said Andy.

Andy took him to the door. He hadn't known Bridges very long. Well, five years.

'I wouldn't get too close to her,' Bridges advised; 'remember you had a pretty bad siege yourself not too long ago.'

'I'll be careful, but she mustn't be alone.'

'Good friend of yours?' said Bridges.

Andy grinned. He said:

'We were married—once.'

'Oh. Sorry, old man,' said the doctor, startled.

'I'm not ... thanks for coming. You'll be in in the morning?'

'Yes. Miss Sims can telephone me tonight if she needs me. I don't anticipate it, of course, but you can never tell.' He looked at Andy with frank curiosity.

Andy went back to Carol. She was crying again. She said:

'I thought you'd gone.'

'I'm here.'

He sat watching her uneasy sleep, holding her hot dry hand. She looked, she was, helpless. She was not now the chic Miss Reid, efficient, clearheaded, able to hold her own anywhere. She was merely Carol, ill with flu. She was not especially attractive, dry-lipped, her hair lank from the sponging, her lips cracked.

He thought, You poor little idiot...

Her temperature rose. She woke and looked at him, her eyes glazed, and he was conscious of the sickening fear, a fear he had fought all evening.

She still knew him, spoke his name.

He answered her soothingly, but she began to complain in a hoarse small voice ... 'It wasn't my fault,' she said. 'It was yours. Eva Parsons told me all about it.'

He realized with a pang that she was reliving one of their old, more violent quarrels. The time he'd asked her to go on the house party and she wouldn't. She'd hated Eva Parsons, slithery, sly, always making excuses to put her hands on Andy, on any man. So Andy had gone. There'd been considerable drinking and Eva had a girl visiting her. Eva had told her all about that girl and Andy.

Carol's fault, he'd said, for not going to the party with him.

He sat, listening. The hoarse murmur ceased. She said suddenly:

'But they expect us for Christmas, Andy, how can I face them, how *can* I?' Christmastime and himself coming home, the worse for wear. The house in Ridgefield waiting, the decorations up, the turkey ready

315

to pop into the oven and the two of them standing in the New York apartment saying angry, poisonous, irrevocable things.

'All right,' said Carol on a clear note, 'if that's the way you feel. I don't love you any more. I haven't for a long time.'

What fools we were, he thought. We had so much, we threw it away. Trivial, trivial. He thought of the things each had seen, had faced, since. His struggle for a foothold, Carol's loss of her parents, her personal struggle.

He bent closer to her, and spoke.

'You're dreaming, darling. I love you. I always have. And you love me.'

She heard, she looked at him with eyes that were clear, conscious of him. She tried to smile. She said his name.

The bell rang and Andy went to admit Miss Sims, short, middle-aged, serene, her small black bag in her hand.

'Thank the Lord you've come,' he said, relieved.

He came early the next day, talking to Miss Sims in the living room. Carol was sleeping, he could not see her. He called the doctor, talked to him. He went to the office, and told them that Carol was ill. He telephoned Miss Sims at noon and went to the apartment after work.

Flowers. From Andy, from the office, from Lorna, Lydia and Bill. Andy had called Lorna before her train left, to reassure her.

Miss Sims stayed for ten days. She wouldn't

316

let him remain in the sickroom, she hovered like a watchful hawk. Put his head in, say hello, go away again. She had her orders from Dr Bridges, she said.

On Monday, Bess calling Carol talked to Miss Sims. She'd come to relieve her, she said, every day. And did so, sitting silent and stalwart by the bed while Miss Sims napped in the living room or went for a walk.

On the eighth day Dr Bridges professed himself pleased. On the tenth Miss Sims departed, and Carol was up, sitting in a chair. The management of the house had found her a good maid who would come in temporarily to look after her. She could be alone at night. Now it was a question of regaining her strength.

Miss Sims left in the evening and Andy arrived before her departure. She left him there, with Carol, not without speculation, which she tried to suppress as idle and none of her business. But Mr Morgan was so attentive, and distracted. Perhaps, she thought, they were engaged. Still, she'd seen no ring. It's not your affair, she thought, hoping it wasn't Carol's, as she liked Carol and believed in certain conventional standards, despite her long experience as a nurse. Nurses see everything, few are shocked. Miss Sims wasn't shocked, she was merely sorry if what she feared were true. Such a nice girl, such a nice man. Young people nowadays lived their own lives, she thought, resigned.

Carol was curled up on the living-room couch, making faces at the eggnog Miss Sims had fixed for her. If she saw another eggnog, she'd cackle and moo.

'How do you feel?'

'Wobbly, otherwise all right. The maid comes tomorrow. I can't go back to the office for a week, Dr Bridges said, blast him. I have to eat, sleep, get a little air and coddle myself.'

'That's right, Bridges is a good guy. You scared the daylights out of me, Carol.'

She said, looking too thin, 'I'm sorry, Andy, I've been a nuisance.'

'You always were. I wired Lorna Sheffield today and told her you were as good as new.'

'Thanks, you've been swell. I had such a cunning letter from Lydia.'

He asked, 'Carol, do you remember anything of that—Sunday night?'

'Just you, being here and . . .' She flushed, looked away.

'You do remember!'

She said defensively, 'What of it? I dare say I was wandering. Miss Sims said I did, a lot. You were trying to—to console me.'

'That night,' he said, 'you wandered—back to Eva Parsons' houseparty, and to that damnable Christmas quarrel.'

'How stupid of me.' She wouldn't look at him. 'Forget it, Andy, will you?'

'No. I can't. It means that you still

remember. It's there all the time, under the surface.' He leaned forward, took her hand. 'Look at me, darling.'

Reluctantly her eyes came to his.

'I love you,' he said. 'What idiots we've been.'

'There was Millicent.'

'Damn Millicent. She told me you were going to marry Bill. I believed it. I hoped you wouldn't. I didn't know I was in love with you, Carol. Yet when she told me it was as if the bottom had dropped out of everything. I didn't even care when she announced a nonexistent engagement. It didn't seem to matter. I thought, Hell, what's the use!'

She said painfully:

'I did think I might marry Bill. Chiefly because of Lydia. I had no right, to her or to him. They belong to Lorna. He'll learn that too.'

'Carol,' said Andy, 'I didn't know I loved you until I saw you with Lydia. I saw the way you looked at her. I thought, If we had had a child she would have looked at her that way . . . and I wouldn't have felt out of it, as if I had no business there.'

'Lydia liked you,' said Carol after a silence.

He said, leaning closer:

'I'm in love with you. As you are now. It isn't that I've *stayed* in love with you, Carol, I don't suppose I have. But I'm in love again. Not with you at eighteen, but with you at thirty. I'll

319

always remember that other girl, she had her special place. But it's you I love.'

She began to cry, from weakness, and stirred by an emotion she could not name.

'Carol...'

'Please ... oh, please,' she said, 'go away now.'

He said, rising, looking down:

'It isn't fair. You're not yourself yet. I can wait.'

She heard the door close. Bill had said that, she remembered.

She thought, But I'm not in love with Andy, I can't be. It isn't like it was before—that was love, wasn't it? I don't feel the same way, I'm not the same person. This is just being lonely, and frightened. Realizing for the first time how alone I am, that I won't grow any younger, and that no matter what fun I have I'll always come back to a place like this, alone ... unless I marry again. And as the years go by there will be less opportunity...

Andy did not come to the apartment again. When she returned to the office he looked in at her, unsmiling.

'Feeling all right?'

'A million ... everyone says I've been malingering, they never saw me look better.'

'Don't overdo,' he cautioned her.

'You sound like Dr Bridges. I've enough work to keep me busy for years.'

Andy nodded. He suggested:

'Dinner tonight? You must be bored, cooped up. I'll come get you. That is, if you'll feel up to it, after your first day back.'

'I think so,' she said. 'We'll eat early, I'll go home to bed. All right, Andy. Six-thirty then.'

He called for her promptly, took her to the place where they had dined that first time after her coming to M. and H. and where they had dined many times since.

Carol said, studying the menu:

'I have to be careful for a while. The old appetite isn't what it should be ... No, no cocktail, just sherry. And roast beef, rare.'

Later he watched her cutting off the fat very carefully. He said, annoyed:

'I wish to heaven you'd get over that habit; your plate looks like the sheep and the goats by the time you are through.'

'But I don't like fat,' she argued.

He asked, after a while:

'Have you made up your mind yet?'

'About what?' asked Carol, avoiding fat.

'Marrying me. Good Lord, have you forgotten?' He put his hand up, yanked at his tie. And Carol said crossly:

'Will you leave your tie alone? It drives me crazy the way you—'

His hand dropped, he stared at her and burst out laughing.

'What's funny?' asked Carol. 'For heaven's sake, do *something* about that tie.'

But he let it ride under his ear. He said:

'Don't you see? It irritates you again. My tie, me! And you annoy me, cutting the fat from your meat. Don't you remember? Yet when we had dinner here for the first time since our divorce, we observed each other's old mannerisms and thought them amusing ... remember how we laughed?'

'But—'

'That proves it,' said Andy triumphantly. 'We're in love again or we wouldn't care!'

She asked gravely, 'Do you really think so?' and then, 'Andy, don't look at me like that, everyone will—!'

'To hell with them,' he said gaily. 'Carol, I'm proposing to you.'

She asked slowly:

'How can I be sure? I was ill and frightened and you were there—you were sorry for me, Andy. It might have been that, with us both.'

He said something short, profane, impolite.

'Andy!'

'Sorry. But *I* am sure. Carol, did you want me to marry Millicent?'

'No.'

'Why?'

'She would have made you unhappy.'

'Why would you care?'

'You are my friend.'

'Not to that extent. I didn't want you to marry Dawson. I was damned jealous of him. You couldn't belong to anyone else. I knew that.'

322

She whispered:

'But it's not like before.'

'Of course not. Did you want it to be the same? Isn't this as good, better, isn't this for the rest of our lives?'

'If—if you'd give me ... time, Andy,' she said slowly.

'There isn't enough time,' he said. 'Lydia said we'd wasted time. She was right. But if you like we'll do it the recognized way. Flowers, letters, drives in the country, arguments, pleas. I'll even let my tie alone.'

'I've grown used to working, I like it. I don't think I could go back to doing nothing,' Carol said.

'But when you considered marrying Dawson—'

'There was Lydia.'

He said gently:

'All right. We'll work together. Not too long. I'd like that little place in the country, Carol, and my family.'

'Oh,' said Carol, 'here come Bess and Jerry.'

'Well, damn *them*,' said Andy heartily.

Bess and Jerry came over, and sat with them for a time. Bess looked from one to the other. She had met Andy during Carol's illness. She liked him. She hoped—and kept her thoughts to herself.

Going back to the apartment in the taxi, 'I won't come up,' he said. 'I won't bludgeon you any more. I'll try to behave according to the book. Girls are entitled to courtships. But I want you, woman, if you keep me waiting too long—'

He pulled her to him, held her close. He kissed her, once and then again. Lying against him, her hands tight on his shoulders, she thought, It is as it used to be. The senses remembered, they were wiser than she, this had endured but she had not known it. She had surrounded herself with a barrier of easy phrases, she had disciplined herself, she had not permitted herself to acknowledge that she could fall in love with a stranger whose arms were familiar, whose mouth was known to her.

'Not too long,' he said.

'We'll see,' Carol told him. But she knew that it would not be long. They had ten years, almost, which they must recapture.

She said with her hands in his:

'We'll make a success this time ... we've learned such a lot, we've forgotten so much.'

'But not how to love each other,' he said, content.

'No. And yet,' she added, excitement growing in her, 'we have still more to learn—about each other, about loving—being, as we now are, two different people.'

We hope you have enjoyed this Large Print book. Other Chivers Press or Thorndike Press Large Print books are available at your library or directly from the publishers.

For more information about current and forthcoming titles, please call or write, without obligation, to:

Chivers Press Limited
Windsor Bridge Road
Bath BA2 3AX
England
Tel. (01225) 335336

OR

Thorndike Press
P.O. Box 159
Thorndike, Maine 04986
USA
Tel. (800) 223–2336

All our Large Print titles are designed for easy reading, and all our books are made to last.